EX LIBRIS

12 4 APR 2014

VINTAGE CLASSICS

D1323806

LANDFALL

Nevil Shute Norway was born on 17 January 1899 in Ealing, London. After attending the Dragon School and Shrewsbury School, he studied Engineering Science at Balliol College, Oxford. He worked as an aeronautical engineer and published his first novel, *Marazan*, in 1926. In 1931 he married Frances Mary Heaton and they went on to have two daughters. During the Second World War he joined the Royal Navy Volunteer Reserve where he worked on developing secret weapons. After the war he continued to write and settled in Australia where he lived until his death on 12 January 1960. His most celebrated novels include *Pied Piper* (1942), *No Highway* (1948), *A Town Like Alice* (1950) and *On the Beach* (1957).

OTHER WORKS BY NEVIL SHUTE

Novels

Marazan

So Disdained

Lonely Road

Ruined City

What Happened to the Corbetts

An Old Captivity

Pied Piper

Pastoral

Most Secret

The Chequer Board

No Highway

A Town Like Alice

Round the Bend

The Far Country

In the Wet

Requiem for a Wren

Beyond the Black Stump

On the Beach

The Rainbow and the Rose

Trustee from the Toolroom

Stephen Morris and *Pilotage*

Autobiography

Slide Rule

NEVIL SHUTE

Landfall

A Channel Story

VINTAGE BOOKS
London

Published by Vintage 2009

First published by William Heinemann in 1940

Vintage
Random House, 20 Vauxhall Bridge Road,
London SW1V 2SA

www.vintage-classics.info

Addresses for companies within The Random House Group Limited can be found at: www.randomhouse.co.uk/offices.htm

The Random House Group Limited Reg. No. 954009

A CIP catalogue record for this book
is available from the British Library

ISBN 9780099530053

The Random House Group Limited supports The Forest Stewardship Council (FSC), the leading international forest certification organisation. All our titles that are printed on Greenpeace approved FSC certified paper carry the FSC logo. Our paper procurement policy can be found at: www.rbooks.co.uk/environment

Mixed Sources
Product group from well-managed forests and other controlled sources
www.fsc.org Cert no. TT-COC-2139
© 1996 Forest Stewardship Council

Printed and bound in Great Britain by
CPI Antony Rowe, Chippenham and Eastbourne

Si vous entrez dans une *public house*, n'offrez jamais de pourboire à la *barmaid*, car c'est une dame . . .

ANDRE MAUROIS: *Conseils à un jeune Français partant pour l'Angleterre*

I

THE car, a chilly little open sports two-seater, drew away from the dim bulk of the dance-hall. It accelerated with a crescendo of noise quite disproportionate to its performance and made off down the sea front, its one masked headlamp showing a feeble glimmer in the utter darkness. Presently it took a turning through the park towards the town. The steady rumble of the engine became intermittent; then there was a crashing report and a sheet of yellow flame from the exhaust-pipe. It drew up to a standstill underneath the trees.

In the cramped seat the driver was conscious of the girl's shoulder pressed against his own; only his heavy coat prevented him from feeling the warmth of her thigh. He turned to her. "I don't know what's the matter with it," he said. "It won't go any more."

She said: "Oh yes, it will. Start it up again."

He said: "I'll try if you like. But I don't think it'll go. It does this sometimes."

"Go on and start it."

He pushed the starter. The lights, already dim, went down to a dull red glow and the worn engine turned feebly. "It won't go," he said, and there was a hint of laughter in his voice. "It's the rain or something."

She stirred beside him. "I can get a bus from the corner."

He said: "Don't go. There's a horse coming in a minute."

"What horse?"

"The horse that's coming to tow us home. It won't

I

be long now. You can give it a lump of sugar, but you must hold your hand flat. Otherwise you lose a finger."

There was a light rain falling. In the darkness beneath the flapping fabric of the hood she stared at him. "Whatever are you talking about?"

"The horse. You can stroke its nose, if you like. I'll hold it for you."

"Where are you going to get a horse from?"

He said: "It'll turn up. We've only got to sit here for a little while, and it'll come."

"I'll sit here till the next bus comes."

"All right. What's your name?"

She hesitated. "You want to know everything, don't you?"

"Well, it's not much to ask. You're going to spend the night with me, and you won't tell me your name."

She was startled and upset. "I don't know what you mean," she said. She fumbled for the handle of the door.

There was laughter in his voice. "Well, you said you'd stay here till the next bus came. It's after half-past twelve—there won't be any more till morning. So you'll have to sit here all night. I do think you might tell me your name."

She relaxed. "You do say the most awful things!"

"What have I done now? You've done nothing but pull me up all evening."

"You know what you said."

"I know. I asked you to tell me your name, and you won't tell me. I believe you're an enemy alien and you think I'll put the police on you."

"I promise you I'll take you home the minute the horse comes. In the meantime, I do think you might tell me who you are."

She giggled. "You've seen me often enough."

"I know I have. That's what's worrying me."

"I know who you are."

He turned to her, immensely conscious of her presence. "Do you?"

She nodded. "You come from Emsworth aerodrome. They call you Jerry, don't they?"

"Oh—yes. Everybody calls me Jerry. How did you know that?"

"Never you mind. What's Jerry short for? Gerald?"

"No—Chambers. Roderick Chambers. But you may call me Jerry."

She turned her head. "You do say horrid things."

"Well, you said that one. Tell me, what *is* your name? I've told you mine."

She relented. "Mona Stevens."

"Mona." He paused, and then he said: "That's rather a nice name."

She was pleased. "It is, isn't it? I mean, there aren't so many Monas about. Better than being called Emily, or something of that."

He turned to her. "Tell me, where do you work?"

She laughed at him. "Think hard."

"I am thinking. You aren't the old charwoman who cleans out my bedroom, by any chance?"

"No, I'm not."

"I thought not. It's a pity."

She turned the subject. "I know what you had for supper tonight," she said.

He stared at her. "What did I have?"

"Steak and chips, and then you had a bit of Stilton cheese. And you had about three half cans of bitter."

He said, astonished: "You're clairvoyant." She shook her head. "Then you smelt my breath."

She turned her head away. "Don't be so rude."

He thought for a minute. "Well then, you were in the 'Royal Clarence' tonight, anyway." Recollection came to him in a wave. "Of course. You work at the 'Royal Clarence'—in the snack-bar."

She mocked him. "Aren't you ever so quick?"

He said weakly: "I knew that all the time, of course. I was just pulling your leg."

"You do tell stories."

"No—honestly. You don't think I'm the sort of chap who goes to the Pavilion to pick up girls, do you?"

"Well, what else did you go to the Pavilion for?"

He said loftily: "I went there to dance."

She bubbled into laughter. "I'd like to have seen you dancing with them other officers you came in with."

"You don't quite understand. We had a party all fixed up; the ladies were to meet us there. There was Ginger Rogers and Merle Oberon and Loretta Young— oh, and several others. Greta couldn't come."

She said a little doubtfully: "I don't believe you. What happened to them?"

"They didn't turn up. So then I looked around and you were the only person in the room I knew, so I asked you if you'd dance with me."

"You do tell 'em. You never recognised me at all."

He said: "You hurt me very much when you talk like that."

"It'ld take a hatpin to hurt you."

A little shift of wind blew a few drops of rain from off the dripping hood in on to the girl. "Here," she said. "It's raining in all over me. Go on, and take me home."

"The horse will be here in a minute—then we'll all go home together. You can have a ride on it, if you like. Look, I've got a rug here." He reached round to the little space behind the seats, dragged a rug out between their shoulders, and arranged it over her. It was quite necessary to reach round her back to do so; she moved a little closer to him and his arm remained around her shoulders.

She said: "What do you do out at the aerodrome?"

He said: "Fly aeroplanes."

"That's what them wings on your chest mean, isn't it?

"That's it. I carry them as spares."

"Are you a squadron-leader, or something?"

He said: "Or something. I'm a flying officer."

"What sort of things do you do when you go flying? Have you shot down any Germans?"

"They don't come near these parts, thank God. All we do is to go out over the sea and report what ships we see."

"It must be frightfully exciting."

"We get bored to tears."

He turned to her; they drew a little closer. "You've not been at the 'Royal Clarence' very long, have you?"

"Six months. You don't notice, that's what's the matter with you."

He said: "We won't go into that again. What did you do before that?"

"Worked in the corset factory—Flexo's. I got there when I came away from school, and stayed there ever since. But that's no kind of life, in the factory all day. I was always on to my old man about it, and last year he said, well, I was twenty-one and I could please myself. So then I went to Mr. Williams at the 'Royal Clarence' because my uncle knows him at the Darts Club, and he spoke to the manager for me. So then I started in the snack-bar."

"It's more fun there, I should think, than making corsets all day long."

"Ever so much. But then I wasn't on the corsets. I was on bust bodices."

He said innocently: "What's the difference?"

"Why—a bust bodice is what you . . ." She checked herself. "You know well enough what it is. You're just being awful."

In the warm darkness underneath the rug his arm

reached round her shoulders and his hand lay at her side. He moved his fingers. "Honestly, I don't know what it is. Is this one?"

"No, it's not. Give over, or I'll get out and walk home."

"I only wanted to find out."

"Well, look in the papers. There's pages of them in the advertising."

"I don't read the advertisements. I think they're low."

"Not half so low as what you're doing now. Give over, or I will get out and walk. Really and truly."

"It's raining—you'll get soaked."

"That'll be your fault."

"You'll get double pneumonia, and die. You've not got enough clothes on to go wandering round the streets at this time of night, in a howling blizzard."

"Never you mind what I've got on—it's nothing to do with you."

"Have it your own way. I was going to buy you a beautiful ermine cloak trimmed with—with birds of paradise. Still, if you take that line, I'll have to get you something else. What about a stick of Southsea rock?"

"You do talk crazy. I don't believe you've got a stick of Southsea rock, nor an ermine cloak, either."

He said: "I've got a cigarette."

With a number of contortions they managed to light cigarettes without disturbing the position of his arm, which lay around her shoulders; their movements shuffled them closer together. For a few minutes they sat smoking quietly.

A figure loomed up on the pavement beside Chambers, a figure in a tin hat and a dripping raincoat. It paused beside the little car; from the driver's seat the young man recognised an air-raid warden on his rounds.

The warden said: "I should move on and go home now, if I was you. Getting a bit late, isn't it?"

Chambers said: "I can't. The car's broken down. We're waiting here till a horse comes along to tow us home."

"You don't suppose I'll swallow that one, do you?"

"Well, the lady did. If it's good enough for her, it's good enough for you."

The warden coughed, and spoke in to the car. "I should make him take you home now, miss."

The girl did not speak. Chambers said: "I think you'd better go away and leave off bothering us."

The warden thrust his thumbs into his belt. He was fifty-six years old, and an accountant in his working hours. He said: "No parking allowed on these common roads after black-out. We got to keep them clear in case of fire-engines, and that. You'll have to move along. You can park in the station yard if you're going on all night."

He had played his trump card, and he knew it. Reluctantly Chambers reached out to the starter switch; the engine turned feebly and began to fire on three cylinders; presently the fourth chipped in. The pilot withdrew his arm from the girl's shoulders. "I think he's got us there," he said. "We'll have to go."

She nodded. "He's got a nerve," she said in a low voice. "Nothing to do with him."

Chambers said, equally low: "It's not worth a row. Besides, he's right about these roads. There's a notice up about it."

He let in the clutch and the car moved away. The girl drew the rug about her and sat a little more erect. They drove into Portsmouth in the utter darkness, a town without street lights or lit windows. The dim light of his one shaded headlamp lit the road immediately before them; everything else was black and silent.

He found her house at last, a building at the corner of a shabby street. It seemed to be a second-hand furniture shop in rather a poor way; he drew up by the side door of the shop.

She said: "I had a lovely evening, ever such fun. Thank you ever so much for bringing me home."

He said: "I'm glad Ginger Rogers couldn't come. You dance much better."

"You do talk soft."

"Would you like to do it again?"

"All right."

"What about tomorrow?"

"If you like. Same time at the Pavilion?"

"I'll have to shake off Loretta Young, but I can get rid of her all right. I'll tell her I've got chicken-pox. Half-past ten?"

"All right."

"Is this where I kiss you?"

"No, it's not."

"You're wrong."

Presently she got out of the car and stood for a moment in a shadowy doorway, slim and erect, waving him good night. He started up the worn engine of the little sports car again and drove out of the city on to the country roads.

The girl pulled the door behind her and bolted it, turned out the flickering gas-jet, and went up the narrow stairs to her room. She trod softly on the oil-cloth and shut her door furtively behind her, because she did not want to wake her mother. Her mother never minded whom she went about with, but liked her to be home by midnight.

She had a room to herself, being the only one of the children still at home. Her brother Bert was in the Navy, a leading seaman in the *Firedrake*; he was away from England. They thought he was somewhere in the South Atlantic; it was six weeks since they had heard from him. It had had to be the Navy, of course. Her father had served for nearly thirty years, finishing up as a chief petty officer. He had a small pension, and the shop made a profit of a few shillings a week, enough for them to get along on.

Millie, her sister, had shared the room with her till the beginning of the war; she had been working at the corset factory. A panic reduction had thrown Millie out of work with a hundred and fifty other girls; she had then joined the A.T.S. and was doing canteen work at Camp Bordon. She looked very smart in her khaki uniform; Mona sometimes regretted that she had not done the same. But it was more fun in the snack-bar, with everybody having a good time, and all the officers drinking with their ladies, and that.

The room was cold; she undressed quickly and jumped into bed. Was that a bust bodice, indeed! The cheeky thing! Probably he only said it to tease her. She never had heard anybody talk so silly, but it was fun being out with him. She was glad he had asked her to dance again. He was ever so tall, six foot two at least; the long blue greatcoat and the little blue forage cap stuck sideways on his black hair made him look taller still. She thought he was older than she was, twenty-three or twenty-four perhaps. He had a very young face, with pink cheeks.

She liked him. She was glad to be going out with him again; it was something to look forward to.

Jerry, they called him. It was really awful; a typical officer's joke.

Very soon she was asleep.

Ten miles away Chambers turned his noisy little car in at the gateway leading to the officers' mess and parked it in the open-sided garage barn. He draped the rug over the radiator in case of frost and went into the mess. It was a good mess, a solid building of red brick designed by a good architect and put up about ten

years previously. It was overcrowded now; the aerodrome accommodated five squadrons instead of the two
that had been the establishment in peace-time. A cluster
of bedroom huts were springing up on what had been
the tennis-courts, but Chambers had a bedroom in the
original building. He had been there since he had left
Cranwell three years previously.

There was still one light burning in the ante-room;
he crossed the room and studied the operations board.
The weather report for the morning was there; cloud
ten-tenths at a thousand feet. Sleepily he made a
grimace; still, it was December and you couldn't expect
much else. He scanned the other notices on the board.
Battle practice in Area SQ from 1200 to 1400—that
wouldn't worry him. Experimental flying in Area TD
at 1,000—that might be interesting. AA gunnery practice from Departure Point in Area SL—that was off his
beat. There was nothing that concerned him.

He looked at his watch; it was half-past one. He went
up to his room.

His room was comfortable enough, though furnished
with a Spartan simplicity. There was an iron bedstead
with a clean white counterpane; his batman had turned
down the bed and put out his pyjamas. The walls were
cream distempered, and the paint was grey. There was a
small wash-basin with running water, a small radiator,
and a large painted tallboy for his clothes. There was a
double photograph of his father and mother on the
mantelpiece, and a couple of detective novels. There
was a large deal table in the window, and most of his
private life revolved around this table.

He kept his letters in its drawers, and his fountain-
pen, and the bottle of ink, and all the oddments that he
would have liked to carry with him in his pockets if it
had not been for spoiling the set of his tunic. On it
stood his wireless set, a jumble of valves, chokes and

condensers on a plain deal board innocent of any covering. He had put it together himself; it got America beautifully. Beside it was his galleon. He had bought the kit of parts to make the galleon a couple of months previously and he was laboriously rigging the yards with cotton thread according to the book of the words, and painting it with the little pots of brightly-coloured pigments supplied with the kit. It was about half finished.

He ran his eyes over it lovingly; he liked the delicate, finicking work with his fingers. It was fun to work at, in his long leisure hours. He had thought of calling it the "Santa Maria"; that was what the book told you to paint under the stern gallery. "Mona Lisa" would go as well, he thought, and it would leave a little more room for the lettering. Mona.

He switched on all the switches that controlled the wireless set, and tuned it in to Schenectady. He heard a dance band faintly, overlaid with background noise and echoes of Morse, and got his customary thrill out of it. The room was cold; he slung his gas-mask over the back of a chair and started to undress.

In bed, he twitched the string that ran ingeniously round the picture-rail to the switch at the door, and pulled the cold sheets round him. She was a decent kid, that Mona. He had danced at the Pavilion several times before, but had never wanted to meet his partners again; usually he had been only too glad to get rid of them. This one was different. She was dumb as a hen, of course, but all girls seemed to be like that. It would be fun to spend another evening dancing with her, provided no one from the mess happened to see them. He didn't want to get his leg pulled.

Perhaps it was better, after all, to stick to beer.

He thought of her again, remembered the feel of her shoulders, and drifted into sleep, smiling a little.

Five hours later he woke up with a start as his bat-man snapped the light on at the door. The man put a cup of tea beside his bed. "Half-past six, sir," he said. "Been raining in the night, I see, but it's stopped now."

The pilot sat up in his bed and took the cup. "What's the wind like?"

"Blowing a bit from the north-east." The man took his boots and went out of the room, leaving the light on.

Chambers got up, shaved and dressed and went down to the dining-room. At one end of one of the long tables there were three or four young men at breakfast, served by a sleepy waitress of the W.A.A.F. It was still dark out-side and the curtains were still drawn; in the cold light of a few electric bulbs the meal was cheerless and uncom-forting. He pulled a chair out and sat down to porridge.

Somebody said: "'Morning, Jerry. What time did you get home?"

"Half-past one."

The other said: "I saw you—you were doing nicely. I got fed up and left."

The conversation flagged; the pilots ate hurriedly and in silence. They had been on the morning patrol now for a month, and they were sick of it. With the late, dark mornings and the cold weather the patrol over the sea was unattractive, boring in the extreme, and a little dangerous. There had been losses in the squadron, un-romantic, rather squalid deaths of pilots who had mis-calculated their fuel and had been forced down in the winter sea to perish of exposure or by drowning. To set against the black side of the picture there were only long strings of meaningless statistics gleaned each day, the names and nationalities of ships within their area, the course and the position of each. It was uninspiring, clerical work, meaningless until it reached the com-manders R.N. in the operations room, who daily made up the great mosaic of the war at sea.

This was the last morning patrol that the flight were to do. Tomorrow they would have a change of time-table and would take on the afternoon patrol over the same areas of sea.

"Like the bloody threshing horse that takes a holiday by going round the other way," said Chambers. In the three months since the beginning of the war, nobody in the squadron had seen an enemy ship, or fired a gun, or dropped a bomb in anger.

The pilots finished their breakfast, pulled on their heavy coats and went down to the hangar. The machines were already out upon the tarmac with their engines running; grey light was stealing across the sodden aero-drome. In the pilots' room the young men changed into their combination flying-suits, pulled on their fur-lined boots, buckled the helmets on their heads. The machines that they were flying were enclosed monoplanes with twin engines; in summer they would dispense with helmets. Now they wore them for warmth.

Each machine carried a crew of four, an officer, a sergeant as second pilot, a wireless telegraphist and an air-gunner. They carried two one-hundred-pound bombs and a number of twenty-pound, and had fuel for about six hours' flight.

The officers gathered round the flight-lieutenant, armed with their charts, and heard the latest orders. Then they separated and went to their aircraft. The crews were standing by and the engines were running. One by one they got into the machines and settled into their places; the doors were shut behind them. There were four machines in the patrol. Engines roared out as each pilot ran them up, chocks were waved aside, and the machines taxied out to the far hedge and took off one by one in the cold dawn.

Chambers sat tense at the controls during the long take-off. He knew the machine well, but with full load it was all that she could do to clear the hedge at the far end. It was easier than usual today; they had the long run of the aerodrome and there was a fair wind. He pulled her off the ground at eighty miles an hour three hundred yards from the hedge and held her near the grass as she gained speed. Then he nudged Sergeant Hutchinson beside him, who began to wind the under-carriage up with the old-fashioned, cumbersome hand gear.

From time to time, as they gained height, the sergeant paused in his task to wipe his nose. He had a streaming cold in the head, and he was feeling rather ill. By rights he should not have been flying, but the squadron were temporarily short of pilots, having despatched a number to the Bombing Command.

Behind the sergeant the young white-faced wireless operator unreeled his aerial and made the short test transmission that he was allowed before relapsing into wireless silence, only to be broken by orders from his officer in an emergency. He sat with head-phones on his head, searching the wave-lengths with the knob of his condenser, sleepy and bored and cold. Behind him the corporal gunner sat in the turret playing with the gun. As they passed out over the beach, the corporal fired a long burst into the water to test the gun; the clatter mingled strangely with the droning of the engines. Then he sat idly on the little seat in the cramped turret scanning the misty, grey, and corrugated sea.

Chambers passed over the control to Hutchinson and moved from his seat to the little chart-table. He gave a course to the sergeant, who set it on the compass. They flew on out over the Channel, flying at about seven hundred feet below a misty layer of cloud. Very soon they lost sight of the other machines, each having taken its own course.

The young man sat at the chart-table staring out of

the large windows of the cabin. He had an open note-book before him; on the vacant page he had written the date, the time of taking off, and the time of departure from the coast. In the grey morning light the visibility was very poor; unless they were to pass right over a ship it was unlikely that they would see it. They were all on the look-out; there was nothing else to do.

They flew on for an hour, gradually growing cold. The wireless operator was the first to feel it as a bitter privation. He was a pale-faced lad of nineteen with a home in Bermondsey; he had little stamina and hated the monotony of the patrol. He had nothing to do, ever. The rules against transmitting on the wireless were rigorous, and could only be broken in emergency; in the three months of the war they had not suffered an emergency. In three months he had done no useful work at all, and he was sick of it. For this reason he hated the patrol, and felt the cold more than any of them.

Chambers moved back into the first pilot's seat. "See the Casquets pretty soon," he said. The sergeant nod-ded his agreement.

Five minutes later Hutchinson plucked his arm and pointed downwards. The young officer craned over and saw through the grey mist a small black rock awash in the sea, with white surf breaking on it. Then there was a long black reef, then nothing but the sea again.

Chambers said: "For the love of Mike, don't lose it. Shove her round." He moved back to the chart-table and bent above the chart. It might be Les Jumeaux, or a bit of Alderney. He set a new course as they circled round the reef; the sergeant steadied on it. Very soon an island rose out of the mist, rocky and barren, with a lighthouse on it.

The machine turned away and took a course back for the coast of England, flying upon a course ten miles to the west of their flight out. It was their job to cover the whole area in strips, so that at the end of their five-hours' patrol they would have an accurate report of everything that floated in their zone. In theory, that was, for on mornings like the present one they could see barely half a mile on each side of their path.

They saw a ship before they reached the English coast, a collier with the letters NORGE painted upon her side. They circled her and swept low by her stern to read the name, the *Helga*. Then they resumed their flight. The young officer produced a bottle of peppermint bull's-eyes; they all had one, with a drink of hot coffee from the Thermos-flasks. The drink and the hot sweet refreshed them and brought back a part of their efficiency; they were all suffering a lassitude from the raw cold.

They made their landfall and turned back to the French coast. Backwards and forwards they went as the grey morning passed, tired and bored and numb. From time to time they saw a ship and noted the particulars: the name, the nationality, the course, and the speed. In the gun-turret the corporal was sunk into a coma of fatigue. On and on they went, hour after hour. Presently Chambers began to watch the clock above the chart-table; soon he would be able to turn for home.

At half-past eleven they left the area, at noon they crossed the English coast again. As they passed the long, deserted beaches the four machines of the outgoing patrol passed by them on their starboard hand; Chambers waggled his wings in salute. Then they were above the aerodrome. The sergeant lowered the wheels for landing and the pilot put the machine into a gliding turn above the hangars. They made a wide sweep and approached the hedge; the flaps went down and the ground came up to meet them very quickly. The pilot waited his moment and then pulled heavily upon the wheel; the monoplane touched ground smoothly but decisively and ran on at a great speed. Chambers jerked up the lever that controlled the flaps and checked her gently on the brakes. She ran for several hundred yards; then she was slow enough for him to turn into the hangars.

He switched off the engines and an aircraftsman came up and opened the cabin door. In the machine no one was in a hurry to get out. They were too tired and too stiff to make a move at once. The corporal unloaded the gun and put the magazines away; the wireless operator sat listless at his little desk. The sergeant was entering the flying time and details of the flight in the log-books. The pilot made a few pencilled notes in his book and collected his charts.

Back in the pilots' room he slowly stripped off his flying clothing before the stove. The other three were there already, writing their reports. Matheson said: "See anything?"

"Not a bloody thing." The pilot shivered a little as he wriggled out of the combination suit. "A lot of sea and one or two mouldy ships."

He turned to the stove. Behind his back the door opened and the flight-lieutenant came into the little room, a fresh-faced young man of twenty-five called Hooper.

Matheson said: "Jerry didn't see anything. What's it all about, anyway?"

"Blowed if I know."

Chambers turned towards him. "Has something happened?"

The newcomer shrugged his shoulders. "There's a cag on about something—I can't find out what it is. You didn't see anything?"

"I saw one or two ships." He reached for his note-book; the flight-lieutenant looked over his shoulder. They ran down the list of names, times, and locations.

"There's nothing in those," said Hooper. "Nothing unusual?"

"Not a thing."

"Well, something's happened. The Navy are creating about something."

The pilot turned back to the stove and huddled his chilled body over it. "Blast the Navy," he said petulantly. "They've always got a moan."

The flight-lieutenant took the notebook and went over to the squadron-leader's office. "Jerry's just come in, sir. Here's his book. He saw nothing out of the ordinary."

Peterson took the book and ran his eye down the list of ships. "Damn," he said very quietly. "Didn't anybody see the *Lochentie*?"

"The *Lochentie*?"

"Yes." The squadron-leader hesitated. "There's a blazing row going on about a ship called the *Lochentie*. She's been torpedoed somewhere off St. Catherine's."

"This morning?"

The other nodded.

The young flight-lieutenant made a grimace. It was right in the middle of the area covered by the patrol. "Is that what the Navy are raising hell about?"

"That's it. You'd better come along with me."

They left the office in silence and walked down the road towards the wing-commander's office. Wing-Commander Dickens was a small, dark-haired, rather irritable man. He was an efficient officer, but one who was inclined to stand upon his rank in the manner of an earlier day. He believed in discipline, in rigid and unquestioning obedience to the exact letter of an order. He had little or no use for initiative among junior officers; their duty was to do the job that they were told to do, and nothing more.

They went into his office as the telephone bell rang.

He lifted the receiver, nodding to them. A voice said: "Captain Burnaby upon the line, sir."

"Oh . . . put him on." The wing-commander covered the mouthpiece and said: "Wait outside a minute." The squadron-leader and the flight-lieutenant withdrew, shut the door behind them and stood in the corridor.

The wing-commander waited uneasily for a few moments. He had not a great deal of imagination, but he carried in his mind a very clear picture of Captain Burnaby, R.N. A man of fifty, still in the prime of vigour, over six feet in height and massively built. A man with a square, tanned face and bushy black eyebrows, a man outspoken and direct. A man who was inevitably, always right. A man of influence, due to Flag rank; a man who was deep in the confidence of the commander-in-chief. A man who had very little use for the Royal Air Force.

Captain Burnaby was speaking from his office in the annexe to Admiralty House. He said: "Wing-Commander Dickens? About the *Lochentie*. I have a signal from the trawler that is bringing the survivors in. The ship was definitely torpedoed ten miles from St. Catherine's, bearing one nine two."

The Air Force officer said: "They're quite sure it was a torpedo, are they?"

"Certainly—the track was seen. It happened at ten o five. The vessel disappeared at ten-seventeen, leaving some wreckage and a boat which my trawler got at eleven-eighteen. Will you please tell me what reports you have from the aircraft?"

The wing-commander shifted awkwardly in his chair. "So far, the reports to hand are negative."

"So far? Have all your machines got back?"

"The last one has just come in."

"Is his report negative, too?"

"Yes. The visibility was very bad."

"This action took place in the area covered by your morning patrol. Do you mean that none of your aircraft saw anything of it at all?"

"Apparently not. The visibility was such that a machine could pass within a couple of miles and see nothing, you know."

"I don't know anything of the sort. My trawlers found the place all right."

The wing-commander said weakly: "It's often clearer right down on the water."

For three months both men had undergone the strain of a responsible command in war-time. In that three months neither of them had had so much as one day of rest.

The naval officer said viciously: "I quite agree with you. That is exactly what I always say whenever the usefulness of air patrol comes up in a discussion."

There was an awkward pause.

The captain said: "What organisation have you got to ensure that your pilots actually patrol the areas they are supposed to?"

The little wing-commander flared suddenly into a temper. "That's a reflection upon my command. We'll get on better if we keep this civil, Captain Burnaby."

The other said directly: "I'll be as civil as the facts permit. I have to make a report upon this matter to the Commander-in-Chief, and I want the facts. So far, I know that a valuable ship has been torpedoed, right under my nose. I know that there are thirteen survivors living and that nearly a hundred people have been killed, including several women. I know that my trawler found the ship and saved the thirteen lives. I know that my application for more trawlers have always been turned down, because it was said that air patrol could do the work more efficiently. You tell me now that your patrol saw nothing of this wreck because of the bad visibility. Now, have you got any more facts upon this matter that you can give me?"

"No, I've not."

"All right, wing-commander. I shall put in my report upon those lines."

He rang off; the wing-commander put down the telephone, white with rage. It was not the first time he had had a brush with Captain Burnaby. With his reason he knew that the visibility had been too bad that morning to expect results; with his quick temper he felt bitterly that he had been let down. The duty of the pilots was to get results. They hadn't got them.

He crossed to the door and opened it. "Come in," he said, and went back to his desk. "Now, what about this ship? Has anyone reported her?"

Squadron-Leader Peterson said: "Nobody saw anything of her, sir. Are you sure that she was in our area?"

"The Navy say that she was fifteen miles from St. Catherine's, bearing one nine two."

The flight-lieutenant said: "What time did it happen?"

"At five minutes past ten." The little wing-commander stared arrogantly at the young officer. "Whose zone was that?"

Hooper thought for a minute. "That'ld be Matheson, I think."

"And he saw nothing of the ship?"

"Not a thing, sir."

"Nor of the boat that was picked up?"

"He didn't see anything at all. The weather was very thick."

The wing-commander said: "Well, I think that's a pretty bad show. This squadron has been given the job of doing the patrol. It's not been done. Say it's the weather, if you like, although it's not too bad for flying.

Whatever the reason is, the squadron hasn't done the job that it was told to do."

There was a tense silence in the office.

Dickens went on: "It's no use coming along now to tell me that the weather was too bad to do your job efficiently. The time to tell me that is before the patrol starts, not after they've made a muck of it. Tell me before you start and I can do something—double bank the patrol, perhaps."

There was another silence of strained nerves. He went on: "Well, that's all for the moment. You'll be interested to know that I've just had Captain Burnaby on the telephone telling me that the coastal patrol's no bloody good to him. Judging from this morning's performance, I rather agree. That's all. You can go."

The squadron-leader set his lips and said nothing. The young flight-lieutenant stepped forward impulsively. "There's just one thing, sir," he said hotly. "I'd like to hear from Captain Burnaby why his ship wasn't in convoy, as it should have been."

"That hasn't got a thing to do with you, Hooper," said the wing-commander. "Your job is the patrol, and I'm not satisfied with that patrol at all. You can go now. Send Matheson to see me."

They left him; the wing-commander remained seated at his desk, tapping a pencil irritably on his blotting-pad. He would have to see the Air Officer Commanding and tell him all about it—no good letting Burnaby get his tale in first.

He brooded darkly for a time. That flight-lieutenant had a nerve . . . although why hadn't the *Lochentie* been in convoy, anyway? He would put up the A.O.C. to find out that. He'd been too open with these lads like Hooper; the result was that they all thought that they could run the war. They'd have to learn that they'd got just one job to do, and one only, without reasoning too much, or digging into everybody else's job. He'd see in future that his orders were framed for their job alone.

In the pilots' office the four pilots wrote their short reports. Presently Matheson was summoned to see Wing-Commander Dickens; the others went over to the mess. Chambers went up to his room and had a wash, yawned for a few moments before the glass, and went down to the ante-room for a beer before lunch.

He found Hooper brooding sullenly alone over a tankard. "Dickens tore me off a strip just now," said the flight-lieutenant. "I'm fed up with this job. Think I'll put in for a transfer."

Chambers said: "Where was the ship, anyway?"

"Bung in the middle of Matheson's zone. Thank your stars it wasn't yours. There's the hell of a row going on."

"Am I out of it?"

"So far."

"That's a bloody miracle," said Jerry, and went in to lunch.

He went into the Junior Mess-room after lunch, got himself a cup of coffee and a copy of *For Men Only* and stretched himself in an arm-chair before the fire. He turned over the pages of the little publication and looked at the pictures, smiling a little. Presently the eyelids drooped over his eyes and he slept, his long legs reaching out towards the comfortable glow, his slim body at rest.

He woke an hour later, rested and refreshed. He had grown accustomed to this sleep after his lunch since he had been on the morning patrol. He stirred in the chair and planned the remainder of the day. Tomorrow was the change-over of patrol; he would not be flying till the afternoon. Therefore, another late night wouldn't hurt him. He had arranged to meet the girl friend in the evening; he looked forward to that with some pleasure. He might pick up Matheson or Hooper and take in a movie, and go on to the "Royal Clarence" for ham and eggs in the snack-bar. In the meantime, he would have an hour or so for working on the galleon.

He spent the afternoon in his room threading minute cords through little blocks upon the yards and securing them with tiny dabs of seccotine. He was pleased with his work. His imagination showed the ship to him as she would have been; she became real to him, magnified. Studying the bluff lines of her hull, he felt that he could hear the bubbling of the bow wave at her stem, see the long trail of eddies in her wake. He could feel her deck heaving gently beneath his feet. He could hear the yards creaking and complaining as she rolled. To him she was a real little ship. He was immensely pleased with her.

Presently he went down to tea, then got his car and drove into Portsmouth. He had one or two small items of shopping to do. For one thing he wanted an electric torch; he was tired of falling over bicycles each time he parked his car. But torches were scarce. He tried three shops without success; the black-out had created a demand that had swept torches off the market.

Finally he went into a large chemist's and stood looking around him for a moment, uncertainly. It did not look a likely place to buy a torch. It was largely devoted to soap and perfumes, and all manner of feminine cosmetics. He stood irresolute, a tall figure in an Air Force blue greatcoat, pink-cheeked and rather embarrassed.

A girl came up to him from the beauty stand. "Can I get you anything, sir?"

He said: "I'm not quite sure. I wanted an electric torch."

"I think we're out of torches. We have lamps."

He brightened. "A lamp would do. Could I see them?" He followed her down the shop. "I didn't really think you'd keep that sort of thing. Like trying to buy a lipstick at the ironmonger's."

She said: "We always keep a fancy line." She opened a carton. "This is the only lamp we have at the moment."

It was a moulded glass rabbit with red eyes. It stood upon a round chromium base with a little handle; when you turned the switch a bulb lit up inside it and the rabbit glowed with light.

The pilot said: "My God, that's wizard. Just look at its eyes! What sort of battery does it use?"

He made her take it to bits to show him; then he bought it and took it away, very pleased with himself. He went on to a cinema and sat for a couple of hours watching a gangster melodrama; at about nine o'clock he was in the snack-bar of the Royal Clarence Hotel.

It was the busiest hour of the day; the long room was crammed with people. Most of them were young, most of the men were in uniform. There were naval officers, a fair sprinkling of naval surgeons, a good many sub-lieutenants and lieutenants of the Royal Naval Volunteer Reserve, the Wavy Navy. There were lieutenants and captains of Marines, and anti-aircraft-gunners, and young Sapper officers. There were young Air Force pilots with the drooping silver wings upon their chests, and young Fleet Air Arm pilots with the golden wings upon their sleeve.

The room was filled with smoke, a smell of grilled food and a great babel of conversation. There were two bars serving drinks, and a snack bar with stools arranged around a grill. The centre of the room was filled with tables and the walls were lined with settees. There were perhaps a hundred people there, all talking and smoking and eating and drinking.

Chambers took off his coat and hung it on an over-loaded stand and pushed his way to the bar where Mona was at work. There were two other barmaids with her, all immensely busy. She gave him a swift smile and served him deftly with a gin and Italian.

He said: "Dancing?"

She smiled brilliantly and nodded. He took his glass and elbowed backwards from the crowd into a corner.

A man behind his back said: "We never got that signal. I got it from Purvis in T.87. He flashed it to me by lamp round about one o'clock."

Chambers turned; there was a little knot of R.N.V.R. officers standing beneath a blue poster warning them not to discuss naval matters in public places. He judged them to be off the trawlers that came into harbour every night. Another said:

"We ought to carry more life-saving equipment. I'd have got more of them if I'd had a couple of Carley floats."

"Couldn't the boats have got them?"

"There were only two proper seamen in the boat. They had all that they could do to keep her head to sea, of course. The ones in the water were just drifted away." The speaker paused, and then said very quietly: "It was a stinking bloody mess. I've never seen anything like it."

"Much fuel oil about?"

"God, yes. They were covered with it—the ones that were in the water. Just choked with the bloody stuff. I'd have picked up a few more of them if it hadn't been for that."

"How many did you get in all?"

"Thirteen in the boat and then we picked up seven from the water. We got three bodies, too."

"The women were all in the boat, weren't they?"

"No—of the seven we picked up, there were three women and four men. But two of the women died within ten minutes and one of the men. They'd been in the water over an hour."

Somebody said: "Christ. I suppose they were practically gone when you got them?"

"Just floating in the life-jackets, you know. To all intents and purposes, they *were* dead."

"What about another?"

"I don't mind."

One of the Wavy Navy pushed his way towards the bar. Another said: "I don't understand why they only got one boat away. They weren't shelled, were they?"

"Not that I know of. We'd have heard it, anyway. But she went down still steaming ahead at about six or seven knots, as far as I could make out from what they said. They never got her stopped to get the boats down."

"She just went on till she went under?"

"That's right."

"Christ!"

Another said: "Who owned her?"

"I've no idea." And then another said: "Sanderson and Moore—Sunderland. They had the *Lochentie*, and the *Glen Tay*, and the *Glen Ormond*."

Chambers turned to them. "I'm sorry—I heard what you said about the *Lochentie*. I'm Coastal Command, patrolling in your sector."

The other nodded. "In an Anson?"

"That's right. Tell me—was it a submarine?"

"Must have been. Too deep for a mine—there's thirty fathoms of water out there."

"Did you see anything of the submarine?"

"Not a smell of it. Did a bit of listening, but she'd been gone an hour. Nothing to go by."

Another said: "She'd slip away ten miles and then lie quiet on the bottom till nightfall. She might be anywhere."

Chambers said: "Can't you get her when she surfaces?"

The trawlerman shrugged his shoulders. "Got a couple of drifters out there now on listening patrol. It's just a chance if they contact her in the dark."

One of the others said: "What are you drinking?"

Chambers said: "I don't see why you should. Well, gin and Italian."

He turned back to the first speaker. "I was on the morning patrol," he said, "but my zone was to the east of you. It was filthy visibility—we couldn't see a thing. I'm afraid the chap who had that zone missed the ship altogether."

The other nodded slowly. "An aeroplane flew near us twice while we were picking up the boat. We heard it, but we couldn't see it."

One of them said: "It's a wonder you come out at all, this sort of weather. Bill Stammers picked one of your Ansons out of the sea on a day just like this about a month ago."

Chambers said: "I know. Chap called Grenfell was the pilot. Flew right in. He and the wireless operator ruined themselves. That's the one you mean?"

"That's right. The other two were in a little rubber boat."

"Too bloody cold for that this weather."

"You're right. Though for December it's not as cold as it might be."

The pilot said: "We could do without all this blasted rain."

He stayed with them for a quarter of an hour and stood a round of drinks. Then he said:

"Well, I must go and feed. I'll keep my eyes skinned for your little friend when I'm out tomorrow."

The officer who had rescued the survivors said suddenly and harshly: "If you see the bloody thing, give it everything you've got."

There was a momentary silence.

The young flying officer nodded soberly. "Okay," he said. "I'll do that, with your love."

He went off to the grill.

II

IN the Pavilion the lights swung and changed colour on the dancers. The floor was crowded. Most of the dancers were in uniform, sailors and officers mixed indiscriminately. There was a sprinkle of khaki and of Air Force blue, but most of the uniforms were naval.

Chambers swung the girl deftly in and out of the crowd of dancers on the floor. They were laughing together in the changing lights. She still wore the plain black frock that she had worn when serving in the bar; he had not allowed her time to go back home to change.

> I like to dance and tap my feet,
>   But they won't keep in rhythm—
> You see I washed them both today
>   And I can't do nothin' with them.

They turned and side-stepped merrily in an open space.

> Ho hum, the tune is dumb,
>   The words don't mean a thing—
> Isn't this a silly song
>   For anyone to sing?

He said: "Don't sing that song. It sends an arrow right through my heart."

She bubbled with laughter. "You do talk soft. What's it this time?"

"I had a date with Snow White. I broke it to come here and dance with you."

"You do tell stories. It was Ginger Rogers last time."

"I know it was. They're all after me because I dance so well."

29

"Do you tchassy in a reverse turn when you dance with Ginger Rogers?"

"We won't go into that again," he said, with dignity. "I do it every time I dance with Snow White. And what's more, Disney makes it look all right."

She laughed again up into his face. "He must stretch out one of your legs to make it look all right, like Pluto's tail."

Presently the dance came to an end. He took her back to the table which they had left loaded with their overcoats to retain it and bought strawberry ices for them both. Presently she said:

"What do you do when you aren't flying?"

He said: "I'm writing my autobiography. It's the right thing to do that when you're twenty-three."

She looked at him uncertainly. "You don't know how to write a book, I don't believe."

"Anyone can write that sort of book. I'm going to call it *Forty Years a Flying Officer*."

The dance-hall was built out upon a pier on the seafront. Beneath their feet the tide crept in over the sand, menacing in the utter darkness. Outside no lights whatever showed upon the waste of waters. On the black, tumbling sea a very few ships moved unseen, unlit, and stealthily. Twenty miles out two little wooden vessels lay five miles apart, with engines stopped and drifting with the tide. In each of them a man sat in a little, dimly lit cabin. Before him was an electrical apparatus; he wore head-phones on his head. From time to time he turned the knob of a condenser.

He sat there listening, listening, all the winter night.

Over her strawberry ice the girl said: "No, but seriously, what do you do when you aren't flying?"

He said: "I build ships."

She laughed again. "No—seriously."

"Honestly, that's what I do. I'm making a galleon."

"Like what you buy in shops, in bits to put together?"

"That's right."

Her mind switched off at a tangent. "Wasn't it terrible about them people in that ship today?"

His mind moved quickly. There had been no mention of the loss of the *Lochentie* in the evening paper. He said innocently:

"What ship was that?"

She said, wide-eyed: "The one you was talking about in the bar. You know."

He said: "I never talk of naval matters in a bar. It tells you not to on the poster."

She said: "Don't talk so soft. You was talking to the officers off the trawlers all about it, the ones what picked the people up out of the water."

He said: "I knew you were a spy right from the first. The next thing is, I threaten to denounce you to the police unless you let me have my way with you."

She said: "If you're going to talk like that, I'm going home."

He said penitently: "I'm sorry. I was only going by the books."

"Well, don't be so awful."

"Did you hear all that we were saying?"

She said: "Not all of it, because of turning round to get the things from the shelves. But you'd be surprised if you knew what we got to know behind the bar."

He nodded, serious for a moment. When old friends in the service meet for a short drink and a meal, not all the posters in the world will stop a few discreet exchanges on the subject of their work. Leaning upon the bar, they say these things in low tones to each other, so low that nobody can hear except the barmaid at their elbow.

He said: "Let's go and dance again."

They went out for a waltz. He was not a bad dancer,

and like most girls of her class she was very good. They were together well by this time, and went drifting round the floor weaving in and out of the crowd in a slow, graceful rhythm. A faint fragrance came up from her hair into his face; he was quite suddenly immensely moved.

He said: "You've done something to your hair."

She laughed. "I had it washed." She paused and then said: "Do you like it?"

"Smells all right."

"You do say horrid things. I never met a boy that said such horrid things as you."

He squeezed her as they danced. "It's the stern brake I have to keep upon myself. If I told you what I really thought about you you'd slap my face and go home."

She laughed up at him. "I'll slap it now just for luck."

"Then I'll have you arrested. You can't do that to an officer in war-time. It's high treason."

Presently they went and sat down again for a time. He lit a cigarette for her, and said:

"What else did you do today besides getting your hair washed?"

"Did the shopping for Mother before going to the snack-bar. We open at twelve-thirty, you know. Then in the afternoon I had my hair done and went home for tea."

"And back to work again."

"That's right. What did you do?"

He considered. "Did a spot of flying. Just scraped clear of a blazing row."

"What about?"

"Only something to do with the work. Then I worked on the galleon for a bit."

"How big is it?"

He showed her with his hands. "About like that."

"What are you going to call it when it's done?"

"Mona."

She was pleased. "You do talk soft—really you do. What else did you do after that?"

"After that? I—oh, my God, yes—I came into Southsea and bought a rabbit."

She stared at him in amazement. "A rabbit? Whatever are you going to do with that?" And then she said: "You're just kidding again."

"You hurt me very much when you say that." He turned and rummaged in the pocket of his long blue overcoat. "You don't deserve to see it."

He pulled out the carton. She bent across the table curiously, her head very close to his. He opened it and took out the lamp, clicked the switch, and the rabbit glowed with light.

She breathed: "Isn't it lovely! Wherever did you get it from?"

He told her. "I went in there to get a lipstick and saw it on the counter."

"A lipstick?"

"I've got it on now." He took the mirror from her bag and looked at himself. "I think it's rather becoming."

"You are the silliest thing ever. You don't use lipstick."

"That's all you know. They told me it was kissproof in the shop. Do you mind if I try and see?"

"Yes, I do."

They went and danced again. The dance was coming to an end; the quick-step accelerated to a wild gallop round the floor. Then the music stopped, the band stood up, the men drew stiffly to attention and the girls tried to imitate them as "God Save the King" was played. Then the gathering of coats and bags, and they were out in the car-park by the chilly little two-seater.

Chambers said: "I'm not quite sure how it's going to go tonight. It's been rather bad recently."

The girl said: "It'll go if you want it to."

They got into it. "I expect you're right," the pilot said. "If it stops we'll just have to sit and wish, and wait for it to start again."

She said: "I don't believe that it'ld ever start that way. The only way to make it start would be to get out and walk home."

He shook his head. "If it should stop—and mind you, I don't suppose it will—we'd better try my way first."

The girl said: "We'll try yours for ten minutes. After that, we try mine."

"All right."

The engine stopped beneath the trees a quarter of a mile away.

Twenty miles out to sea a tired sub-lieutenant shoved his way into the cramped, dimly lit listening-cabin. The man with the head-phones raised his head. "Nothing yet, sir," he said in a low tone, half whispering. "Single screw steamer bearing east-north-east—that's all so far."

The officer put on the head-phones. "Give you a spell."

They changed places and the listener went out; in the dim light the officer sat down before the instruments and turned the condenser slowly, searching round the dial. Outside in the utter darkness the waves lapped against the hull; a small tinkling came from a loose shovel in the engine-room each time the drifter rolled. These mingled with the hissing in the head-phones, and a rhythmic beat at one position of the condenser knob that was the steamer, far away. There was no other sound.

In the imagination of the sub-lieutenant there came a vivid picture of a German listener in a similar, dim cabin curved to the shape of the hull, slowly turning a similar condenser knob upon a similar apparatus.

"Bloody thing must know we're here," the tired officer muttered to himself. "He'll probably stay where he is until tomorrow night. . . ."

In the dark privacy of the little car parked snugly underneath the trees, Chambers said softly:

"The girl told me it was kissproof in the shop. Shall I strike a match and see?"

The girl nestled closer into his arms. "No. You do talk silly."

A thought struck the pilot. "What about yours?"

"My what?"

"Your lipstick. I've got to go back to the mess before I can wash my face."

She rippled with laughter against his heavy overcoat. "Mine comes off like anything. You'll look a perfect sight. All the other officers will know what you've been doing."

"I'll get cashiered."

"What does that mean?"

"Sacked."

She said: "I'll wipe it off for you in a minute, when you take me home."

"In half an hour."

"In a minute," she said firmly.

"Then we've not got much time to waste."

Presently she said: "It's been a lovely evening, Mr. Chambers. I have enjoyed it, ever so."

The pilot said: "My friends all call me Jerry."

"I can't call you that. I'll call you Roddy."

"Jerry."

"All right then. Now go on and take me home."

"Jerry?"

She laughed softly. "Go on and take me home, Jerry."

"When are you coming out with me again?"

"You haven't asked me yet."

"Tomorrow?"

"I can't tomorrow. Uncle Ernest, in the *Iron Duke*—he's coming to see us tomorrow night, and I said I'd be home early. His ship came in yesterday. He's Daddy's brother."

"What about Thursday?"

"All right." She wriggled erect in the seat beside him. "Let me clean your face."

"Better do that when I get you home. It might get dirty again."

The worn engine of the little car came noisily to life and they drove through the black, windy streets to the furniture shop that was her home. There the engine came to rest, and the little car stood against the kerb, motionless and silent. Five minutes later the girl got out on to the pavement, stuffing a soiled handkerchief into the pocket of her coat.

She turned back to the car, and stooped to the low entrance. "Good night," she said softly. "It's been lovely."

"Good night, Mona," he said. "Thursday."

"Thursday," she said. "I'll be there."

She stood for a moment fumbling in her bag for her latch-key; then the door opened and she vanished inside. Chambers sat watching her till she was out of sight, then started up the engine and drove off.

The girl ran quietly upstairs to her room and shut the door behind her. It was not the first time that she had been kissed in a dark motor-car on the way back from a dance, but she had never been much moved by it before. It had never produced in her such a mixture of feelings. She felt safe with him, queerly safe, though with her reason she reflected that his motor-car was hardly a safe place for her. She understood him better than she had ever understood the others; there was no guile about him. His irresponsible talk sometimes puzzled her because she wasn't used to it, but in this his mood was very like her own. She felt that she could fall into his ways very easily. He never worried her at all.

She got into bed and pulled the clothes around her, happy and a little thoughtful. She was not quite in love with him, but she knew that she could be very deeply in love with him if she were to let herself go. She did not quite know if she wanted to do that. She was a sensible girl, and older than her twenty-one years in experience. She knew very little of him, or his background. He had been to Cranwell, the cadet college; she knew that. That meant he was an officer of the regular Air Force, in it for a career, not just a temporary officer for the war. She knew that she was not quite of his social class, and she did not resent it. Her father had risen from the lower deck and kept a little furniture shop in a back street. They were different; you couldn't get away from that. She knew that her father and mother would disapprove of her going about with an officer, especially a regular officer. They'd say that no good would come of it. Probably it wouldn't. But she was going to meet him Thursday, all the same.

She drifted into sleep, happy and smiling to herself.

Chambers drove back to the aerodrome, still tingling with the warmth of the girl's presence. He reflected semi-humorously as he went, that he was probably making a fool of himself. He had no sisters, and he had not had a great deal to do with girls. His family comprised a widowed mother who lived in a suburb of Bristol, and an older brother.

Instinctively, he knew that he was dangerously close to a real love affair. Never before in his life had he thought much about marriage, but he was thinking of it now. His reason told him that marriage was absurd. He was far too hard up on his pay as a flying officer even to think of it; moreover, from all he had heard, you didn't marry barmaids—you seduced them. He shied away from that; he had a poor opinion of it as a hobby, and he wouldn't have known how to set about it. It disturbed him that he should feel rested when he was with her. He could say whatever came into his head without fear of misunderstanding. She was young, and she was healthy, and to him she was very beautiful.

He drove into the car park of the mess, moodily cursing his lot as an officer. He didn't think that it would be a very good thing to marry a barmaid if he wanted to get on in the Royal Air Force. He felt resentment; the world should have been organised upon some different basis.

He parked the car, draped the rug over its bonnet, and lit the rabbit-lamp to find his way through the bicycles. It glowed lambent in the darkness of the blackout, a luminous ghost rabbit. Its red eyes led him to the back door of the mess.

In the ante-room he paused and looked at the operations board. Cloud, it appeared, was to be nine-tenths at two thousand feet during the morning. That was better, but the wind with it was thirty miles an hour from the south-west—not quite so good. Instinctively, he visualised the conditions; a wintry, gusty day, with fleeting glimpses of the sun. He ran his eye over the other notices; there was nothing new but one:

> No submarine is to be attacked tomorrow, December 3rd, in Area SL between 1200 and 1500, in Area SM between 1400 and 1530, and in Area TM between 1430 and nightfall.
>
> A. S. Dickens, Wing-Cdr.

Chambers stared at this for a moment; he would copy it into his notebook in the morning. It affected his own zone. He wondered sleepily what lay behind it; it was

like the wing-commander to keep his own counsel.
Damn silly, Chambers thought, but discipline was
frequently like that. There was nothing else upon the
board to interest him, and he turned away.

Then he remembered the *Lochentie*, and a gust of
irritation at official stupidity swept over him. "Let the
bloody thing get away," he muttered to himself. "Old
Hitler just makes rings round us. . . ."

He went up irritated to his room, his nerves on edge,
suffering a little from reaction after an emotional evening. At school he had read a little poetry of the more
conventional sort, and a familiar stanza came into his
head as he undressed:

> Ah love, could thou and I with Fate conspire
>   To grasp this sorry scheme of things entire—
> Would we not shatter it to bits, and then
>   Remould it nearer to the heart's desire.

He smiled a little as he put on his pyjamas. "Like
hell we would," he muttered to himself. He got into his
bed, still smiling at the thought. Very soon he was
asleep.

Next day was the change-over in patrol. The flight,
under Hooper, were to take the afternoon patrol for
the next month, the variation being designed to break
the monotony of the routine. Chambers was able to
sleep relatively late. He woke punctually at six o'clock,
according to the habit of weeks, and dozed in bed till
eight; then he got up and had a bath. He had finished
breakfast by nine, and walked over to the pilots' room
in the hangar.

Hooper met him there. "Sergeant Hutchinson's gone
to hospital," he said. "What about it, Jerry?"

Chambers grunted. "Good job, too," he said. "He's
been breathing influenza germs all over me for the last
two days. Who can I have instead?"

The flight-lieutenant said: "Nobody."

"Well, that's a bloody fine show. Am I supposed to go without a second pilot?"

"I don't know who there is to send with you. Do you?"

There was a momentary silence. There had been a spate of transfers from the station to the Bombing Command in the past week, to fill vacancies that had resulted from an injudicious raid on Heligoland Bight. The reinforcements from the Flying Training Schools were due to reach them in a day or two, but in the meantime there was a shortage of second pilots.

Chambers said disconsolately: "I suppose that means I'll have to take the thing alone."

"Send Corporal Sutton with you, if you like?"

The flying-officer shook his head. "I've got Corporal Lambert for the back gun, and the wireless operator. He can pass me up the charts."

The flight-lieutenant understood this well enough. The presence of a fourth man in the aeroplane who was not a pilot or a navigator was a hindrance rather than a help; he tended to get in the way of the quick movements of a pilot who was flying the machine and navigating at the same time. It was better to make the radio-operator hop around a bit.

Hooper said: "O.K. If you go alone today I'll let you have Sergeant Abel for tomorrow." The offer meant that he himself would fly alone on the next day.

Chambers said: "We'd better have a round of Santiago for it after dinner." They were great hands with the poker dice.

He set to work to copy out the orders for the day into the notebook that he would strap on to his thigh in the machine, including the order prohibiting the bombing of submarines. "Thank God it's better visibility today," he said when he had finished.

The flight-lieutenant nodded. "Don't want any more *Lochenties*."

Jerry said sourly: "The whole sea might be stiff with *Lochenties* and submarines, for all it matters to us. We're not allowed to bomb the bloody things if we do see them."

He left the hangar and went back to the mess, irritated and a little depressed. The mention of the *Lochentie* had brought back to his mind the memory of the conversation of the night before in the "Royal Clarence" bar. He heard again the voices of the trawler officers describing what they had seen. In his mind's eye again he pictured what had been described. Old women in life-belts and battered in a rough grey, breaking sea, dying of cold and choked with fuel oil. . . . And then on top of that, this order about not attacking submarines!

He had a cup of Bovril and a few biscuits in the mess at eleven o'clock, since he would miss his lunch. Then he went back to the hangar. The aircraft were out upon the tarmac with the engines running to warm up; the crews were moving about them. In the pilots' room the six pilots were putting on their flying clothing, two for each of the other three machines. He joined them, put on his flying-suit, boots, helmet and muffler, and strapped his notebook to his thigh. Then he went out to meet his crew.

They took off at eleven forty-five; the strong wind helped them off the ground. From a thousand feet the visibility was about five miles, uneven and much influenced by streaks of sunlight that came down occasionally through the patchy clouds. The flight kept a loose formation till they reached the coast, passing the morning patrol on its way back to the aerodrome. At the coast they split up, each proceeding independently to his own area.

Behind him, Chambers heard the clatter of the gun as
Corporal Lambert fired his usual burst into the sea to
test the gun. He turned in his seat and motioned to the
radio operator; the lad left his seat and handed him the
chart that he required. The pilot spread it awkwardly
upon the folding seat beside him and picked off his
course for the French coast. He set it on the verge ring
of the compass and climbed up to fifteen hundred feet,
the lower limit of the clouds.

All afternoon they swept backwards and forwards
above the cold grey sea, coming down near the surface
to inspect each ship they saw, noting her name and
nationality, her course and speed. Once in each half-
hour they approached the coast; the French coast to the
south of them, and the English coast to the north. They
did not cross the land; they came near enough to
establish their position accurately upon the chart, then
turned to a reverse and parallel course. After three or
four of these flights Chambers had gauged the wind
correctly, and each succeeding flight took place exactly
down the plotted line upon the chart.

The machine swept backwards and forwards over the
grey sea all afternoon. The crew grew gradually colder;
they sucked peppermint bull's-eyes, suffered the cold,
and watched the clock. At this time of year, in
December, darkness would release them before their
allotted time; that was a compensation for the cold.
Sunset that day was at 3.53. They would land at about
4.15.

As evening drew on the brief patches of sunlight disappeared and the sky became wholly overcast. The light
began to fade. They reached the English coast at about
3.25 and turned seaward once more; they would not
have time to do a full trip over to the French side, but
it was too early to go home. They droned out over the
darkening sea, flying at about sixteen hundred feet, very

close below the cloud ceiling. From time to time they swept through a thin wisp of cloud.

Ten minutes later Chambers saw a submarine.

He blinked quickly and looked again. It was a submarine all right. It seemed to be about two miles ahead of him, going slowly in a north-westerly direction, a short line upon the sea with a lump in the middle. Something turned over in the pilot's chest as he looked at it, and the thought flashed through his mind that he was within thirty miles of where the *Lochentie* had been destroyed. God had been kind to him. He was to be the instrument of retribution.

He pulled heavily upon the wheel and shot the monoplane up into the cloud base immediately above him. He throttled his engines in the dark fog of the cloud and slowed the machine as much as he dared; they must not hear him if it could be helped, or they would dive beyond his power to harm them.

The sudden changes startled the crew from their semi-coma. Corporal Lambert slid down from the gun turret into the cabin and started forward; the radio-operator woke up with a jerk. The pilot turned in his seat, his young face crimson with excitement.

"Submarine!" he yelled. "Up on the surface, about two miles dead ahead of us!"

The corporal nodded, and slid back into his turret; he had the gun to tend. The pilot turned feverishly to the chart. In spite of the excitement, he must mind his orders. Area SM, up to 1530. . . . He shot a glance at the clock upon the panel in front of him; it was 1539. They had turned at 1527—twelve minutes on the new course since they turned. Say twenty-six sea miles. He slapped a ruler down upon the pencilled line that he had drawn upon the chart. They were in Area SM still. Area TM was a good two miles over to the west.

It was all right to attack.

In spite of having throttled back the engines the
machine had climbed to nearly two thousand feet,
thickly enveloped in the cloud. The speed was down to
less than a hundred knots. The pilot pressed the stick
a little, and swung round for a quick glance up and
down the cabin. In the gun turret the corporal stooped
down to look forward at him, and held one thumb up
cheerfully. Chambers turned forward, settled into his
seat, and pressed the machine into a dive.

She gained speed quickly. She broke from the clouds,
diving forty degrees from the horizontal. The pilot
looked round frenziedly to find the submarine.

He saw her still upon the surface, well over to his
left, a thin pencil on the dark grey, corrugated sea.

The rush of air along the windscreen rose to a shrill
whine. He could not drop his bombs upon a turn and
hope to hit; it was essential to come down on her in a
straight dive. He muttered: "Damn and blast!" and
swung the monoplane in its dive over to the right. He
leaned forward and tripped two switches on the bomb-
release control, selecting a stick of four of his small
bombs and making the firing-switch alive.

He shot a glance at the air-speed indicator. Beneath
the notice which said, SPEED MUST NOT EXCEED
200 KNOTS IN DIVE, the needle flicked between 230
and 240 upon the dial. He glanced again at the submarine and judged his moment, then swung the monoplane towards her in a turn to port, easing the wheel
towards him very slowly as she did so.

The submarine loomed up ahead of him. She was
nearly bow on to him, a good position for attack, but
one which hid the sides of the conning-tower from his
view. He concentrated desperately upon identification
marks. He dared not bomb unless he could see something to distinguish enemy from friend. He could see
no one in the conning-tower; already she was lower in

the water, and she was moving ahead. She was going down.

British submarines carried identification marks upon the hydrovanes. He could see the hydrovanes ploughing in a smother of foam as she moved ahead in the rough sea; they were turned to press her down. In the split seconds of the final stages of his dive he watched in an agony for the colour of the metal in the foam. Then the trough of a wave came, deeper than the rest. For an instant the port forward hydrovane was bare of foam, streaming with water that showed grey paint underneath.

He cleared his mind of that, and for less than a second concentrated all his being upon levelling the machine off. Then, as the bow of the submarine passed out of view beneath the bottom of his windscreen, the gloved hand on the throttles moved to the firing-switch and jabbed it firmly. The first stick of four bombs fell away as the monoplane swept forty feet above the low grey hull.

The machine rocketed up to three or four hundred feet, and the pilot threw her round in a steep turn. Behind him he heard the rattling clatter of the gun as Corporal Lambert blazed away at the steel hull. Then the submarine swung round into the pilot's view again as the monoplane banked steeply round her.

One of the bombs had landed near the foot of the conning-tower, or on it; the superstructure was all wreathed in smoke. A stick-like object, mast or periscope, had fallen and was poking sideways from the conning-tower; the pilot got an impression that the submarine had stopped her engines. The deck was awash by this time; she was quickly going down.

There was no time to be lost. He had not hurt her seriously, and she could still submerge beyond his reach. He swung his body brutally on the controls and forced the monoplane towards her in a dive again. He leaned forward quickly to the switchbox and selected four more of his little bombs and one of his two big ones.

Again she loomed up very quickly in the windscreen. He pulled out of his dive just short of her and jabbed the bomb switch viciously. There was an instant's pause, followed by the clatter of the gun again, and the detonation of the bursting bombs behind him. Then came a more thunderous explosion as the big bomb with delay action burst under water.

Again the pilot forced his machine round in a violent turn. As soon as the submarine came in view he saw a change. She was higher in the water than when he had last seen her over the greater portion of her length, but the stern was down. Beside the stern there was a great subsiding column of water from the explosion of his big bomb; a great mass of foam and bubbles was showing all round her.

He thrust the monoplane into a dive at her again. She was now end on to him, badly damaged; he was attacking from the stern. He selected the last of his big bombs and four more little ones, and came at her once again. As the stern passed below his windscreen he pushed hard against the button on the throttle-box.

He rocketed up from her, and turned. His heart leaped as she came in view. There was a great column of water close beside her, rather forward of the conning-tower; the bow was rising from the water. As he watched, fascinated, the bow rose clean out of the water, grey and dripping, like the nose of a monstrous, evil reptile. It was wholly repulsive, a foul, living thing.

He stared at it for a moment, circling round. Suddenly a jet of brown liquid gushed out from the nose, falling into the sea and completing the illusion of a reptile. Chambers stared down with disgust and loathing. It had ceased to signify a ship to him, ceased to have any human meaning. It was something horrible, to be destroyed.

His upper lip wrinkled as he forced his machine round. From the look of the thing he guessed that it was holed; he leaned forward and pressed down all the remaining switches on the selector-box. As he swept over it again he pressed his bomb switch for the last time, and the whole of his remaining bombs left the machine.

He swung the monoplane round more gently this time; he could do no more. When the target came in sight again the bow was practically vertical; the conning-tower was well submerged. The sea was boiling all around her, in part from the explosion of his bombs and in part from the air that now was blowing from the hull. Slowly the bow slid down into the sea. The light was fading; it was too dark to make out much detail. Now there were only six feet left above the water.

Now there were three feet only. Now just the tip.

Now it was gone.

There was nothing left except a great circle of white, oily water on the grey, rough sea.

He relaxed for a moment. The wireless-operator was by his side, looking over his shoulder through the windscreen. Chambers said: "That's finished him."

Above the roaring of the engines the boy yelled: "Good show, sir. First in the squadron!"

The pilot nodded. "It's probably the one that got the *Lochentie*!" he shouted.

He turned and looked behind him. The corporal was leaning down from the gun ring, crimson with pleasure, beaming all over his face, and holding up both thumbs. The pilot grinned and held a thumb up in response, then turned back to his work again.

At some time in the incident he felt that there had

been a ship. He circled round for a minute, peering into the gathering night. At last he saw her. She was a trawler, painted grey, in naval service. She was about three miles to the south of him, headed towards the scene at her full speed.

He swept low over her and circled round; from the little bridge above the chart-house an officer was waving at him. He waved back in reply and flew ahead of her, to dive on to the scene to show her where it was. There was nothing there to see now except a circle of oily water with a great mass of white bubbles coming up. The trawler would buoy the place and pick up any wreckage that there was.

He flew back to the trawler and stayed with her for ten minutes, till she reached the spot. Then, in the dusk, he set a course for home.

The corporal left the gun turret and made his way along the cabin to the pilot. He was bursting with pride. "Poor old sergeant, he won't half be mad when he hears about this," he shouted. "Fair kicking himself, he'll be."

Jerry broke into a smile. "Too bad he wasn't with us," he shouted in reply. "After all this time."

"Serve him right. Shouldn't go catching colds."

He squatted down behind the pilot, staring ahead through the windscreen. Presently they crossed the land; ten minutes later they approached the aerodrome. The corporal wound the under-carriage down as the machine swept low over the hangars; as they crossed the tarmac they saw men stop and stare at them.

The corporal laughed. "They've seen our bomb racks empty," he said gleefully. "That's what they're all looking up at."

The pilot brought the machine round to land; the flaps went down. The hedge slid below them and the ground came up; Chambers pulled heavily upon the wheel and the machine touched and ran along. It slowed and came to rest; Chambers looked round behind and turned into the hangar.

It was practically dark when he drew up upon the tarmac. One or two aircraftsmen came running with unwonted energy; the corporal hurried down the cabin and jumped out of the machine.

One of the men said: "What happened to the bombs, Corp?"

Corporal Lambert swelled with pride. "Fell on a bloody submarine, my lad," he said. "Proper place for 'em, too."

The news ran from mouth to mouth. "Did you sink it, Corp?"

"Where did it happen?"

"Were there any ships about?"

"Did any other aircraft have a hand?"

"Did you get fired at?"

The crowd swelled quickly round the corporal. "Officer sunk it, lads," he said. "Mr. Chambers. I didn't do nothin' but fire the bloody gun, and that's no flaming use against a sub."

"Was it the one what sunk that ship what was torpedoed yesterday, Corp?"

"I can't tell you that, lad. Officer thinks it was."

Chambers got down from the machine, clutching his maps. There was a thin, spontaneous cheer from the crowding men. He was embarrassed, and stood there in his flying clothes, blushing a little, taller than most of them.

"Thanks awfully," he said awkwardly. "We had a bit of luck this afternoon. Pity Sergeant Hutchinson couldn't have been with us."

They cheered him again, more loudly this time. He pushed his way through them and went towards the pilots' room; a dozen of them followed after him. It was practically dark. Hooper came running out to meet him. "Jerry—is this true?"

"True enough, old boy," he said. "We plastered it good and proper."

"Did you sink it?"

"Sunk it all right. It went right up on end; the bow was vertical."

"Bloody good show! Did anybody else see it?"

"There was a trawler about three miles away. I showed her where it happened."

They went together to the pilots' room. There was a surge of pilots round Chambers as he got out of his clothes, with a volley of questions. He changed in a babel of voices and discussion; in the middle his squadron-leader, Peterson, came in.

There was a momentary hush. The squadron-leader said: "Is this true, that you got a submarine?"

The young pilot straightened up. "Yes, sir. I don't think there was any doubt about it."

He told his tale again. The squadron-leader said: "Well, that's all right. I'll just ring Dickens, and see if he wants to see you now, or after you've made out your report."

He lifted the telephone, but the wing-commander's line was engaged.

Hooper said: "I vote we go and break open the bar."

The surged over to the mess in a body, gathering other officers to them as they went. The news spread through the camp like a running flame. It was dark by this time, and work was over for the day. In the ante-room Chambers stood flushed, and embarrassed, in the middle of a crowd of officers, a pint pot of beer in his hand, besieged by questions.

In the babel of talk and congratulations the mess waiter pushed into the crowd. "Wing-Commander Dickens on the telephone," he said. "He wants

Squadron-Leader Peterson and Mr. Chambers over in his office."

Chambers drained his can, and followed the squadron-leader out of the room. They put on overcoats. Outside the night was very dark, with a thin drizzle of rain.

The groped their way over to the wing-commander's office with some difficulty; neither had thought to bring a torch. In the corridor they paused for a minute and tapped on the door. Dickens said: "Come in."

He was alone, seated at his desk. He got up slowly as they entered. He said gravely: "Good evening."

He turned to Chambers. "I understand you sank a submarine this afternoon?"

The young man was a little daunted by the heavy manner of the wing-commander. Surely there could be nothing wrong? He said: "I attacked one, sir. I think she sank all right."

The wing-commander took a paper from his desk and handed it to him. "This signal has just come in."

Puzzled, the squadron-leader looked over his shoulder and they read it together. It was despatched from trawler T.383. It read:

> Submarine destroyed by Anson aircraft 1541 area SM/TM. Recovered floating two British naval caps, one British naval jumper, two empty packets Players' cigarettes. Returning to port immediately. Position buoyed.

There was dead silence in the office.

Dickens said heavily: "I'm afraid one of our own submarines is overdue. H.M.S. *Caranx* isn't answering any signals."

The telephone bell rang. The wing-commander crossed to his desk and picked up the receiver.

The operator said: "Captain Burnaby upon the line, sir."

III

CAPTAIN BURNABY, as usual, was direct and to the point. He said: "I have spoken to Fort Block-house, Wing-Commander. They are sending Commander Rutherford over to my office at once. Will you please come in immediately, and bring the pilot with you? You'd better come to my office, in Admiralty House."

Dickens said: "Very good. I have the pilot with me now."

"Then I shall expect you at about a quarter to six." The wing-commander glanced at the watch upon his wrist; it gave a bare half-hour with fifteen miles to go, mostly in traffic, in the darkness of the black-out. The naval officer went on: "What has he to say?"

"He's only just come in, Captain. I haven't heard his story yet."

"Well, we won't waste time with it on the telephone. Get a car and bring him in with you. In the meantime, I have warned a salvage vessel to be ready for sea at midnight, and I have a drifter standing by the buoy. It's possible that some of them may still get out with the Davis escape gear. T.383 should dock in an hour's time, and we shall see then what they've got."

"Is there still no answer from the *Caranx*?"

"The last signal was received at two o'clock. She should have passed the Gate an hour ago."

There was a pregnant silence. The wing-commander said quietly: "I'm very sorry to hear that."

Captain Burnaby said shortly: "Quite so. I am sure that we are all very sorry, Wing-Commander. Now will you please get straight into a car and come to my office, with the pilot of the aeroplane."

Dickens hung up the receiver, and turned to Chambers. "What letters did the thing have on its conning-tower?"

The pilot hesitated. Then he said: "I never saw them, sir."

Beside him the squadron-leader said gently: "Why not, old boy? Didn't you look?"

The pilot turned to him, flushed and anxious. "I never got a chance. When I got out of the cloud he was over on the left, and going down quick. I had to take him from the bow in the first attack. You can't see the letters when you're on the bow."

Dickens said: "But after the first dive—you made several, didn't you?"

"Yes, sir."

"Didn't you see his conning-tower when you came round?"

"No, sir. There was smoke all round it. I got a direct hit with the first stick."

"But how did you know it wasn't a British submarine, then?"

"It had nothing on the hydrovanes, sir. No identification marks at all."

The wing-commander stared at him. "But you said it was going down. Could you see the hydrovanes?"

The boy hesitated miserably, irresolute. After a time he said: "Yes, sir. I saw them clearly."

The wing-commander got up from his chair. "We'll have to get along," he said. "Come on. We'll walk down to the Transport."

Chambers said: "May I go and get my coat, sir?"

"Yes—be quick." The boy turned to leave the room. Dickens called after him: "Bring a torch, if you've got one—the battery's run out in mine. Can't get about the dockyard without a torch in the black-out."

"I'll bring mine, sir."

He left the room, and managed to slink in unnoticed through the back door of the mess to fetch his coat. In the office that he had left the wing-commander put on his own coat. Then he turned to the squadron-leader.

"It doesn't look so good," he said.

Petersen shook his head. "It doesn't." He turned to the other. "Be careful you don't get him rattled," he said. "He's a good lad, you know. I should be surprised if he'd made a mistake like this."

The wing-commander bit his lip. "It's the Navy I'm afraid of. They're liable to tear him in pieces."

The squadron-leader nodded ruefully. They left the office and walked down towards the transport yard; a car was waiting for them there. The squadron-leader said:

"I suppose that notice about not bombing submarines this afternoon was because *Caranx* was coming in?"

"Yes." The wing-commander hesitated. "I suppose I should have made it clearer."

"We usually do let the pilots know what's going on," the squadron-leader said deferentially.

The wing-commander bit his lip, and they walked on in silence. He had framed his notice in that way because he had been irritated with Hooper, because he thought that the junior officers were getting insubordinate and should be disciplined to concentrate solely upon the job that they were told to do. He reflected that his instructions had been carried out to the letter. Chambers was blameless, technically. The notice had said that no submarine was to be bombed in Area SM up till 1530; the action had taken place at 1541 according to the trawler's signal. *Caranx*, if it were she who had been sunk, was late upon her schedule; she should have passed that spot an hour before.

Still, if the pilot had known *Caranx* was expected he might have taken special care. . . .

That was absurd. You could fight a war if every order had to be explained, to everybody. In this thing the whole fault lay with the Navy. If *Caranx* was dangerously late upon her schedule she should have sent a signal; he could have changed his orders then.

His heart sank as he contemplated the future. If *Caranx* really had been sunk there were the makings of a blazing row that would go straight up to the Cabinet.

Chambers was waiting for him at the car; they got into the back seat together in the utter darkness and were driven into Portsmouth. They said very little on the drive. The flying-officer was frightened and confused. He was not certain of himself. He was sure in his own mind that the submarine he had sunk was not a British ship; he could not satisfy himself with proof. Once Dickens said:

"You're quite sure that you saw the hydrovanes?"

The boy said: "I saw one of them, sir—the port one at the bow. It was painted grey—not coloured, like ours are."

"But you saw it properly—clear of the water?"

"It had water on it, sir. But I saw the colour of the paint."

"You're quite sure of that, Chambers?"

"Yes, sir."

They lapsed into silence again. The wing-commander sat brooding in his corner. Ten minutes later he said:

"How did you know which area you were in?"

The flying-officer explained the steps that he had taken. The wing-commander nodded in the darkness; it was reasonable. Still, it was very near the knuckle. The pilot reckoned he was two miles to the east of area TM, but two miles wasn't much deviation in the thirty miles that he had flown from his last known position. The older officer was sick with apprehension. If this thing had occurred in Area TM their goose was cooked.

The trawler evidently had not known where she was, for she had signalled Area SM/TM.

The car drew up at the dockyard gate and put them down; no cars could move about the dockyard in the black-out. That rule had been made for safety, following on the discovery of a terribly battered car upon the concrete bottom of an empty dry dock, with two dead naval officers in it. They were stopped at the gate by the dockyard police, who telephoned to Captain Burnaby for authority to pass them through.

Inside the dockyard the darkness was intense. The wing-commander said: "Got that torch?"

Chambers pulled out the rabbit-lamp and lit it. The white rabbit glowed luminous in the darkness; by its light they made their way over railway lines and between railway trucks, past docks lined with empty, deserted ships, past the caissons of dry docks sheltering the monstrous bulk of great vessels ablaze with welding torches and vibrant with the clatter of the riveters. Presently they turned down a quiet alleyway and came to the Georgian building where their meeting was to take place.

Captain Burnaby occupied an office of an antique style. It was a tall, white-painted room, with high windows between straight white columns with clean, vertical lines. It was a room that had heard the affairs of many frigate captains in its day. It was still redolent of them. The framed charts upon the wall themselves were anything up to a hundred years old; a coal fire burned brightly in the Georgian grate. A modern touch was given by the battery of telephones upon a wide, old-fashioned desk.

There were three naval officers in the room, who came forward from the fire as the two Air Force officers came in. Captain Burnaby said grimly:

"Good evening, gentlemen. We've been waiting for

you. Wing-Commander Dickens—this is Commander Rutherford, from Blockhouse. And Lieutenant-Commander Dale."

Dickens bowed slightly. He said: "This is Flying-Officer Chambers."

The captain moved toward a green baize-covered table, laid out with paper and pencils for a conference. "This is not a formal meeting," he said succinctly. "But I think we shall get on more quickly if we take it as such." He seated himself at the head of the table, in the position of a chairman, and motioned to the wing-commander to take the seat at his right. Chambers hurried to sit down beside the wing-commander, leaving his hat upon the captain's desk with the lamp inside it. The other naval officers sat on the captain's left.

For a moment Chambers studied the naval officers, and his heart sank. The massive, square-cut features of the captain were set in a grim mould; the iron-grey hair and the bushy eyebrows were those of a martinet, a hard, efficient man. In comparison, he thought he saw a gleam of kindliness and understanding, even of sympathy, in the appearance of Commander Rutherford from Fort Blockhouse, the submarine depot. The last of the three was a dour, scornful young man with raised eyebrows.

Burnaby said: "Well now, gentlemen, we're here to get the facts of what occurred this afternoon. That's the first thing, before we can decide what action we must take." He turned to the commander from the submarine depot. "Rutherford, will you tell us first what orders *Caranx* had?"

The commander said: "She had orders to proceed here from Harwich, sir."

"Quite so. On the surface, I suppose?"

"Oh yes. She wouldn't dive unless there was a very

good reason for it. She was coming round to have——"
He checked himself.

The captain said: "I don't think that's material." He
turned to Dickens. "She was coming back for certain
work to be done?"

The wing-commander nodded.

The captain turned again to Rutherford. "Now, tell
us her scheduled route and times."

The commander took a paper from his attaché case
and laid it on the table. "This is the operation-order I
made out," he said. "It's rather long." He turned its
pages over. "She was due to pass from Area SL to Area
SM at 1430 and from Area SM to Area TM at 1500.
In the order for closing the areas against attack I gave
her half an hour margin each way on those times." He
paused, and then said: "She should have passed the
Gate between 1600 and 1615. If she was later than that
she'd have to anchor in the Roads."

The captain said: "Exactly." He picked up the sheets
of buff typewritten paper, and glanced them over
rapidly. "This is a copy of what you sent me? Yes." He
scrutinised the list of copies sent out at the head of one
page. "I see. And this sheet went to Coastal Command
of the Royal Air Force."

He turned to Dickens, and put the paper before him.
"This is the sheet that you received, Wing-Commander?"

Dickens nodded: "That's right."

The naval officer, pressing his point home, passed the
paper to Chambers. "And you saw this before you went
out on patrol?"

The pilot took the paper. It began with a short statement that a British submarine was to proceed upon the
surface in a westerly direction. Then followed a string
of areas and times restricting submarine attack.

The pilot said: "I've never seen this."

Captain Burnaby's mouth set into a thin, hard line; the bushy eyebrows drew together. He stared grimly at the young man. He said: "Can you explain that, please?"

The pilot blushed and hesitated. Dickens interposed. "You saw a shortened version of it on the notice board?"

Chambers said: "Yes, sir. I took a copy of it in my notebook."

Rutherford said: "I don't see how it could be made much shorter than it is."

The captain said mercilessly: "In what way was the notice that you saw different from this sheet, Mr. Chambers?"

The young man said: "It was the same, I think, except for these first sentences." He pointed to the typescript.

The wing-commander said: "I think that's right. We left out that for secrecy."

The naval captain stared at him for a minute. He was about to say that he was not accustomed to his orders being hacked about, but he thought better of it. Instead, he said to the pilot:

"Was the notice that you saw intelligible to you, Mr. Chambers?"

The flying-officer hesitated. "I understood that no attacks were to be made in certain areas at certain times," he said. "I didn't know why."

The commander from the submarine depot leaned forward. "You didn't know that one of our submarines was coming in, then?" he said kindly.

The boy turned to him gratefully: "No, sir. I didn't know that."

There was a tense, pregnant silence for a few moments. Then Captain Burnaby said: "Well, the Court of Enquiry will go into that, no doubt."

He picked up another paper from the table. "The signal from T.383 gives 1541 as the time of the attack, in Area SM/TM."

Chambers interposed. "It was definitely in Area SM, sir."

"That is what I want to hear about next, Mr. Chambers. If she was in Area SM you were clearly within your rights in attacking, subject to reasonable care. In Area TM you could not attack at all."

The boy said: "No, sir. But she was in Area SM all right."

The naval captain eyed him keenly. "How did you establish that?"

"I set out the course and distance run from my last known position, on the chart, sir. She was a good two miles inside Area SM."

"Have you got the chart here?"

"I'm afraid not, sir."

The sour-faced young lieutenant-commander spoke up. "How far away was your last-known position?"

The pilot turned to him. "I made it about twenty-six sea miles."

Lieutenant-Commander Dale raised his eyebrows slightly higher. "Two miles drift wouldn't be much of an error in the sort of navigation that you do, would it? I don't see how you can be so sure about the area."

Chambers said: "I wasn't two miles out."

Dale shrugged his shoulders. "The trawler doesn't seem to be so certain, or she wouldn't have signalled Area SM/TM."

Burnaby turned to the pilot. "I take it that you plotted the position carefully upon the chart?"

The boy hesitated awkwardly. The three naval officers sat staring at him. At last he said: "I didn't pencil the position in. You can't do that when you're flying the machine."

The captain said: "I understand you have a second pilot."

"I hadn't got a second pilot today, sir. He'd gone sick."

Lieutenant-Commander Dale spoke up again. "How did you do the chart work, then, if you couldn't leave the helm?"

"I had the chart on the seat beside me. I laid off the course and distance run with a parallel ruler."

The young naval officer's upper lip curled slightly. "Working with one hand?"

"Yes."

Dale turned to Captain Burnaby. "I don't see any proof of the position here, sir," he said sourly. "You might be anywhere, working like that."

The captain said: "I quite agree with you."

There was an awkward silence. The pilot stared at the glass ash-tray on the green-baize tablecloth flushed and miserable. He began to feel that they were all hostile to him; their minds were made up. He knew his navigation methods hadn't been according to the book, but he had faith in his position. He was used to rapid chart work under difficulties.

He tried to explain to them. He said: "I really don't think I was two miles out in the position, sir. I made decent landfalls all through the patrol."

The young lieutenant-commander raised bored eyebrows slightly higher. Rutherford, from Fort Blockhouse nodded, but said nothing.

Captain Burnaby said: "Well, the trawler buoyed the place, so we shall know before long where it actually happened. Now, Mr. Chambers, will you tell us just what occurred, from the time when you first saw the submarine until the moment when she sank."

The boy said: "I saw her first about two miles away. It was beginning to get dark. I couldn't make out any detail—just that there was a submarine there. Then I went straight up into the cloud."

They sat staring at him, silent, as he told his story.

The lieutenant-commander, Dale, listened with all the overbearing confidence of youth. He had little knowledge of the Air Force, or of anything outside the Navy. He had entered at the age of fourteen and had lived in, and lived for, the Navy ever since. He was efficient. He hated inaccurate, slovenly work. He never made mistakes himself; they were unnecessary, beastly things. Only damn fools made mistakes. Here was this blushing, stammering young ass who had the insolence to say that he could work out a position accurately, working with one hand upon a chart that was sliding about on a seat cushion. The result was that he had made mistakes—not one, but a whole flock of them, and one of them had caused the *Caranx* to be sunk. He listened in a cyncial cold rage.

Rutherford listened sympathetically. He was closer to the disaster than the others. He knew all the officers of *Caranx* intimately, had messed with them for months. Most of his service life had been spent in submarines and he had known several disasters. He had come to realise this one only an hour before, but already he had accepted with a numbed acquiescence that never again would he meet Billy Parkinson, or play a round of golf with Stone, or drink a beer with Sandy Anderson. Presently he would have to write the letters to Jo Parkinson and Dorothy Stone, and to Anderson's mother at Dalry. From his experience he knew how these things happened. Good men, honest, competent chaps, made a mistake—a hatch had been left open one time. As a young lieutenant he himself had very nearly sunk his own submarine by doing the wrong thing with a lavatory flush. If it were true that *Caranx* had been lost by this young pilot's mistake, the fault was rather in the

system that put such power into the hands of inexperi-
enced young men. There was no blame in his mind
for Chambers. He had been older than that when he
had had his trouble with the lavatory.

Captain Burnaby listened with a mind overlaid with
policy. Throughout his service life the strategy and
tactics of reconnaissance had been his speciality. He had
been in destroyers for much of his time, and had risen
to the command of a flotilla. Now he was in this shore
job and in intimate liaison with the Royal Air Force.
For the first time in his life he drew reports from a service that he did not control. He felt like a horse in
blinkers. He could not reach out quickly and pull in his
information as he had done all his life; he must ask
another service if they would get it for him, and they
would only do so if they had the time to spare, or so he
felt. He was perpetually maddened and infuriated with
the restraint. He believed, with all his heart and soul,
that the existing system was totally wrong, that the aeroplanes patrolling the narrow seas should be under naval
control, staffed by the Navy, part of the Fleet Air Arm.
Most of the Admiralty, he knew, agreed with him. Dual
control was inefficient, and mistakes were bound to happen. One of them had happened now, and a valuable
unit of the Navy had been sunk by this young fool.
Perhaps after this the Cabinet would listen to the Admiralty case. The *Caranx* was a bitter and a serious loss,
but if, through her, the Navy were to gain control of its
own air service, she would not have been lost in vain.

Dickens sat warily watching, sitting on the fence. He
knew all that passed in the simple, direct mind of Captain Burnaby; he realised the political aspect of the
matter to the full. He could not help his pilot and he
did not much want to. If Chambers had really sunk
the *Caranx* it was a bad show, a piece of inefficiency
discreditable to the Royal Air Force. The pilot would

have to suffer, as a matter of course. It was much more
important that the relations of the Navy and the Air
Force should not be impaired; in time of war there
must be no internal quarrels. He knew the Navy wanted
their own coastal patrol; he believed that they had too
little experience of aeroplanes to take it over, especially
in time of war. Dickens sat quiet, watching the naval
officers and their reactions, biding his time.

They heard him to the end in silence; only from time
to time the captain prompted him. He finished and sat
staring round at them unhappily. "That's all I can remember," he said at last.

Captain Burnaby said: "I take it, then, you never saw
the letters on the conning-tower at all?"

The pilot said: "No, sir—I didn't. I never bothered
about them once I saw that there was no identification
marking on the hydrovanes." He paused, and then said:
"I did look for them once, but there was smoke all
round the conning-tower."

The captain said: "Didn't you think it worth while to
make certain?"

Chambers said: "I was certain, sir. It never entered
my head that it could be a British submarine. We're
usually told when our own submarines are in the
Channel."

Rutherford said kindly: "You get notices about our
own submarines pretty frequently, do you?"

The pilot turned to him. "Almost every other day.
That's why it never occurred to us that this had anything to do with our own submarines. It wasn't in the
usual form." He paused, and then he said: "I'm quite
sure this was a German. There was definitely nothing
on the hydrovanes."

Lieutenant-Commander Dale said: "I wish I could
be as sure as you are. You said that one of the hydrovanes washed clear as she was going down?"

"Yes—it was free from foam."

"But it was clear—out of the water, I mean?"

Chambers said: "It wasn't dry, of course. There was water on it, but there were no bubbles—no white foam."

"How deep would you say the water was upon it? Five or six inches—or more?"

The pilot strained his memory to recall the instant flash that he had seen in the last stages of his dive. "Not so deep as that. There might have been an inch of water on it."

"It was getting dark, though, wasn't it?"

"There was light enough to see the colour of the paint."

"Even under water, seen obliquely as you saw it?"

The pilot hesitated. "What I saw was grey paint."

There was a short silence. Burnaby said: "Well, we shall have to leave that point."

Rutherford leaned forward. "May I ask him a few questions, sir?"

The captain leaned back in his chair. "By all means."

The submarine officer turned to Chambers. "Did you notice how many jumping-wires she had?"

"That's the wire that runs from bow to stern over the conning-tower, isn't it?"

"That's right. Did she have one or two?"

The pilot stared at the ash-tray in concentration. Then he raised his head. "I can't say, sir," he said. "I didn't notice."

The commander pushed a paper and a pencil over to him. "Draw us a picture, showing what she looked like, broadside on."

They leaned across the table and watched him intently as he drew. When it was finished, Rutherford pulled the sketch towards him and examined it critcally.

"The one gun forward fits with *Caranx*," he said pensively, "but so it does with most types. Are you sure this prolongation of the conning-tower towards the stern was there?"

The pilot hesitated. "I think it was like that."

Captain Burnaby said: "Is that similar to *Caranx*, Rutherford?"

The submarine officer shook his head. "*Caranx* goes like this." He sketched a line upon the drawing; the modification was not very great. He turned to Burnaby. "Unless you know submarines, they all look much the same," he said. "This doesn't look like *Caranx*—but then, who can say?"

Burnaby said: "I'm afraid we're rather wasting our time, Commander. A sketch like this would only be of use if it showed something definite—two guns instead of one, or something like that. The rest of the evidence is overwhelming."

The man from Fort Blockhouse nodded slowly. "One more question, sir." The captain inclined his head. "What colour was this submarine you sank? Was she light grey or dark grey?"

The pilot said: "She looked very much like any of our submarines—about the same colour. She wasn't very light grey, like a battleship that's been out in the Mediterranean. She was a sort of medium grey—on top, that is to say. She was all rusty underneath."

The commander leaned forward. "She was what? Rusty?"

"Yes, sir. When she put her nose up, just before she sank—the bottom was black paint all streaked with rust."

Rutherford turned to the captain. "*Caranx* was only docked six weeks ago," he said. "She shouldn't have been rusty after six weeks."

Burnaby stared at the pilot. "Are you quite sure of that?"

"Yes, sir. She was definitely rusty underneath."

The captain turned to the commander. "Is that very unusual, Rutherford?"

"It is, rather, sir. They go rusty very quickly in the tropics, of course. I've seen it happen in home waters when they've had electrical defects—you get electrolytic action sometimes. But it's quite unusual to have a hull go rusty in so short a time. They're just like ordinary ships."

"I don't see that we can get any further with this point, Commander. Have you any other questions?"

"I can't think of anything else, sir."

Dickens looked up. "May I raise a point?"

"Certainly, Wing-Commander."

"Somebody said that *Caranx* didn't answer any signals after two o'clock. That's an hour and forty minutes before she was sunk."

Rutherford said: "That's right. At two o'clock she reported herself off Departure Point."

"When did she fail to take a signal?"

The submarine officer glanced at a paper in his hand. "She was sent a signal asking her estimated time of arrival at the Gate, at 14.13. There was no reply to that one. The last signal received from her was sent at 1403 reporting her position."

The Air Force officer said keenly: "So that you must have been worried about her before 1541?"

Rutherford nodded. "In a way, we were. We should have been very worried if she had been diving. But there was no reason for her to dive on a passage of that sort. We thought it was probably a temporary wireless failure. We kept on sending to her till we got the signal from T.383."

Dickens turned to the captain. "It's a point to remember, sir."

Burnaby nodded. "Certainly. I think there is no doubt that she was late on her schedule, and that she became late after passing. It looks to me as if she had some accident or mechanical trouble which delayed her, and cut the current off from her wireless. Is that likely, Rutherford?"

The submarine officer shook his head. "I don't think that quite fits. The wireless feeds straight from the battery."

There was a tap at the door. A signalman entered and laid a slip of paper in front of Captain Burnaby.

"The captain of T.383 is outside, gentlemen," he said. He turned to the signalman. "Ask him to come in."

They all rose from the table as the new officer came into the room. He was a burly man, in shabby uniform. He wore sea-boots and a thick, dirty white sweater that rolled heavily around his neck beneath a very old monkey jacket stained with salt. On his sleeve the blackening gold braid ran in the undulating rings of a lieutenant in the R.N.V.R. In his hand he carried a half-empty seaman's kitbag with some articles in it.

Burnaby said: "Good evening, Mitcheson. Is that what you picked up?"

The man said: "That's right, sir. I brought it right along, soon as we docked, because I thought you'd want to see it. Hope you'll forgive me coming in like this."

He spoke in an undefinable manner as a civilian, which, in fact, he was. Twenty-one years before, as a young man, he had commanded just such another trawler as the one that he had now, on just such duties. In the years between he had longed for his naval uniform. He had had ups and downs of fortune. He had been in the motor trade in Bournemouth and in the wool trade in Bradford; for a time he had managed a laundry in Cheltenham. He had managed a road-house near London, on the Great West Road, and he had travelled in haberdashery. None of these ventures had been a great success, none of them utter failure. All the

time he had longed passionately for the sea. He knew
that he had been better as a junior naval officer than in
any of his other jobs. As war drew nearer he made all
his preparations, pulled all his strings and got himself
back into the Volunteer Reserve. War came and he was
called up. Twenty years slipped off him like a cloak.
Gieves, the naval tailor on Portsmouth Hard, gave him
another sort of cloak, on tick. The Admiralty gave him
Rosy and Kate, of Grimsby. God gave him happiness,
and he went to work.

Burnaby said: "That's all right, man. Let's see what
you've got."

The burly man looked round. "Where will you have
them? They're all over oil and water still."

Beyond the carpet there was a patch of linoleum by
the window. "Put it there."

The trawler officer untied the neck of the kitbag and
turned it back. He put his arm in and drew out carefully some pieces of sodden pasteboard. Without a word
he gave them to the captain.

Soaked through with fuel oil and wet with salt water,
there was no mistaking them. They were the cartons of
two packets of twenty Players' cigarettes, more or less
intact. Burnaby turned them over in his hand.

"Can you be sure these came out of the submarine?"
he said.

Mitcheson said: "When I got there, there was a great
deal of air coming up from something on the bottom,
and there was a lot of oil about. These were floating in
the middle of the slick, near the clothing."

He turned the kitbag upside down and tipped its contents out on to the linoleum. A dark blue mass that was
a seaman's jumper fell out with a sodden flop, and a
seaman's cap rolled over to a corner. He reached into
the bag and pulled out another cap. "That's the lot, sir."

A smell of fuel oil penetrated the room. Rutherford

picked up the jumper. "Has it got a number on it?"

The trawler officer said: "I looked for that, but I couldn't find it."

Dale said: "It's probably a new issue."

They turned over the articles. There were no numbers on them, though one of the caps had the initials A.C.P. inked on the leather band. All were sodden with fuel oil; they dripped little pools of it upon the floor.

Rutherford said: "I can't see how they got so soaked in oil." He glanced at Dale. "Funny, isn't it?"

The other nodded. "Looks as if they'd been blown into a tank by the explosions."

Burnaby said: "Anything might have caused that."

Rutherford glanced at the trawler captain. "Is this all there was? Just these things?"

The man said: "That's all we could see. It was just on dark, you know." He hesitated, and then said: "As soon as I saw these I put a spar buoy down, right in the middle where the air was coming up."

The submarine officer nodded. "What's the depth?"

"Thirty-five to forty fathoms at low springs."

Rutherford said very quietly: "Christ. We'll never get a diver down to her." He turned to Mitcheson again. "Did you hear anything upon the hydrophones?"

"Not a thing. We listened for a quarter of an hour before the drifter came up to take over. We heard the sound of air blowing out of something on the bottom. But nothing else."

"No tapping?"

"No, sir. Nothing at all."

Burnaby said: "*Redeemer* has been warned. She's loading two air-compressors now. She'll be ready to sail at midnight, with six divers on board."

Lieutenant-Commander Dale said quietly: "There's a gale warning, sir. Came through about an hour ago."

There was a momentary silence.

Rutherford said wearily: "I doubt if it's much good. Keep the drifter there, in case some of them get out with the Davis apparatus. But if there's no more sound from her, I shouldn't think it's going to be much good to send out the *Redeemer*. You'd need a flat calm and slack water to put down a diver to that depth."

The captain said: "I know." He bit his lip; there was the risk to the *Redeemer* to be thought about. Salvage vessels were at a premium with ships being torpedoed daily round the coast; it would not do to have *Redeemer* anchored in the middle of the Channel, a sitting target for all passing German submarines. If there were any prospect of salvaging *Caranx* the risk must be taken; he dared not send the vessel out upon the slender hope of salvage that appeared at present.

He said: "I shall keep *Redeemer* standing by." He turned to Dale. "Send *Redeemer* a signal, ordering steam at half an hour's notice from midnight onwards."

"Very good, sir." The young man left the room.

The captain turned to the trawler officer. "I don't think you need stay, Mitcheson. You can leave that stuff there."

The man said: "All right," and turned to go.

"Let me have your written report as soon as possible."

"Very good, sir."

The door closed behind him. The captain turned to his desk, away from the sad heap of sodden clothing on the floor beneath the window. The smell of fuel oil filled the room, a reminder in this quiet place of the grim facts of war. For once Captain Burnaby was tired. He was tired of being responsible for the safety of ships. He was worn out with his anxieties. He was tired of being stern with men to make them careful. All he had done could not avert disaster. First *Lochentie*, practically right beneath his nose in spite of his patrols, and

now *Caranx*. God knew, he had tried hard enough. He
had not spared himself.

The two Air Force officers and the commander from
Fort Blockhouse waited patiently for him to resume the
meeting.

Mechanically the captain reached for a cigarette from
the silver box upon his desk. His sleeve brushed an Air
Force cap and overturned it. There was a metallic clatter
on the desk. An object rolled over on to the blotting-pad
and miraculously became alight. A moulded glass
rabbit glowed suddenly upon the writing-desk, staring
at the captain with illuminated crimson eyes.

Burnaby stared at it, startled from his mood. *Caranx*
was lost, and this rabbit was a grotesque joke. It was no
time for jokes. The swift, choleric anger rose in him;
he stared round at the officers beneath the beetling,
bushy eyebrows. "Who does this thing belong to?"

Chambers said: "I'm sorry, sir. It's mine." He
stepped forward and picked it up, switching it off.

The captain said icily: "I might have guessed that,
Mr. Chambers." He strode over to the green baize
table and sat down again at the head of it, suddenly
furious. The others sat down in their chairs again.

Burnaby said: "Well, gentlemen, I shan't keep you
much longer. You've heard what has been said. I shall
report to the C.-in-C., and he, of course, will order a
Court of Enquiry to be convened."

He stared grimly at Dickens. "I don't know what
your view is, Wing-Commander. In my mind there is no
doubt that *Caranx* was sunk by this young gentleman
with you, who does not seem to me to be sufficiently
responsible to carry out the duties you entrust him with.
The Court of Enquiry will settle where the blame
should lie for the accident, whether with the captain of
Caranx or with the pilot. And we must try to get the
Court to make some recommendations that will prevent

such valuable vessels being lost like this in future. I
think that's all. Is there anything else before we dis-
perse, Wing-Commander?"

Dickens said slowly: "I don't think so. From what
I've heard I feel that the blame does not rest solely on
Mr. Chambers for this accident. The only other thing I
have to say is what I am sure you know already—that we
in the Air Force regret the accident most deeply."

The captain said coldly: "Thank you, Wing-Commander." He got to his feet and the others rose with
him.

Chambers said hesitantly: "I'd like to say one thing.
If I did make a mistake, I'm most frightfully sorry." He
paused and then said: "It's sometimes a bit difficult
when you've got to act very quickly."

The captain nodded shortly, a grim, square-jawed
figure; the iron-grey hair and bushy eyebrows were
more formidable than ever. "No doubt, Mr. Chambers,"
he said curtly. "But when you act quickly you've got to
be right."

He bowed to them as they left the room. At his side
the commander from the submarine depot gathered up
his papers. The captain stood staring at the closing
door and then relaxed. "A bad business," he said
quietly.

The submarine commander said: "Yes, sir." The
only thing to do was to look upon one's mates as ciphers,
figures that left no more regret than figures on a black-
board when they were rubbed out. Deep personal
friendships were no good in time of war. They were
luxuries of peace-time, like the ski-ing holiday in
Switzerland that he ached for in these black months of
the winter.

His mind reverted to the technical aspects of the case,
and his brow wrinkled in perplexity. "I can't make out
why *Caranx's* hull should have been rusty," he said. "I

wonder if any of this new de-gaussing stuff is doing it? I hope to goodness we're not in for trouble there."

The captain nodded. Technical matters were impersonal and easy, a relief to talk about. "You might have a word with Simmonds in the *Vernon* about that." He was silent for a minute, and then said: "Funny the way those things were soaked in fuel oil."

They glanced down at the sodden heap on the linoleum. The commander said: "I suppose in a mixture of oil and water they take up the oil in preference to the water."

The captain said directly: "Well, I thought it was the other way about. I thought the surface tension of oil was greater than water, and that in a mixture they would take up water rather than the oil."

The commander smiled. "I'm afraid you've got me there, sir. I should have to look up the text-books."

Captain Burnaby turned away, a little heavily. "I must be wrong about it—anyway, it doesn't matter." There was a little pause. Outside the rising wind whipped round the building with a faint moan in the utter darkness. "We can't send out *Redeemer*," he said quietly. "I don't think it's justifiable."

The submarine officer inclined his head. "I don't think it is." Thirty miles away, deep under the black, wintry sea, young Sandy Anderson must be already dead. That letter to his mother was going to be the worst one of the lot, much worse than the ones to the wives. It would be foolish to expose *Redeemer* to the risk of a torpedo. Burnaby was right.

He said heavily: "The only thing to do now, sir, is to see that this can never happen again."

The captain's lips set in a thin line, the bushy eyebrows drew together in a frown. "I'll do that," he said grimly, "if I've got to put a naval officer in every aeroplane of the Coastal Command."

IV

IN the car on the way back to the aerodrome, creeping at slow speed through the utter darkness, Chambers said to the wing-commander beside him:

"I know it looks bad, sir. But I'm still absolutely positive that there was nothing on the hydrovanes."

From the blackness of the seat beside him Dickens said: "I wonder if the paint could have got rubbed off?"

"No, sir. I saw grey paint—definitely."

"I'm afraid you'll have a job to convince the Navy of that, in face of all the other evidence."

The boy shrugged his shoulders hopelessly. "I can only tell you what I saw."

They drove on in silence. In the chill blackness the wing-commander sat huddled up in his coat in his corner of the saloon, thinking ruefully of the enquiries that would follow. He would not escape censure for his modification of the order about *Caranx*. He had done it for the best, or so he had thought at the time, but it would be chalked up against him in the service. This static war might last for ever; peace might come and find a surplus of wing-commanders in the Royal Air Force. He might be forced into retirement at the age of forty, all through this young fool Chambers.

He must see the A.O.C. and get his word in first, before the Navy.

They got back to the aerodrome at nine o'clock. The wing-commander said:

"The A.O.C. will want to see you in the morning, Chambers. You'd better get to bed now. I expect you're pretty tired." He hesitated for a moment. "You won't be going out upon patrol tomorrow."

The boy said quietly: "Very good, sir."

75

Dickens was suddenly compunctious. "Don't take it too much to heart," he said gruffly. "These things do happen, but they're soon forgotten. Especially in war-time."

"Thank you, sir."

They separated outside the mess. Chambers went round to the back and in by the back door, and went straight to his room. In the corridor and on the stairs he passed one or two of his fellow-officers; he brushed past them quickly with averted head, and they pretended to be too busy themselves to stop to speak with him. He bolted into his bedroom and shut the door.

At the same time Wing-Commander Dickens was telephoning to the Air Commodore from his office. "I've just got back from the dockyard, sir," he was saying. "I'm afraid there's no doubt about it—they got clothes and stuff up from her. But I think she was late on her schedule, so that the pilot was quite justified in attacking. No, sir—as a matter of fact, I've sent him up to bed. He really isn't fit for further questioning. I thought perhaps you'd see him in the morning, when he's had some sleep. Very good—I'll come right along now."

In his room, Chambers threw off his coat and gas-mask and sat down upon the bed, utterly miserable. It seemed to him to be incredible that this thing should have happened to him. Accidents like this did occur from time to time, he knew. Anti-aircraft-gunners sometimes got our own machines confused with enemy raiders and shot them down. Single-seater fighters had been known to do the same. More similar still, he had heard a story of a submarine who had wirelessed to her home port:

> Estimated time of arrival 1500 if friendly aircraft will stop bombing me.

Always before he had been scornful of these incidents,

had considered that appalling carelessness had caused them. But he had not been careless. At least, he didn't think so.

To add to his unhappiness he was very hungry. He had eaten nothing since the Bovril and biscuits that he had had before starting out on the patrol, though he had sucked a few sweets in the machine and he had drunk a mug of beer when they were congratulating him in the mess. He did not care to go downstairs and forage round for food; he might meet somebody and have to talk. In the room there was nothing to eat except a bottle of malted milk tablets, sent to him by his mother to take out with him upon patrol. He settled down, depressed, to empty the bottle.

It was too early yet to go to bed; he would not sleep. He turned to his wireless set, the jumble of valves and condensers on a bare baseboard that he had put together himself from an article in a magazine. He turned it on, and the American voice brought him comfort. The words, "This is station WGEA, an international broadcast station owned and operated by the General Electric Company at Schenectady, New York," consoled him with a sense of achievement; he himself had conjured this statement from the ether. Presently a talk for schools upon the work of the W.P.A. in reducing distress in South Carolina penetrated his consciousness and took his mind from the submarine.

After a time he sat down at the table and pulled the galleon towards him on its stand. It was very nearly finished now; the sails were bent, and there was little more than touching up left to be done. As the woman's voice told him about the difficulties of the poor whites in the South, his hands reached out mechanically for the brushes and the little pots of paint.

There was a red cross of St. George to be painted on the lateen sail, perhaps with a gold border. There was

the name to go on the stern gallery—*Mona*. He plunged
into another gloomy train of thought. It was very
probable that he would never again see Mona, after
the *Caranx* episode. He could not face the bar of the
"Royal Clarence," filled as it always was with naval
officers. He could not show himself dancing at the
Pavilion, the man who had sunk *Caranx*. It would be
impossible for him to carry on in Portsmouth. If he
were not cashiered—and that was quite a possibility—
he would have to put in for a transfer. He would apply
to be posted right away from the district. He would try
and get to the Bomber Command, and see some real
war in Heligoland Bight.

For the name of the galleon it would be better to
stick to *Santa Mría*. But he grew tired before he came
to paint it in. Dance music from Schenectady lulled
him to a doze; the fine lines that he was painting on the
sail began to waver. Presently he put away his paint-
pots, turned in to his bed and slept heavily for the first
part of the night.

Over his head the thunder rolled that night. In
Whitehall, at about ten o'clock, there was a bitter row
between an Admiral of the Fleet and an Air Marshal,
which ended by each in turn seeking a private audience
with the Prime Minister, which neither got. All evening
a string of questions from the Air Ministry came to Air
Commodore Hughes; he sat up with Dickens until after
midnight. On one point the Air Commodore was
adamant; he would not rouse the pilot to interrogate
him again that night.

At a quarter to twelve Operations had enquired how
many hours the pilot had done on Ansons. The Air
Commodore swore softly. "What on earth's that got to
do with it? Tell the bloody fools, a hundred and fifty.
It's a good round number. Do they think I'm going to
get him out of bed to ask him that?"

Dickens gave the information and replaced the receiver. "The Navy must be raising merry hell."

The air officer nodded. "I'm sorry now I didn't go to Admiralty House with you and see Burnaby myself."

In the morning, after breakfast, he sent for Chambers. He greeted him kindly. In the last war he had himself been a sub-lieutenant in the Royal Naval Air Service; he knew a good deal about the difficulty of identifying ships from the air.

"Good morning, Mr. Chambers," he said. "You had a bit of bad luck yesterday, I hear."

"Yes, sir."

The air commodore took in the white, strained appearance of the boy. "Sit down, Chambers. Tell me just what happened."

The pilot told his story once again, this time to a more sympathetic audience. At the end of it the air commodore said:

"One of the most important points seems to be the position—whether you were really still in Area SM."

Chambers said: "I'm quite sure I was, sir. I'd got the wind correction taped. I'd made half a dozen good landfalls in the patrol. I'm quite sure the position was in Area SM."

The wing-commander said: "Well, the Navy buoyed the place. They'll waste no time in checking the position; if it's not in Area SM they'll raise a scream fast enough."

The A.O.C. nodded. "Burnaby must know by this time. We'd have had him on the telephone before now if it was out of Area SM."

Chambers said: "Has anyone spoken to Corporal Lambert to find out what he saw?"

Dickens said: "I have. He didn't see the hydrovanes at all. For the conning-tower, he said what you said: that it was all covered with smoke after the first attack.

He thought he saw it once, and he thought that there was nothing on it in the way of lettering. But he won't say for certain that he didn't see a film of smoke, mistaking it for the side of the structure."

The A.O.C. said: "His story really doesn't take us any further."

He eyed the pilot sympathetically. "I'm afraid there can be no doubt that it was *Caranx*," he said quietly. "The clothing alone shows that. But in my view, the Navy are alone responsible for this. You've got nothing to reproach yourself with. The submarine was in the wrong place at the wrong time, and either through negligence or accident she did not advise anybody of her change in schedule. Further, it seems very doubtful if her identification marks were properly in order."

The wing-commander raised his eyebrows. "Are you going to say that, sir?"

"Certainly I am. If the Navy want a row, they can have it. I'm getting rather tired of being blamed for their mistakes." He paused, and then said: "We still haven't heard the reason why the *Lochentie* wasn't in convoy."

There was a short pause. Then the pilot said: "There's one thing, sir." He hesitated. "I think it would be better if I put in for a transfer."

The air officer looked at him kindly. "Not so far as I'm concerned, Chambers. If the Court of Enquiry dig up any more evidence, it may be different. But from what I've heard so far, you have no reason to transfer."

Chambers said in a low tone: "That's terribly nice of you to say that, sir. But I don't think it would be very comfortable for anyone if I stayed on after this."

The wing-commander nodded. The air officer said: "That may be so. If you go, where would you like to go to?"

"I'd like to go to the Bomber Command, sir. Somewhere away from this district—in France, or in the north of England."

The air officer absently made a note upon his blotting-pad. "I'll see to that. You'd better go on leave until the posting." He thought for a moment. "The Court of Enquiry opens at three o'clock this afternoon, in Fort Blockhouse. I shall come to that with you."

"Thank you, sir."

"I expect it will go on tomorrow. I'm not putting you under any form of arrest, because I don't see any reason for it. Stay about the place in case you're needed, but you won't go out upon patrol. As soon as the court is closed, you can go off on leave until your posting. I shall want to see you again before you go."

"Thank you, sir."

The Court of Enquiry sat that afternoon in a big lecture-room opening upon the garden quadrangle of the submarine depot. In the dark winter afternoon a light snow was falling, powdering grass and flower-beds. The Court met under the presidency of a Rear-Admiral, with Captain Burnaby and a captain from the depot to support him. Air Commodore Hughes attended for the Royal Air Force, with Wing-Commander Dickens, but they were admitted by courtesy and not by privilege. This was a naval enquiry into the loss of a naval ship.

All afternoon the Court considered evidence. The witnesses were not admitted to the hearing, but sat in constrained silence in an ante-room. Rutherford gave evidence of the movements of *Caranx*. Chambers was summoned, and told his tale once more, faltering a little under the cold scrutiny of the naval officers. He answered several questions uncertainly and with much hesitation; the enquiry produced nothing new. At last they released him and sent for Corporal Lambert, who faced them with cheery nonchalance.

"Never crossed my mind but what she was a Jerry," he said breezily. "What's more, I still believe she was." But, pressed upon that subject, he had nothing to substantiate his confidence.

The wireless operator followed him, diffident and ignorant. He had seen little or nothing of the submarine, being occupied in winding in the aerial and hanging on to his seat. He had never seen a submarine before, except once in the distance, and he knew nothing of identification marks. He thought that Mr. Chambers was a very careful pilot.

Lieutenant Mitcheson, R.N.V.R., followed, and told the Court how he had heard the sound of bombing and had seen the splashes three miles to the north of him in the fading light. He had turned towards the scene, winding in his sweep as he went. Far away, he had seen the bow of the submarine rear up till it was vertical and slowly disappear, but he could not distinguish details. The aeroplane had guided him to the spot. When he got there, there had been a mass of escaping air-bubbles coming to the surface, and there was a great deal of oil upon the water. On the hydrophones he had heard the rush of air escaping from something on the sea bottom, but he had heard no other sound. He had immediately dropped a spar buoy on the spot.

He had recovered certain objects floating in the middle of the slick, the objects that he now saw on the side-table. Those objects were all that he had seen. When he recognised the objects as the clothing of a British seaman, he had sent a signal on his wireless. Yes, that was a copy of the signal that he sent.

Questioned by the president, he did not know the position accurately at that time. It was somewhere near the boundary of Areas SM and TM.

By leave of the president, Captain Burnaby interposed that the position of the buoy had since been accurately fixed. It was in Area SM, eleven cables from the boundary.

Air Commodore Hughes half rose from his seat and caught the eye of the president. "May I draw the attention of the Court to the fact that that position is very close to the point estimated by Flying-Officer Chambers?" he said. "It confirms our own opinion that Mr. Chambers is a careful and reliable officer. I should like the Court to give full weight to the accuracy of his evidence on the position when they consider his evidence upon the marking of the hydrovanes."

The Rear-Admiral nodded. "I accept that point, Air Commodore. I was about to call for evidence upon the painting of the hydrovanes."

But Rutherford, recalled, said that he had been on board *Caranx* sixteen days previously at Harwich. He clearly recalled that the paintwork was in very good order. He recollected the appearance of the hydrovanes, and they were clearly marked. He did not think it possible that the paintwork could have suffered very greatly in the meantime. It would be possible to get Harwich on the telephone and confirm that no work had been done upon the hydrovanes or on the hull that would have obliterated the marks.

The Court then adjourned till the next morning.

Chambers drove back in silence to the aerodrome with the two senior officers, creeping along in the darkness in the Air Force car that had waited for them outside the court. In the blackness of the transport yard they separated, and the pilot went up to his room. It was only about six o'clock.

There was nothing for him to do, nothing to read. He shrank from going downstairs to the mess to meet with other officers, perhaps be questioned. He sat down at his table wearily and drew the model of the galleon to him. But it was practically finished, all barring the name.

Then he remembered it was that night he had a date with Mona, to dance with her at the Pavilion. He'd have to break it; he could be seen dancing at the Pavilion—the man who had sunk *Caranx*. At that same time, he longed to talk to her. He wanted to be with her, to tell her of the fearful mess he'd got himself into. She might agree to meet him somewhere else.

At that time Mona was taking off her coat in the passage behind the snack-bar. She was looking forward to the couple of hours of dancing that would come after her four hours of work. She had made considerable preparations for her evening. She was wearing new shoes and new ribbed rayon stockings. She had bought herself a little blue bottle of scent in Fratton Road called "Bal Masqué", and she had used it with discretion. She had spent some time upon her finger-nails, and she had bought a little bunch of violets for the front of her dress. She walked into the bar and began to arrange her glasses, humming a little tune.

Her friend Miriam said: "My aren't we all got up tonight? Going dancing?"

She nodded, eyes sparkling. "Mm."

"Got a date?"

"Mm."

Miriam, deeply curious, said: "Who is he? Is he a sailor?"

It was on the tip of Mona's tongue to say he was an officer, but she refrained. Instead she tossed her head, smiled brilliantly, and said: "Just somebody I know."

Her friend said "My!" again. And then: "Where did you get them stockings, dear? I think they're ever so chick."

The first customers began to come into the bar, and they had no more time for gossip. Once opened, the snack-bar quickly filled with officers with their wives or with their girls, or else in parties of three or four, all gravitating for a drink and a cheap meal before the last house of the pictures. To the girls behind the bar, each evening had a character of its own. Saturday night was always crowded and hilarious, Friday was usually busy. The other nights took their colour from the events of the day, or of the war. Gloomy nights of bad news alternated with riotous nights when there was good news to report; the night of the *Graf Spee* had equalled any Saturday there ever was.

This was a curious, sullen evening. The officers stood about in little groups discussing something in low tones, not drinking very much. In the first hour it was evident that something had happened. Mona, out in the passage to chase the bar-boy to come and wash the glasses, met Miriam looking for a new case of Four X.

Mona said quickly: "What's the matter with them all tonight? They're like a lot of stuffed dummies."

Miriam saw her case and darted for the bottles. "It's a submarine been sunk or something," she said hastily. "One of ours. Here, give me a hand with these, there's a dear. If you take two I'll bring the other four."

They went back into the bar and served the waiting crowd. The six bottles of Four X were for a little crowd of six officers from the trawlers that docked each night in the dockyard. They took their glasses and resumed their conversation in the low tones that had spread a furtive, sullen atmosphere into the grill that night.

One of them said: "I can't see why they didn't send out divers if they've really got the place."

"Too deep, isn't it?"

"How deep can a diver go to, anyway?"

"Three hundred feet's about the record, isn't it?"

"I thought they went deeper than that."

"The truth of it is, they don't know where she is at all."

There was a faint, general smile. "As a matter of fact,

they do know that. Maynard said that there's a drifter standing by—Kitchen's drifter. The one with the pink funnel."

Another nodded. "They know the place all right. It's in Area SM."

One said: "That's not what Rugson said. He said it was in Area SL."

"How did Rugson know? He only docked tonight."

"Rugson couldn't have known anything about it."

"Well, he did. He closed with Porky Thomas, T.192, in the forenoon, and Porky said he sailed right through the place this morning just after dawn, and there was oil still coming up."

"Was Kitchen there?"

"I don't think Porky said anything about a drifter. Rugson didn't say so."

"It could have been the place. I know, because Maynard said that Kitchen was standing by all night in case any of them got out. I think he's out there still."

Somebody laughed shortly and turned away. "Not much bloody hope of any of them getting out now."

"Where did Rugson say this place of Porky's was, then?"

"Off Departure Point somewhere. In Area SL."

Somebody said: "That couldn't have been anything to do with *Caranx*. They know where *Caranx* is all right. They got clothes up from her."

"Who said that?"

"I overheard Dale saying something about it. He said Mitcheson had brought in clothes and stuff that came up in the boil when she went down. I think that's right. Mitcheson came in yesterday, but he wasn't due to dock till Friday."

"Where's Mitcheson now?"

"I don't know."

Somebody said: "They opened the Court of Enquiry over in Blockhouse this afternoon."

Behind the bar, in a pause between the serving, Mona said quietly to Miriam: "You was right about that submarine. I heard them talking. *Caranx* they said the name was. One of our own. Isn't it awful!"

The other girl said: "Did you hear them say one of our own chaps did it?"

"You don't say!"

"I thought I heard them say that. One of the Air Force aeroplanes that bombed it by mistake."

"Not really?"

"That's what they was saying just now."

"But how could that happen? They got markings to show they're English, haven't they?"

"I dunno. That's what one of them was saying just now."

There was a momentary silence. Then Mona said: "Did *Caranx* commission here, do you know?"

"I couldn't say, I'm sure. Submarines do mostly, don't they?"

"I don't know."

A fresh spate of orders came and stopped their chat.

Towards nine o'clock Chambers crept into the city through the black-out in his little sports car with the dimmed headlights. He had finished the galleon, had painted MONA under the stern gallery in a wave of sentiment. He had not cared to face the ordeal of dinner in the mess, and he was very hungry. It was with difficulty that he had nerved himself to go into the snack-bar of the "Royal Clarence", but he knew no other way to get hold of the girl. If he nipped in and out quickly he probably would not be recognised.

He parked the car and went into the bar, cap in hand, his heavy grey-blue greatcoat pulled up round his ears. He thrust his way directly to the bar, blushing a little, and confused. Mona smiled at him, and he took comfort from it.

"Half a can," he said. She turned and brought it to him.

"Look, Mona," he said quietly, "I can't go dancing tonight." He saw the look of disappointment on her face. "I'm frightfully sorry, but I can't make it." He hesitated and looked at her appealingly. "Is there anywhere we could go and have supper, or something, instead?"

Out of the corner of his eye he saw, or thought he saw, one of the Wavy Navy staring at him. He said: "I want to have a talk to you."

"But why can't we go dancing, then?"

He said urgently: "I don't want to do that. I'll tell you afterwards."

She said: "We could go to the Cosy Cot, if you'd rather."

He knew the road-house at the entrance to the town, though he had never been there. "That's all right," he said. "Where shall I meet you?"

"You know the back entrance round behind in Clarence Lane?"

He said: "I'll find it. What time?"

"Five past ten."

The naval officers were talking in a little group and looking at him. He said urgently: "I'll be there. Thanks awfully, Mona." And with that he turned and made his way swiftly through the crowd towards the door.

She stared after him, puzzled and disappointed. The Cosy Cot wasn't half so much fun as the Pavilion, with the music and dancing, and the lights, and all. At her side Miriam said mischievously: "He ain't half nice-looking, Mona. You never said he was an officer."

The girl said: "He doesn't want to go dancing after all. He just wants to go somewhere and eat."

"Well, dearie, he's got to eat some time. Perhaps he hasn't had any tea."

She said discontentedly: "He could have had something to eat here, and then we might have gone to the Pavilion. I can't make him out."

Her friend said: "Never mind, dear. I think he looks ever so nice." A fresh wave of orders stopped their conversation.

Chambers shot out into the street again in fear of meeting anyone in the black, unfriendly street. He was intensely hungry. It was three-quarters of an hour before he could meet Mona, and it was snowing a little in the darkness. He did not dare to go back into the grill-room for a meal, nor to any place where he might possibly meet naval officers. He got into his car and sat uncertain for a few minutes, wondering where to go to. Finally he drove up to the railway station, parked the car, and went into the buffet for a stale ham sandwich and a glass of beer.

By five minutes to ten he was standing in the deeper blackness of the lane behind the hotel, waiting for the girl to come. He stood muffled to the ears in his greatcoat, cold and lonely, and uncertain of the reception that he would get from Mona. It now seemed to him to have been a piece of great foolishness to have come here at all. He'd only get a flea in his ear from her—another flea to join the many fleas that his ear now contained. He should have stayed in his room, taken an aspirin, and gone to bed.

She came to him presently, within a minute of her time. He saw her first as a slight, dim figure in the doorway and stepped forward.

She said: "Is that you, Jerry? It's ever so dark."

He said: "It's me all right."

"Where are we going to? The Cosy Cot?"

He said suddenly: "Mona—look, there's something

you ought to know about. I mean, you may not want to come out with me when you know, so I'd better tell you now."

She stared up at him, dimly seen; a little flurry of snow swept about them. "Whatever are you talking about?"

He said: "Do you know anything about submarines?"

"They was talking about one of ours that had been sunk tonight in the bar. *Caranx*, or some name like that."

"*Caranx* was the name." He hesitated, and then said: "Mona—I sank it."

She said: "Oh, Jerry . . ." There was a pause; she moved impulsively a little closer to him. "You poor thing!"

There was a momentary silence between them, as if to mark what she had said. In that minute they both realised without words that their relationship would never be again the casual, happy-go-lucky matter it had been before she had said that.

She said: "Was it an accident?"

"A sort of accident." He hesitated. "I didn't want to go to the Pavilion . . . in case people saw me. Would you rather I just took you home?"

She said: "But you want supper, don't you?"

"Oh, I'm all right."

"Have you had any supper?"

"I've just had a sandwich while I was waiting for you."

The meals of officers were not very familiar to her. Tea did not bulk so large in their life as it did in hers. She said a little doubtfully: "Did you have tea?"

"Not today."

"Do you mean you've only had a sandwich since dinner? You must be hungry."

He smiled down at her; there was infinite relief for him in her concentration on mundane matters. "I dare say I could do something with a steak and chips."

"I should think so. Let's go to the Cosy Cot. You wouldn't mind that, would you? I don't think officers go there very much."

"I'd like that. Are you sure you don't mind?"

"Of course not, Jerry."

They turned and walked towards the little car. The flying snow had blown into it a little and a thin powdering lay on the seat. It did not worry either of them very much. The thin layer on the road made driving easier in the black-out, and they made fair speed out to the Cosy Cot.

He drove into the car-park and stopped the little car outside the blackened building, from which no light shone. He got out and helped the girl out from her side.

"Before we go in," he said huskily, "I wanted to say 'Thank you.'" He took her in his arms and kissed her; she strained up on tiptoe and kissed him back.

"Poor old Jerry!" she said softly. "Now that's enough. Remember you're hungry."

He released her, laughing. "I am so."

They went into the Cosy Cot. It was a long, panelled hall completely filled with small tables and thronged with people eating inexpensive food and drinking beer. Most of the men were in uniform, sailors and soldiers and airmen; Chambers was the only officer to be seen. There was a clamour of conversation and a haze of smoke; it was the non-commissioned counterpart of the snack-bar of the Royal Clarence Hotel.

They found a table with some difficulty and ordered a steak and chips for Jerry and a fish and chips for Mona, with beer and cider respectively. It came presently, poorly cooked, but Chambers fell upon it ravenously.

The girl watched him in bewilderment as he ate. What he had told her was that he had sunk the submarine, and it had been an accident. She did not know exactly what he did, or what his duties were. But in her

short life she had met many men; she knew men far
better than girls of a more exalted social class. She knew
and could distinguish good men from bad men, silly
men from flippant men, competent men who would get
on from the charming inefficient ones. She could have
put nothing of this into words, but she knew well
enough. It was extraordinary to her that Jerry should
have made that sort of mistake. In the terms that she
had gleaned from the movies, it didn't make sense.

Twenty minutes later they were sitting very close
together over cups of coffee, smoking cigarettes. Not
far away from them a radio-gramophone was churning
out a long sequence of records that made private conversation possible even in that crowded room—

> South of the Border,
>   I rode back one day . . .
> There in a veil of white by candlelight
>   She knelt to pray . . .
> The Mission bells told me
>   That I mustn't stay—
> South of the Border,
>   Down Mexico way . . .

She said: "Jerry, what happened?"

He turned to her. "I sunk it with bombs," he said.
The strained, haggard look that had left him for a little
while came back as he spoke. "I thought it was a German one. And later they found out it wasn't. It was one
of ours."

"How awful! Didn't it have any marks on it to tell
the difference?"

He said: "I'm quite sure it hadn't—I'm sure of that
still. But I suppose it must have had. You see, they got
clothes out of it."

"Clothes, Jerry?"

"Yes, and a couple of packets of Players'." And then,

in a flood, the story all came out. For the first time somebody heard the whole story, unrestrained and unedited
in the pilot's mind, told without fear or thought of con-
sequences. The girl listened without interrupting very
much, trying to understand the work he had to do. She
was unused to mental concentration. Other people had
always done her thinking for her. Here she felt instinctively, with all her being, was something she must try to
understand if she was to help him, and she wanted most
terribly to help him. She bent all her energies to the
task of understanding.

Presently she said: "Where did it happen, Jerry? Was
it by Departure Point?"

He stared at her. "No—it was much more towards the
island. What made you think that?"

"There was some officers talking tonight. They
thought it was there."

"Well, it wasn't." He hesitated. "Did they know who
sunk it?"

"They knew it was an aeroplane what did it. I don't
think anyone knew it was you."

He said bitterly: "They'll all know about it before
very long."

There was a silence.

She said timidly: "They couldn't do anything to you
for that, though, could they? I mean, it was an accident."

He smiled a little. "I won't be able to stay on here,
after this. I don't suppose I'll be able to stay in the Air
Force after the war's over."

"Oh . . ." She said: "Will they send you away?"

He nodded. "I got it in before they did. I asked to
be transferred away from here to some other job." He
turned to her, miserable. "That's why I wanted to see
you tonight, Mona. I'm going away."

She looked up at him, bitterly disappointed. "When
are you going?"

"Very soon—as soon as the Court of Enquiry is over. It'll close tomorrow. I expect I'll be going the day after that."

"Where to?"

"I'm going to the Bomber Command. Either to France or somewhere in the north of England."

"You won't be round Portsmouth any more?"

He shook his head. "Not for some time. It's better to get away and make a new start somewhere else."

She said: "I suppose it is."

He turned to her. "It's been fun going out together," he said quietly, "and dancing. But for that I should be glad to get away."

She said: "I've loved going out with you." Tears welled into her eyes, but it would be absurd to cry.

He said awkwardly: "You know I told you I was making a galleon?"

She nodded.

"Would you like to have it?"

"I'd like it ever so, Jerry."

Desperately he sheered away from sentiment. "I mean, it's rather an awkward thing to take in the car because it's so delicate, you see. And I thought you might like to have it."

She said: "It's terribly nice of you to think."

He said: "I'll bring it to your house tomorrow."

She nodded. "I'll be home tomorrow afternoon."

For a time they sat disconsolate over the litter of their meal, not talking very much, depressed by rather mournful dance tunes from the radio-gramophone, all about thwarted love. Presently he paid the bill and took her home.

In the black street outside the furniture shop the car stopped for a few minutes; then she got out and went indoors, and went up quickly to her room. It was silly to be crying. He was a nice boy, terribly nice, but she hadn't known him long. Not nearly long enough to cry about him just because he was in trouble, and because he was going away.

Chambers drove back to the aerodrome, tired and resentful. He had passed the stage of being appalled at the loss of *Caranx*. He was still positive that the submarine carried no markings, but, marked or not, she had been out of position. In an impersonal way he was sorry for the people in her, but he was beginning to be sorrier for himself. He felt that he had not been careless, that he had done his job as well as anybody could. He felt that the Navy were making a scapegoat of him for their own ends. A great deal of criticism had been given to his own efficiency, but very little had been said of the undoubted fact that *Caranx* was in the wrong place.

He felt that he was being used unjustly as a pawn in a political intrigue, that he was being disgraced and made to change his squadron without proper cause. In normal times the change would not have worried him at all, but leaving Mona hurt most damnably. Desperately seeking to comfort himself, he reflected that in time he might feel that he was well out of it. She wasn't his sort, really. He was getting dangerously fond of her. He felt at home with her; that he could talk to her freely and she would understand.

To hell with everything! If he had to go, let it be quick. If the Navy had to blacken his career, let them get it over and done with, and then let him get away.

He drove into the yard, parked the car, and walked in the glow of the rabbit lamp to the back door of the mess. Up in his room he turned on his wireless to America and got a peculiar religious service, in which the Glory of God and the merits of Bergson's Baking Powder were given equal prominence. It brought him comfort by diverting his mind to a trail of wonder, and in time he slept.

Next day the Court of Enquiry sat in private, hearing no more witnesses. At the end of a couple of hours their findings were committed to typescript and sent by special messenger to the Admiralty, who in due course approved them. The findings were:

That H.M.S. *Caranx* was sunk with all hands at 1541 on December 3rd, 1939, by the action of an Anson aircraft under the command of Flying-Officer R. Chambers, R.A.F.

That the captain of the submarine was to blame for having departed from his time schedule without notification.

That sufficient care had not been exercised by Flying-Officer Chambers in identifying the submarine before attack.

That no useful purpose would be served by attempting salvage operations before the conclusion of hostilities.

Captain Burnaby came out of the court-room and walked with Rutherford across the grassy quadrangle of the submarine depot to the commander's office. Rutherford said heavily: "Well, that's the end of that." He must get those letters written now, and then it would be over.

Burnaby said: "There's one more thing. The Admiral wants us to draft the terms of the announcement for the Press Department."

The commander made a gesture of distaste. "All right, let's get that over now."

They went into his bare little office. He took a signal pad and a pencil from the desk. "How shall we put it?"

Captain Burnaby drew his brows together in a frown. "An accidental explosion, I should think."

"I suppose that's the thing to say." The commander turned the pad over and wrote rapidly upon the back of it. "Something like this?"

> The Admiralty regrets to announce that H.M.S. *Caranx*, a submarine of the 1933 class, has been lost with all hands due to an accidental explosion while at sea.

Burnaby took the pad from him and read it over for himself. "That'll do," he said. "It's true enough. The Press Department can re-word it if they don't like that."

He folded the sheet and put it in his pocket. Then he turned aside. "The thing to do now," he said grimly, "is to make quite sure that this can never happen again."

They discussed the methods of issuing time schedules for a few minutes. At the end, the captain said:

"What's this?"

The object was a large glass jar with a ground glass stopper, of the sort that small confectioners use to keep sweets in. It stood upon the desk. It was half full of a mixture of fuel oil and water, with a few bits of cloth submerged and floating in the liquid.

Rutherford said: "You know we were talking about surface tension the other night?"

"I remember. Whether cloth would take up oil or water from a mixture. Is this an experiment?"

Rutherford took up the jar. "I thought it would be interesting to see."

"Which do they take up?"

"Water." The commander took off the stopper, put his hand in and pulled out a piece of cloth. He squeezed it, and a little stream of water ran out.

Captain Burnaby stared at it for a moment. Then he said: "What does that mean?"

"I don't know, sir. There are several points about this thing that I don't understand."

The captain turned away. "In any case, it's all over now."

The commander thought: all except those letters.

V

MARKET STANTON is a village on the Yorkshire Wolds, ten miles from the North Sea. In 1934 the population was about four hundred people, and there was some talk of an aerodrome to be constructed on the undulating farm-land of the district. The population has increased of recent years, and now stands at about two thousand five hundred, mostly airmen.

It lies seven miles from Beverley, the nearest town of any consequence. Chambers got there in his little car in the fading light of a mid-winter afternoon and thought that he had never seen a place so desolate.

Caranx to him now was only a dulled, shameful memory. His leave had extended over Christmas; he had been at his home in Clifton for over three weeks. It had not been a happy leave. He had not dared to tell his family about *Caranx*, and he had had to submit to a certain amount of mild hero-worship in consequence. His mother had been particularly trying. She had taken him shopping with her in the mornings, trailing along behind her, tall and blushing, in order that she might show him off to her friends.

She was very proud of him. "You remember Roderick?" she would say. "He goes out flying every day to protect the convoys, looking for submarines, you know."

Usually the friend would say: "I hope he sinks them for us," or words to that effect.

His mother would say triumphantly: "Of course he does. But, you know, they aren't allowed to say. We can't get a thing out of him."

This usually got him an admiring look.

She arranged tea-parties for him, two hours of the

same purgatory. He was fond of his mother and bore with it stoically, but he wished she wouldn't.

No, it had not been a happy leave. He had been restless and distracted over Mona. Their parting had been stilted and unsatisfactory. Immediately the Court of Enquiry had risen he had been seized with a blind urgency to get away, and there had been nothing to keep him. The Air Commodore had seen him for a quarter of an hour and had wished him luck.

"I'm not entirely in agreement with the findings of that Court," he had said. "I shall forward a note of my own with the papers for attachment to your personal record."

Chambers had said: "Thank you, sir."

"The best thing you can do now is to get off at once and forget about it."

He had anticipated that, and had made all his arrangements. He had driven down to Portsmouth with the galleon balanced on the seat beside him. In daylight the little furniture shop looked squalid and depressing; the snow was melting on the pavement under a steady, persistent rain. He rang the bell of the side door and her mother had answered it, an untidy, pleasant-looking woman in a dirty apron, bulging out of her clothes.

He had felt foolish, and had said: "I'm sorry—could I speak to Mona?"

In a quick, shrewd glance she had taken in the tall figure in the blue-grey coat, the fresh pink-and-white complexion, and she had approved. She had said: "Half a mo', sir. I'll just give her a call."

The word "sir" had depressed him more than ever.

In a minute or two the girl had come to the door. He had said: "I'm going off this afternoon, Mona. I just brought you down the galleon."

Desperately she had searched her mind for somewhere where she could see him alone. But there was nowhere; her father was in the shop and her mother in the kitchen. There was no parlour to the house. She had said: "It's ever so sweet of you to give it to me, Jerry."

He had taken it from the car and put it into her arms; she cradled it like a baby. "I can't ask you in," she had said unhappily. "There's nowhere to go."

"I couldn't stay. I'm just going off on leave."

"Going home?"

"Yes. I live in Bristol, you know."

"Will you be coming back here after that?"

He shook his head. "I don't think so."

There had been an awkward, unhappy pause. The rain dripped steadily upon the pavement at his feet.

He said: "If I get down to London any time, would you like to come up, and we'd do something together?"

She hesitated. The fare would mean that she would have to draw upon her tiny savings, but her mother might be able to help. She said: "I'd love to do that."

He had smiled. "I'll write to you and fix up something."

So they had said good-bye, and he had driven off back to the aerodrome in the little sports car, to collect his bags and start for Bristol. Mona had taken the galleon up to her room and put it on the dressing-table, where it was in the way. Later in the day her mother, wistful for a daughter's confidence, had said a little timidly: "I did think that officer looked ever such a nice boy, Mona."

She had turned away. "I shan't be seeing any more of him. He just came round to say good-bye. He's going away."

She had gone out to be alone, and had walked for two hours through the streets and down the rain-swept, deserted sea-front till the gathering darkness and the rain had driven her home, to change her shoes and stockings for her evening's work in the snack-bar.

It had not been possible for Chambers to get to London before Christmas without worrying his mother, and his posting to Market Stanton came at a day's notice.

He found Market Stanton cold comfort. The aerodrome was deep in snow and mud, alternately hard with frost and miserable with the thaw. The mess was a brick building reasonably warm and comfortable; the bedrooms were in wooden huts separated into cubicles of beaver-board, tiny and bleak and quite unheated. Chambers suffered it for a couple of nights, then motored seven miles into Beverley to buy a paraffin heating-stove and a can of oil. This warmed his cubicle sufficiently to enable him to unpack and erect his short-wave wireless set and re-establish radio communication with America. The occupation eased the lonely ache that he had suffered since he had left Emsworth. Presently, settling down, he wrote to London for the kit to make a model caravel.

He did not find the work exacting. The aerodrome accommodated several squadrons of Wellington heavy bombers, faster than the machines that he was used to, and a good deal larger, but intrinsically much the same. He flew one dual with a flight-lieutenant for a couple of hours and learned to land it in the swept lanes of the aerodrome; then he flew it solo for a few hours more. Presently he was flying it confidently by night as well as by day, and was ready to go on service as a second pilot.

Towards the end of January he flew over Germany.

The flight was curious to him, because it was almost completely uneventful. It was just like any other night flight, lasting about eight hours. The squadron chose a fine, frosty, starry night for the raid, with a light northerly wind. The machines were loaded up with leaflets printed in German for distribution over enemy territory. Each Wellington had a different course to take. The full crew of five were on board and full ammunition, but the bomb-racks were empty and the machines were loaded in the fuselage with the brick-like packets of the propaganda. Past raids of that sort had shown them that it was unlikely that they would encounter much resistance.

The pilots were amused and scornful of the job they had to do. "Hitler doesn't give a . . . for the stuff," was the general opinion. "It's not worth his while to waste his petrol sending up his fighters." They expressed the view that the Führer welcomed the paper for sanitary reasons.

Nevertheless, there was excitement and tension in the aeroplanes as they took off.

They left the ground at about eleven o'clock at night, taking off singly at intervals of about three minutes. Each of the big monoplanes taxied to the end of the runway in practically complete darkness, guided only by the flicker of flash-lamps. Engines were run up for a last test with the machines facing down the long swept path, the exhaust-pipes streaming long spears of blue flame in the cloudless, starry night. Then, when all was ready, the dim lights came on which showed the runway, and the machine took off; immediately it was clear of the ground the lights were extinguished till the next machine was ready.

Chambers was in the third machine to go, serving as second pilot to a flight-lieutenant called Dixon. The flight-lieutenant piloted the monoplane for the take-off; Chambers sat beside him in a little folding seat in the passage that gave access to the bomb-aimer's position in the nose. Beside them were the wireless operator and the corporal gunner, the latter sitting on the piles of propaganda leaflets. In the gun-turret at the very tail of the machine a sergeant gunner sat alone.

They came to the end of the runway and swung round as the lights were extinguished and the second machine climbed slowly from the ground, vanishing into the starry night, its tail-light visible as a wandering star among the other stars. Dixon settled in his seat and slowly pushed one throttle forward. In the shaded orange lights over the instrument panels both pilots watched rev counter and boost gauge, the cylinder head temperatures, and the many pressure gauges. They tested the controllable propeller, and then closed down that engine and ran up the other.

In the end, Chambers raised his thumb. The pilot nodded. Chambers glanced back over his shoulder and nodded to the men behind, then flashed the signalling-lamp on the underside of the fuselage. Immediately, the lights came on, and the long runway stretched out straight ahead of them, nearly three-quarters of a mile in length.

The pilot pressed the throttles forward, and the machine began to move. She gained speed slowly for the first few seconds; then the propellers took hold of the air and they went trundling down the runway, heavy with the fuel and load on board. At five hundred yards they were doing eighty on the air-speed indicator, and the big monoplane was starting to feel light upon the ground. The snow flew past them on each side. At ninety the pilot eased the wheel towards him with a firm, slight pull; the vibration from the runway ceased and they climbed very slowly from the ground. They crossed the hedge with about ten feet to spare and flicked the undercarriage switch; the hydraulic pumps groaned and clattered as the wheels retracted. Then the lights behind them were extinguished, and they went climbing up into the blue vault of the starry night. .

Chambers left his seat, and went to the navigating table, stayed there for a moment, and came back and set the course upon the compass. Each of the machines had its own route to follow in the operations of the night, independent of the others. Chambers set a course direct for Cuxhaven.

They went climbing up into the night. Two or three minutes after they had crossed the coast they turned out the navigating lights and went on out over the sea, a dim shadow moving across the firmament. Already it was very cold in the machine. They shut up all the windows and turned on the heating full; even so the temperature in the cabin fell below freezing very soon. Chambers changed places with the flight-lieutenant and took over the piloting. At fifteen thousand feet they adjusted the oxygen-masks upon their faces and turned on the supply; immediately they felt warmer. At twenty thousand feet they levelled out, stopped climbing, and took up their normal cruising speed.

As they crossed the sea, seen dimly beneath them as a corrugated sheet, the moon came up ahead of them. Its light shone upon the cockpit and the wings and made them feel conspicuous; they would have preferred the shadow of the night. Once they saw a ship upon the water, heading roughly north-east; they had no means of telling whose it was.

They saw land ahead of them at about a quarter to one, and picked up the outline of the estuary of the Elbe at Cuxhaven. They followed the river, checking their navigation by the ground to settle the direction of the wind, until they came to Hamburg.

There was no doubt about the city. All round it the snow covered the countryside; the city appeared as an untidy, speckled blotch upon a field of white. In the bright moonlight they could see the docks and the line of the river, and they made an effort to count the ships in sight along the quays. The streets were faintly lighted. There were no searchlights visible. They strained their eyes into the darkness for enemy fighters, but in vain. Each minute they expected gunfire, but no gunfire came.

To Chambers it was fantastic and unreal. It was incredible that that big town below him should be full of Germans, fanatically devoted to their Führer, hating England and the English with all the force of their warped, virile souls.

Dixon leaned his head towards him and moved the oxygen-mask from his mouth. "Not much wind," he said. "Get about five miles over to the west, and we'll drop the stuff there."

He showed Chambers the map of the locality. The pilot nodded and swung the bomber round, staring intently at the dim ground below. Presently he found the wood that he was looking for and circled over it. He glanced over his shoulder. Dixon and the corporal were shoving the brick-like packets of leaflets down the chute. The pilot glanced over the side, but he could see nothing of the paper cloud.

The flight-lieutenant came along to him. "Berlin next stop," he said. He set the new course on the compass for the pilot. "We'll probably run into searchlights pretty soon. Like me to take her?"

Chambers grinned: "I'm all right. You take a spell after Berlin."

"All right."

Half an hour later, sure enough, the searchlights blazed out ahead of them from somewhere near Spandau. Most of them were white in colour, one or two were pale-green and one or two violet. The machine flew on steadily towards them, flying at about twenty-two thousand feet. At that height they were very largely safe from searchlights; when the beams caught them, as they did from time to time, the illumination of the machine was not very great. The young man kept a keen, in-

cessant look-out for enemy fighters. They saw nothing.
Swiftly they passed above the line of searchlights, dis-
covered a river and a dark, faintly-glowing mass ahead,
and so came to Berlin.

They made a wide circuit of the city, tense and
anxious. There were no searchlights, no gunfire, no
fighters. The main streets seemed to be faintly illuminated by shaded street lamps, and away on the outskirts
to the east there was a pattern of light that they took
to be the landing lights laid out upon an aerodrome.
They flew towards the west again, discharged their
leaflets at a spot where the wind would carry them down
into the city, and set a course for Leipzig, relieved and
faintly disappointed.

They got to Leipzig at about three o'clock in the
morning; by that time the moon was high. There they
were fired upon, without searchlights. Below them they
could see the flashes of the guns, the long trails of tracers
from the shells, and the vivid bursts about their level.
Dixon was flying the machine, and climbed and dived
alternately to change the height by a few hundred feet.
The others concentrated intently on the work they had
to do as the machine circled the city. None of the shells
came near. Chambers watched the flashes of the guns
intently from the forward gun position, marking the loca-
tion of each battery upon a large-scale plan of the city.
They scattered their leaflets and set a course for Kassel.

Kassel was dark and silent; they circled it, dropped
their leaflets and turned northwards for home. At Han-
over and Bremen there were searchlights, and between
Bremen and Wilhelmshaven there was an intense
barrage of searchlights and of gunfire. Dixon was still
at the controls and went through it in a series of dives
and climbs coupled with forty-five degree turns to port
and starboard, designed to confuse the sound locators
and the gunners. One or two bursts came near them,

and next day they found a small gash in the fabric of the rear fuselage where a splinter had passed through, but they suffered no damage and set a course for home over the North Sea.

It was a little after five o'clock in the morning. In spite of the heated cabin they were all stiff with cold; with the relaxation from the strain of being over Germany they began to feel their fatigue. Chambers took over the controls and brought the bomber down to a more reasonable height—about ten thousand feet; they took off their oxygen-masks and breathed naturally once again. Dixon got out the thermos flasks and passed round mugs of coffee and a tin of boiled sweets; the drink refreshed them.

Presently, as they flew, a faint tinge of grey came into the sky behind them and the stars grew paler in the east.

They approached the coast of Yorkshire in a long descent, with navigation lights alight and with their Very pistol charged with a flare cartridge showing the colour of the day. They made their landfalls at the mouth of the Humber and flew north a little up the coast before turning inland towards Market Stanton. In the grey light of a frosty dawn they came to the aerodrome and circled round it at a thousand feet. Dixon was at the controls; he brought the big monoplane in low over the hedge and put her down upon the runway.

They taxied into the hangar and cut the engines. The duty-officer came out to meet them, muffled to the ears in greatcoat and muffler. He asked: "What was it like over there?"

Dixon said: "Bloody cold."

They handed over their notes and wrote a short report. Then they went back to their respective messes. Chambers was cold and sleepy; about them the camp was coming to life. He went to the breakfast-table in the mess and had a cup of coffee and a plate of very sweet porridge. Then he went over to his bedroom, un-dressed and tumbled into bed, and slept till lunch.

There followed ten days of stagnation, of routine duties and short test flights, of reading the papers and waiting for orders. In this time Chambers made a start upon his caravel, decarbonised his little car, and brooded restlessly about the mess. It ended in a summons to the group-captain's office.

Two other pilots came with him; none of them knew what it was about. They stood in a row before the C.O.'s desk, a middle-aged officer, rather portly and going a little bald.

He said: "Good morning, gentlemen. I sent for you because I've been asked to supply a volunteer for special duties. I don't know what the work is, except that it's some sort of testing to be carried out on Wellingtons."

He paused and smiled a little. "I want a volunteer," he said, "because I understand that it's not quite so safe as—as flying over Germany, shall we say. I sent for you three because you all have the basic qualifications for the work, because you're none of you married so far as I know. It's the sort of job that might lead to something. On the other hand, it may go flat after a week or two."

One of the flying-officers said: "Can we have some idea what sort of work it is, sir?"

"Not much. It's out over the sea, and that's about all I know. I picked you three because you've all had a good bit of experience over water, and because you're all adequate pilots on the Wellington."

Chambers said: "Can you tell us what the establish-ment is?" It was important for a regular officer to know that, to avoid stagnation in promotion.

"I don't think there is any establishment. The pilot who gets this job will be the first. He should be quite all right in that way."

One of them said: "Unless he falls in the drink."

The group-captain said: "Unless he falls in the drink." He eyed them for a minute. "I want a volunteer for this," he said, "because I understand that it's a tricky sort of business. You'd better go away and let me know this afternoon if any of you want it. If more than one of you are keen to have it I shall have to choose somebody; I'll have to choose somebody if I don't get any volunteers." He paused. "That's all for the present."

They filed out of the office and walked over to the mess. Chambers said: "Well, what does anyone make of that?"

The other two were lukewarm. One of them said: "I put in a month ago for posting to a fighter squadron. I was put down for fighters at the F.T.S., and then they sent me here. I'm not so stuck on going on on Wellingtons, myself."

The other was silent. His home was in York, and Market Stanton was near enough to York for him to get home at week-ends and on half-days of leave, especially when the days got longer and one could motor later before black-out. He said presently: "I'd rather go on here."

He turned to Chambers: "Do you want it?"

The young man shrugged his shoulders. "I don't care much either way. It sounds as if it might be interesting."

"Bloody sight too interesting, if you ask me," said the first. "Fighters are the thing to go for. Nice to fly, and you get a chance of acting on your own. They're safe, too. Ruddy great engine in front of you to keep the bullets off, and eight guns for you to hose him with. Safest job in the war, these Hurricanes and Spitfires. I wish to God they'd ask for volunteers for them."

The other said to Chambers: "Are you putting in for it?"

"I might do. Do you want it?"

The other shook his head. "I'd go if I had to, of course—if the C.O. picked me. But I'd rather stay here." He hesitated, and then said: "I'm getting married in the spring."

Chambers said: "Are you? Have a beer. The young people—they will do it. Can't stop 'em. That lets you out of it, anyway."

The other said: "You want to get into a fighter squadron if you're getting married. Safest job in the war, old boy."

Chambers sat down in a long arm-chair before the fire with a copy of *Picture Post*. He did not dislike the idea of a change. The monotony of sitting on the ground week after week waiting for orders for a raid was irking him, as it was irking all of them. After the continuous patrol that he had been used to on the Coastal Command the inactivity was galling. The thought of more work was attractive, and test flying should be interesting. He had been at Market Stanton for about six weeks, and he did not care for the station. It was too far from a picture-house for his liking. It was twenty miles from a decent grill-room. As he thought about it his heart ached for the Portsmouth scene, where there had been grill-rooms and pictures, and Mona, all within ten miles of the aerodrome.

To hell with it. This place was no damn good. He'd put in for this job and get away.

He presented himself before the group-captain that afternoon. "I think I'd like to put in for that job, sir," he said. "Can you tell me where it would be?"

The C.O. said: "I don't know that myself, Chambers. I rather think it's on the Clyde."

The boy nodded. Anything was better than Market Stanton. "I think I'd like to have a stab at it," he said.

"All right. Are any of the others putting in for it, do you know?"

"I don't think so, sir. Neither of them seemed very keen."

"I'll give them the rest of the afternoon. If they don't show up by then I'll put you forward for it."

"It means going pretty soon, sir, I suppose?"

"Almost immediately, I should think. We'll probably get a postagram about it in the morning."

"I'd better start putting my things together, then?"

"I should think so. I know they want somebody quite urgently."

Chambers went back to the bedroom-hut and began to collect his scattered belongings ready for packing. Before dinner he met the group-captain in the mess. "I put you in for that job, Chambers," he said. "I sent off a signal about it. We should hear by the morning."

The boy said: "I'll get ready to go, then, sir."

The C.O. said: "I'm sorry you're going, Chambers. You've done quite well here. I was going to send you as first pilot, in charge of a machine, next time we had a show."

"It's very nice of you to say that, sir."

"I mean it. I'm sorry you're going."

Chambers went back to his bedroom and began to dismantle his wireless set.

Next morning he was summoned to the C.O.'s office. The group-captain said: "I've got the postagram about your posting, Chambers. You're to report to Titchfield aerodrome at once, to the Marine Experimental Unit. Titchfield—that's somewhere down by Portsmouth."

The pilot swallowed something. "I—I've just come from there, sir."

"Have you? I thought you came from the Coastal Command."

"Yes, sir. I was at Emsworth aerodrome."

The group-captain smiled: "Well, you're going back again to the same part of the world. I hope you've enjoyed your trip to Yorkshire."

The boy stood dumbfounded. It was clear to him that

the group-captain knew nothing of the reasons that had caused him to be moved from the Portsmouth district. Now the die was cast, and he was shifted back there again. In the stress of war the papers in his personal record had been overlooked by Postings, if indeed his personal record had been consulted at all before the appointment had been made.

Now was the time to make a protest, if one was to be made.

He thought of Market Stanton, and he thought of Portsmouth. It was two months or more since *Caranx* had been lost. There would be embarrassment, perhaps, but he would be with a different unit on a different aerodrome. In all probability he would meet none of the same people. He hesitated, irresolute.

The group-captain eyed him keenly. "What's the matter?"

"I didn't much want to go back to Portsmouth, sir. For a personal reason."

The commanding-officer said: "Well, it's done now, Chambers. Is your reason very serious?"

The pilot hesitated again. If he braved it out and went back to Portsmouth, he would see Mona. He said slowly:

"I don't think so, sir."

The older officer stood up. "Well, you'd better take it and get off to your new job. I'm sure you'll do well in it. In war time we can't pick and choose the postings as we used to do, you know. I'm sorry if it's not quite what you wanted, but one has to take the rough with the smooth."

Chambers nodded: "I know." And then he said: "What does the Marine Experimental Unit do?"

"I haven't an idea—you'll find out when you get there. I've never heard of it before."

"Is it a new unit, then?"

"It must be. It certainly wasn't in existence before the war."

"It sounds as if it might be interesting."

He said good-bye to his commanding-officer, and went over to his bedroom-hut. His packing was very nearly finished. He strapped his bags, and gave a tip to his batman; then he drove the little sports car round and loaded everything he had into it. He went over to the mess and paid his mess bill, and then to the adjutant's office to get petrol coupons for his journey south.

He got on to the road directly after lunch.

Although his little motor-car made a good deal of noise, it did not get along the road very fast. It was getting dark when he arrived at Barnby Moor; he stopped there for the night. Next day he went on down the Great North Road, skirted round London in the early afternoon through Watford and Slough, and came to Titchfield aerodrome on the edge of the darkness. He drove straight to the adjutant's office and reported.

The adjutant said: "You're the Wellington pilot for the Marine Experimental Unit, then?"

Chambers said: "Yes, sir. Can you tell me what it is I have to do?"

The squadron-leader said: "I'm not supposed to know anything that goes on over in that hangar. But I can tell you, more or less."

He did so. What he said really doesn't matter a great deal. It was very technical, difficult to understand, though interesting in its way. So far as I know Chambers never spoke of it to anyone, even to Mona. It was purely by chance I came to hear what he'd been doing. I found it in a file at the Air Ministry when I was looking for something else, and my tea got cold while I went chasing up that side alley. But the file was marked SECRET and I had to sign for it; and so I think we'll let it rest. It had nothing to do with *Caranx*, anyway.

That evening Mona walked to the snack-bar in the grey dusk. It was the first time in months that she had gone to work in daylight, but it had been a fine light evening, and she was a little early. As she went she was wondering whether to change her job. The snack-bar was all right, but since Jerry went she had been restless. Now, with the prospect of light evenings once again, specially when daylight saving came in in the coming week, it did not seem to her a good thing to be starting work at six o'clock.

She was restless with the spring. It might be fun to try it in a shop. If she could get into a big shop, now, in the perfumery or the ladies' gowns. . . . It might even be she could become a mannequin, and that led to the films, or so she thought.

She arranged her glasses behind the bar. A few officers came in at six o'clock and she was mildly busy; by half-past six the place was starting to warm up. There was a lean, saturnine lieutenant in the R.N.V.R. there that she knew as Mouldy James; she was not sure if the mouldi-ness was his nature or whether it meant that he had specialised in torpedoes. As a Portsmouth girl, born and bred, she knew it might be either.

Mouldy was with one or two others; they had a paper in their hands that they were laughing over. At first sight she took it for a rude story in typescript, such as she knew men liked to circulate. Then she saw it was a cutting from a newspaper. She caught the eye of Lieutenant James, who grinned at her.

Business was slack for the moment. She said: "What's that you've got there?"

The officer took the cutting and flipped it across the bar to her. "My uncle in America sent it to me," he said.

She took it, wondering. "Is this a bit of an American paper?"

"That's right. He lives in Norfolk, Va."

"Just fancy." She looked at the print. "It's really just the same as our papers, isn't it?"

"God forbid."

She smiled politely, not quite understanding what he meant. "What did you mean by saying that your uncle lived in Norfolk, Va?"

"Virginia. Just like you might say Portsmouth, Hants."

She said again. "Just fancy . . ." Then she read the cutting.

ACE WAR-TIME SKIPPER SAW BRITISH SINK NAZI U-BOAT.

Alex Jorgen, blue-eyed red-haired captain of Dutch motor-ship *Heloise*, told *Star* reporter of hairbreadth escapes in England's blockade zone.

Traversing English Channel on December 3rd, said Dutch captain, we saw a U-boat sunk by British off Departure Point. Violent explosion about two miles in-shore broke glasses in the steward's pantry, then bow and stern of U-boat appeared separately before vanishing for ever.

Jorgen said British were as bad as Nazis in the war on neutral shipping. On last voyage was forced to jettison 600 tons of rubber at Weymouth, British contraband control port, following navicert trouble.

Somebody came up to the bar, and said: "Two half-cans, please."

She served him and returned to the cutting. "I don't see what the joke's about."

Mouldy James took the cutting back and put it carefully into his notecase. "There isn't any joke, really," he said. "Only, I know that captain. I was in the Contraband Control when they brought him in. He's the biggest liar that we ever got. He said the rubber was for contraceptives."

She sniffed. It was the sort of joke the barmaid has to sniff at.

One of the others said: "His U-boat story is a bloody great lie anyway. We never got one in these parts till January."

Mona opened her mouth to speak, and then shut it again. In a sickening moment she realised that the date was the date when *Caranx* had been sunk: December 3rd. These officers had not appreciated that; quite possibly they had none of them been in the district at that time. She must keep her mouth shut, because of Jerry. He had gone out of her life and she would never see him again, but she would not rake his trouble up in idle talk.

She turned away and began rinsing out her glasses.

When she turned back to the bar, Mouldy James and his friends had gone away; she saw them sitting up at the grill-bar, eating. She served her drinks listlessly, depressed. For some time now she had forgotten about *Caranx*; the reminder of the submarine increased her restless urge to make a change. Outside in the street there might still be a faint glow of sunset in the blackness of the sky. It was too bad to be cooped up in the snack-bar every night.

In a slack moment Miriam said: "You look proper down, tonight. Anything wrong, dear?"

She said: "Everything. I'm getting to hate this work."

The other girl said: "Well, I don't know about that. It's regular. I thought you liked it here."

"I did used to. I don't now."

She looked round the long room. In a far corner a group of three young ladies, officers of the Women's Royal Naval Service, sat together at a table, looking a little out of place, and self-conscious. Mona said: "That's what I'd like to be. Join the Wrens."

The other girl followed her glance. "You won't get a uniform like them. The ordinary uniform isn't half so nice as the officers'. I do think they look ever so smart."

Mona considered this. There was good sense in what Mariam had said. After all, it would be lovely if she got a job in the perfumery. . . . She had a great craving for beautiful things, for silks, perfumes, and beauty creams in elegant white alabaster pots, all wrapped in cellophane. She was sick of handing sloppy cans of beer across the bar.

Miriam was still looking at the Wrens. "You see that one in the middle? That's Miss Hancock."

Mona looked idly across the room. "Who's she?"

"Her pa works in the dockyard, or used to do before the war. He was captain of the navigating school. They lived inside the gates, just this side of Admiralty House."

"How'd you know that?"

"My cousin Flora—she's in service with them. Before the war, I used to go and have tea in the kitchen. But they won't let you in the dockyard now, not without you've got a pass."

Mona was mildly interested. "What does an officer do, like that Miss Hancock?"

"I dunno what they do, I'm sure. She works in Admiralty House, along with the Commander-in-Chief, so Flora says."

Mona said: "They get all the good jobs, officers' daughters and that. I believe I'd like to try it in a shop, in the perfumery or something."

Her friend said generously: "Well, you might get in that. You make up ever so pretty, really you do."

Mona shot a brilliant smile at her. "You do talk soft." A very shy young pilot in the Fleet Air Arm saw it, and his heart turned over. But his grill was ready, and in any case he would have been far too shy to go and talk to the barmaid. Romance was still-born.

The evening wore on, not very busily. In the intervals of serving Mona's thoughts drifted more and more from beer; in the bitter aroma of the bar she savoured all the perfumes of Arabia. There were ever so many different sorts of colours of lipstick and of powder; she did not know them all, but she could learn. It would be lovely to get a job and go round all the big shops demonstrating facial make-up, helping people to look nice. A job in the perfumery would be the start, if she could land one. She wondered what was the best way to set about it.

The bar closed at ten. At about a quarter to ten she saw a tall young Air Force officer come in through the swing doors, dressed in a long grey-blue overcoat and forage cap, with black hair and pink cheeks glowing with the sudden warmth of the room. She stared amazed. Jerry was up in Yorkshire, or so she had thought. He couldn't be back here again. But there he was.

He grinned at her across the room; she put a hand up to shoulder height and waved at him. Then he hung up his coat and came to her through the naval officers.

"Jerry!" she cried. "Whatever are you doing here?" Behind her, Miriam watched entranced.

He said: "I came for half a can."

"But what are you doing down here?"

He looked into her eyes, laughing. "Buying half a can."

"Oh, you and your half-can!" She served it to him. "Are you just back on a holiday?"

He raised it to her. "All the best." He set it down again. "How've you been?"

"I'm fine. How are you, Jerry?"

He said: "I got rid of my ringworm, but my cancer's troubling me a good deal. I don't think I've got very long to live."

She said: "You look like it. Tell me, are you back at Emsworth?"

"I'm at Titchfield now."

"How long have you been there?"

"Three and a half hours. Nearly three and three-quarters, now."

She said happily: "And you come right along. . . ."

He nodded. "That's right. I couldn't miss my beer."

There was an interruption, and she left him to serve three double-whiskies and a crème-de-menthe for the lady. When she came back to him, he said:

"Doing anything afterwards?"

She smiled. "Nothing special."

He set down his can. "I don't want to go dancing at the Pavilion," he said quietly. "Not just yet. And it's too late for a flick. Would you like to go and eat something at the Cosy Cot?"

"I'd like that ever so."

"Five past ten, round by the back door?"

"That's right."

He grinned at her. "I'll be there."

He moved away, beer-mug in hand; Mona went on with her work, humming a little song about rolling down the cotton on the levee down south, which she did not fully understand, but which seemed to express what she was feeling. Miriam came up and smiled at her.

"Got the boy friend back again?" she said. "You might have told me."

Mona said: "I didn't know he was coming. He went away to Yorkshire."

"You don't say. I thought he just went off, like."

Mona shook her head. "He got shifted away."

"What's he doing here now?"

"He got shifted back again."

"My! Going out with him?"

The girl nodded.

Miriam sighed a little. Some girls got all the luck. She herself had been sedulously to the Pavilion, year after year, but she had never "got off" with an officer like that. All she got were awkward sailors who danced badly, smelt of beer, and never even made a dubious proposal, such as she had read of in books. Some girls had all the luck.

She said: "You be careful. He's got a naughty look about him."

Mona laughed. "You're telling *me*!"

The other sighed. "I'd leave home for him, any day," she said.

Chambers stood in the darkness of the alley, waiting. It was a fine bright moonlit night, frosty and with a keen wind. In the shadows of the alley the darkness was intense. He held the rabbit-lamp in his hand. When he heard Mona at the gate that led into the yard of the hotel he flashed the rabbit suddenly at her, and said: "Boo!"

She jumped back with a little squeal. He caught her in his arms, and kissed her in the darkness of the alley. She said breathlessly: "You and your rabbit! I didn't know what it was."

He held her to him and said: "Me."

"I know that." She wriggled in his arms. "Give over now. You'll get me all mussed up."

"That's the object of the exercise. Are you glad to see me?"

She stopped wriggling and said quietly: "Ever so glad, Jerry."

He released her. "Let's go and get something to eat."

They walked across to the little car parked by the roadside. "You've got the same car still," she said.

"That's right. Look out how you sit down. The bottom's coming out of that seat."

They drove out to the Cosy Cot, sitting more closely together even than was warranted by the cramped nature of the car. The road-house was only moderately full; they got a table in a corner and ordered ham and eggs and beer.

She said: "How long will you be here, Jerry?"

He shrugged his shoulders. "I don't really know. Some time, I should think."

"Is it flying out over the sea, like you did at Emsworth?"

He hesitated. "It's not much like that. It's a sort of an experimental job."

"One of them you're not supposed to talk about?"

"That's it."

"I see." There was nothing new to her in that. When her father had been working in the dockyard towards the end of his career in the Navy, there had been a period of four whole years when they had not known what work he did when he went off each day. Those four years in his life were still a sealed book to his wife and family.

He said: "Been dancing much?"

She smiled at him impishly. "Went to the Pavilion two or three times, but I never got another officer."

"One's enough."

"That's right," she said. "Once bit, twice shy." They both laughed. "No, I've not been there much."

"Still liking it in the bar?"

She shook her head. "It's all right, but I'd like to have a change. With the summer, and the long evenings, and all."

He nodded. "What would you want to do?"

"I thought it might be nicer in a shop." She looked at him doubtfully, wondering how he would react to that; he might regard it as a step down in the social scale.

"What sort of a shop?"

She said: "I'd like to sell perfumes, ever so."

He nodded. "Not bacon, or split-peas?"

"Don't be so silly. I don't mean a shop like that."

He said: "I was joking—sorry. Tell me, why per-fumes?"

"I don't know, Jerry. Only, that's what I'd like to do." He nodded with understanding. She leaned for-ward to him. "Things like silks, and evening gowns, and perfumes, and face-powder. It'ld be lovely to be hand-ling them sort of things all day." She considered for a moment. "Of course, it's all right in the bar."

He smiled. "But you're getting restless."

"That's right."

He said: "It's the war. Nobody really settles down to any job."

Behind them the radio-gramophone was playing dance tunes, softly and continuously.

She said quietly: "War is a fine time for men. I mean, all them chaps that get called up. They get fun, and games, and work outside in the sun instead of working a machine all day in the factory." She looked up into his face. "I walked along the front today, and there was dozens of them in the Fort, sitting about and smoking in a patch of sun, out of the wind. They seemed so happy. I was ever so glad for them."

• He smiled at her. "It may be a fine time for men, but it's a rotten time for women."

She shook herself. "We're getting mouldy, Jerry. We'll be weeping salt tears next."

"I know. It's all this beer we're drinking does it. We'd have been merry as a grig if we'd been drinking gin."

She laughed. "Says you."

"We'll go and dance, next time."

She eyed him for a minute. "You wouldn't want to go to the Pavilion yet, would you?"

"I don't know that I mind much, now." He stared across the room, absent-minded for a minute. His new job with the Marine Experimental Unit rather altered his diffidence about the Pavilion. The work, so far as he had been able to assimilate it in an hour's discussion, was definitely dangerous and of the highest value to the progress of the war. One pilot, who was married and whose wife was having her first baby, had asked if he might be excused from it. That was why a pilot had been sent from Market Stanton. Chambers was pleased and proud to have the chance of doing it; only a strong sense of discretion had prevented him from pouring his news out to Mona. With this job he had walked straight into the status of a test pilot, and a pretty responsible one at that. It made a difference to dancing at the Pavilion, in his view. It gave him back self-confidence. To hell with what the Navy chose to think of him. He was one of the test pilots from the Marine Experimental Unit.

Mona said gently: "Did you hear any more of that submarine thing, Jerry?"

He shook his head. Behind them the radio-gramophone was churning out its grievances—

> Tonight, I mustn't think of him—
> Music maestro, please—
> Tonight, tonight I must forget
> Those happy hours, but no hearts or
> flowers—
> Play that lilting melody:
> Ragtime, Jazztime, Swing—
> Any old thing
> To help to ease the pain
> That solitude must bring . . .

He said: "It's all over now and best forgotten. I suppose I sank it. I must have done. But it was an accident, and it really wasn't my fault. The thing was ten miles out of its position." He stared at her. "I shall be sorry about it all my life," he said quietly. "But one must go on. There's still work to be done."

He used to like waltzing—
   So please, don't play a waltz—
He danced divinely
   And I loved him so
   But there I go . . .

They sat together, without talking much. Mona did not pursue the subject of the submarine; she listened absently while he told her of the flight that he had made across Germany. There was something in her mind that puzzled her; she could not exactly place it. Seeing Jerry and talking to him in the Cosy Cot had brought back to her mind the details of the time before when she had sat with him, listening to the same tunes on the same radiogram. That was the time when he had told her about *Caranx*, when she had sat straining to assimilate the story in order that she could help him in his troubles. She sat there listening to him as he talked, and the conviction grew in her that there was something inconsistent, something wrong. She had heard of *Caranx* again that evening, and it was different. *Caranx* was sunk by a number of bombs, some large, some small; Jerry had told her all about it, and she had strained to memorise the details. But the cutting in the newspaper had said there was one big explosion. And what was that about the bow and stern coming up in two separate parts? That wasn't what Jerry had told her.

She would not worry him by raking it all up again. He had said that it was best forgotten, and it was. American newspapers were bound to be all wrong about the war; she had seen half a dozen movies of American newspaper offices in which the heroine solved the mystery and married the District Attorney. They had left her pleasantly thrilled, but with a poor opinion of the American Press.

Jerry was right. *Caranx* had been an accident that was best forgotten.

VI

CAPTAIN BURNABY sat in conference in his office in the dockyard. He sat at the head of the long green table, his massive, iron-grey eyebrows knitted in a frown as he battled stubbornly with unfamiliar problems. A stern pride had made him master every technicality that had come to him in a long career. It was bad luck that electronic theory should have crossed his path so late in life.

He turned to the civilian on his right. "If you can calibrate the circuit in the trial runs, that's good enough," he said. "I don't see where the difficulty arises."

The professor cleared his throat. He was a grey-haired, serious man of fifty, dressed in a dark-grey suit. He was not yet at home in the naval atmosphere to which his work had led him. He did not understand their processes of thought, and he was ill at ease.

"We can calibrate for any given frequency," he said. "The difficulty lies in assessing the conditions as the aircraft nears the ship."

"But as I understand it, every ship has its own frequency."

"Yes—every ship of the same class has similar characteristics."

"And the frequency is always the same, from month to month and year to year."

"That is so. But, of course, it will be modulated by the direction of the ship relative to the meridian."

"Oh . . ." The captain stared at the blotting-pad before him in a giant effort of concentration. It was impossible for him to admit that once again he was out of his depth. The wing-commander on his left came to his aid.

"The course corrector deals with that, sir. The pilot sets the course of the target ship upon the dial, you remember."

"Yes—yes," said Burnaby. "I see that." Now that his memory was refreshed, he could recall that point.

The professor said: "But that's a relative correction, not an absolute one. It has no bearing on our difficulty."

There was a short silence.

Burnaby turned to the civilian. "You say it's going to take three months to do these calculations?"

"At least that, I'm afraid. It means we've got to plot the influence round several known ships, in three dimensions. From that we can construct the diagrams for any other ship."

The naval officer cut through the difficulty with a swift question.

"Suppose we haven't got the time for that," he said. "Suppose I tell you that this thing has got to be in service in three months from now? I understand there's no production difficulty."

The wing-commander nodded. "It could be used in three months' time," he said. "Deliveries will be starting in a week or two."

The professor of physics looked helplessly from one to the other. "We must find out the conditions before we can make it work at all," he said.

The captain looked at him. "Can't we fly it over a known ship and poop it off?" he said. "Poop off half a dozen of them, each with a different setting?"

The wing-commander said: "Surely we can bracket it like that?"

The civilian said slowly: "I don't think you can go at it in that way. You see, you have to have a bursting charge to free the satellites. You can't do it with a dummy."

Burnaby said: "I'm afraid I don't quite get that point."

"Well, if, in fact, the frequency is lower than the setting, it probably won't work at all. If the frequency is high, then there's a danger that the bomb will go off in the aeroplane. We can't take out the bursting charge, you see."

The naval officer said slowly: "I see that."

There was a short silence. Burnaby sat marshalling his rather scanty knowledge of the subject that they were discussing. Not for the first time he cursed these new-fangled weapons. Things had been easier in the last war. You got a bomb and stuck a simple fuse in the end of it. If you hit it with a hammer, it went off. It was as simple as that. But things were very different now.

He said: "I suppose if the bomb exploded in the aeroplane we'd lose both the machine and the pilot?"

The wing-commander nodded. "We mustn't let that happen." He paused, and then he said: "But I don't think it need. We can go at this from the low-frequency end and work up gently. It should be all right that way so long as we don't make any mistakes."

Burnaby said: "That seems all right, so long as we go carefully."

The civilian listened uneasily. For fifteen years he had worked in the seclusion of a Cambridge laboratory upon the research that war had switched to a new weapon. He was a practical man, and fully understood the urgency with which the Navy drove on the development. But with that understanding he had other understandings of his own. He knew that they knew so little of the influences round a ship; such things had never been plotted or explored. He had made estimates, and if his estimates were right, the weapon would work. If not, either it wouldn't work at all or else it would be set off prematurely in the aeroplane.

He said: "I don't think we could possibly do that."

Burnaby stared at him. "Why not?"

"Well, think of the risk."

The wing-commander said: "If we get it wrong, of course we lose the aeroplane. But I don't see any reason why we should go wrong."

The civilian said stubbornly: "It seems to me that we'll be taking very great risks if we go at it that way."

Burnaby laid his arms down on the table and stared straight ahead of him. "Let me get this quite clear in my mind," he said. "This is the last stage of our development, isn't it? When these calibration trials are done— however they are done—it can be used against the enemy. That is right?"

Professor Legge said: "That's quite right."

The captain raised his head. "Mr. Winston Churchill was talking to the Admiral about this yesterday," he said. "It's very important that this thing should be in service in the spring. He wants three squadrons fitted up with it."

The wing-commander said: "We could do that, all right."

Burnaby turned to the civilian. "In time of war one has to take certain risks," he said. "One has to rush through experimental work in a way that one would never do in time of peace. I grant you, we may lose the aeroplane in these trials. But we should save three months."

Legge nodded. "Well, that's outside my sphere, of course. If you go at it this way, we shall learn a great deal very quickly. But we may have accidents."

The wing-commander turned to Burnaby. "I agree with you, sir. I think there's a case here for taking a bit of a chance."

The naval officer said: "Well, we'll take that as a decision then." He swung round on the paymaster-lieutenant at the desk behind. "Put that into the minutes."

The young man nodded without speaking.

Professor Legge said: "The pilot must be very well instructed before anything is done."

The naval captain nodded. "You must have a good, steady pilot for the work."

The wing-commander said: "The pilot came down yesterday from Market Stanton. I had a talk with him this morning. He seems quite all right."

"Good. Of course, you'll do whatever can be done to safeguard him, if there should be an accident."

The wing-commander made a grimace. "Not very much," he said. "But I don't think it's so bad. There *is* some risk in it—we all know that. But if he were bombing ships in Heligoland Bight he'd have to take risks of the same order. It's a different sort of risk. That's all."

Burnaby straightened up in his chair. "That's settled, then. Now for the programme. I take it that you want to calibrate upon a battleship first?"

The civilian nodded. "We shall have to have the biggest ship you've got, lying across the meridian. That's the least sensitive combination. A big ship going east or west."

"I can't let you have a battleship before Tuesday of next week."

Legge said: "The more time I can have for computation between now and the first trial, the safer we shall be."

They began to discuss the details of the programme.

That night Chambers picked up Mona at the back door of the Royal Clarence Hotel when the snack-bar shut, kissed her in the darkness of the mews, and took her to the Pavilion. They went in a little furtively, glancing suspiciously from side to side, prepared to leave at once if they attracted any attention. Nobody took the least notice of them. They sat for ten minutes at one of the tables, warily alert; then greatly daring, they got up and danced.

They were very careful to avoid the floor until it was well crowded. Presently they gained confidence, as no one paid the least attention to them. It became a game.

"You're not that important, after all," she said.

"There's nobody from Emsworth here tonight," he replied. "Or nobody I know."

"It wouldn't matter if there was."

"No. As a matter of fact, they've been shifting people round a good bit in the Coastal Command; there may be nobody there now that I know. And I don't think very many people in the Navy knew me by sight."

She said comfortably: "Anyway, nobody's paying any attention to us."

He grinned at her. "They will be soon."

She glanced at him suspiciously. This was the old Jerry come to life again.

He said: "We'll dance the next one as an Apache dance."

"Not with me."

"It's quite easy; I'll show you the steps. It goes side step, chassé twice, reverse. Then I take your right arm and right leg and swing you round."

"I dare say."

"It's quite easy—honestly."

"You can do it with that fat girl over there—the one what squints."

He said persuasively: "I'll buy you a strawberry ice afterwards."

"You'll buy me a strawberry ice before."

"You'll be sick if you have a strawberry ice before my Apache dance."

"I'm not going to. Go on and buy me an ice."

He called the waitress and she brought them ices. Presently he said:

"Are you doing anything on Sunday?"

She said: "Sometimes we go to church." That was quite true. Her father and mother went each Sunday to the Cathedral, sometimes dragging an unwilling daughter with them.

He said: "That's a pity."

"Why?"

"I thought it would be nice to take the car and go up on to the Downs and have a walk."

"All day?"

"That's what I had in mind. Take a few sandwiches for lunch and have a real walk." He grinned at her. "I'm sorry you've got to go to church."

She said: "I'd have to be back by six, anyway. I'm on duty in the snack-bar then."

"Swop your day off with Miriam. She can do your church for you, too."

Mona said: "I know what it'll be. I'll go and get her to change her day, and then you'll have to work, or something."

He shook his head. "I shan't be doing anything this week-end. After Tuesday I shall be working every day." He was silent for a moment. Then he said: "A walk'll do you good."

"It'll rain all day."

"No, it won't. I've arranged that."

She said: "You think of everything, you do."

At midnight the dance ended, and they went on to the Old Oak tea-room. The Old Oak was an establishment that served teas languidly in the afternoon, grills and ham and eggs later, and which really came to life about eleven o'clock at night. After the pictures young men and young women went there to prolong the evening; it was unlicensed, but there was generally a gallon or two of beer in a white enamelled jug beneath the counter.

They sat there smoking and drinking coffee for an hour or more, listening to the radiogram, reluctant to go home. He told her about his radio set, and about the caravel that he was just beginning to build, and about the place in Cornwall where they had spent summer holidays when he had been at school. She told him about the pictures that she had seen since he had been away, and about Millie who was in the A.T.S. at Bordon, and about the lovely time that she had had last summer in the holiday camp in the Isle of Wight, all on two pounds ten. And all this was real and exciting to them; they could have gone on with it all night.

A hundred and fifty yards away a man sat in a sitting-room alone. A gas fire hissed gently in the grate. One shaded light flooded the big table at which the man was working, littered with sheets of paper, files, and books. A little black calculating machine stood upon the table at one side of him, an open attaché-case was on his other hand. Only the scratching of his pen and the hissing of the stove broke the long silence. The man was working quietly and methodically, covering sheet after sheet with close rows of figures, pausing now and then to tot up columns on the calculating machine. Slung casually across the back of a chair were the general arrangement blue prints of a battleship; upon the table were more confidential drawings.

In the stillness of the night he went on steadily, hour after hour. Professor Legge was working against time.

The little car drew up outside the furniture shop at about a quarter to two. In the room above the shop Mona's mother jogged her husband with her elbow.

"Stevie," she said. "Stevie—wake up."

He stirred and rolled over. "Ugh—what's the matter now?"

"There's Mona coming in. It's ever so late."

"What time is it?"

"Nearly two. She did ought to be in before this."

They lay and listened. There was no sound from the car that had stopped before the shop.

"Fine goings on," said her father.

Presently they heard her come in at the door, heard soft footsteps on the oilcloth as she slipped up to her room. Then the car started noisily and went away.

He said: "Who is it, Ma?"

"I think it's that young officer, Stevie—the one in the Air Force."

"I thought he went away."

"I believe he's back, if you ask me. But Mona never tells me nothing."

He grunted. "She'll tell me something when I get her in the morning. Coming in at two in the morning after being out with an officer! Fine goings on!"

She said: "If it's the one I think, he's the one what gave her that ship."

He was silent. He had seen the galleon when Mona had first had it; from time to time since, when she had been out, he had crept up to her room to look at it again. He admired it very much. As a young man in the Navy he had once made ships himself, full-rigged ships inserted miraculously into whisky bottles. He had been taught the art by an old boatswain, who himself had learned it from an older man. Now his fingers were too stiff and clumsy for such delicate work; it was twenty years since he had put a ship into a bottle. The galleon had stirred memories in him. It was a bigger ship than he had ever tackled, and more complicated, though it hadn't got to go into a bottle, of course.

He felt that Mona wanted checking. Two o'clock in the morning was no time to come home. It made a difference, certainly, that the young man had built a galleon. If it had been anyone else, he'd have been really angry.

He drifted into sleep, thinking of ships.

He caught her next day in the middle of the morning as she was dusting out the shop.

He said: "Here, girl, what time did you come home last night?"

She stared at him, surprised at this attack. Then she relaxed and smiled. "I dunno, Dad. The milkman hadn't been."

"Well, I can tell you what the time was." He eyed her sternly. "It was two o'clock. That's no time to come home. Your mother was proper fussed. Where had you been to?"

She tossed her head. "Dancing at the Pavilion. After that we went to the Old Oak. There's no harm in that."

He felt himself about to be defeated by his daughter, not for the first time. He said: "Who was you with?"

She said curtly: "An officer."

He said: "Well, two o'clock's too late for you to come home, Mona. You got to think of your mother and what the neighbours say. You know the way they talk. Make him bring you home by half eleven—anyhow, by midnight."

"That don't give much time for anything," she said discontentedly. "I don't get off till after ten." She turned to him. "If he works all the day and I got to work all evening, where are we, Dad?"

He hesitated. It seemed to him to be a reasonable point; she should have time to meet a young man if she wanted to. He said:

"Who is this officer? Is he the one what gave you the ship?"

"That's right."

"I thought he went away."

"He came back again."

There was a little silence. The old man felt himself to be getting out of his depth. In the interval when this young man had been away Mona had been out very little, and when she had been late she had been home before midnight.

He said weakly: "Well, two o'clock's too late."

She smiled at him. "Don't worry about me."

He was silent. He want to say all sorts of things to her, but could not find the words to express himself. He wanted to tell her that it was no good for her to get ideas into her head about an officer, especially a regular officer, as he understood the young man was. He wanted to tell her that there were still classes in England, that there could be nothing but pain to come to her from an association with an officer—a real officer with a regular commission.

She realised something of all this that he was struggling to say, perhaps. In regard to classes, her knowledge was more up to date than his. She said gently:

"You don't want to worry about Jerry. He's all right."

"Flying-officer, isn't he? With a regular commission?"

"That's right."

"Does he make many of them ships?"

"I dunno, Dad. He's making a caravel or something now."

His mind drifted from the subject, as an old man's mind is apt to do. He asked: "Did he ever put one in a bottle?"

"I dunno. I'll ask him, if you like."

He considered for a minute. "'Tain't so difficult to make a ship the way he done it," he said at last. "Not but what he made a good job of it. But putting it in a bottle—that's what's difficult."

He drifted into reminiscences of ships and bottles, and the matter lapsed.

At the aerodrome that morning Wing-Commander Hewitt and Professor Legge explained in detail to the pilot what the trials were to be. "It's quite all right," the wing-commander said, "so long as we go at it carefully. But it's a bit tricky, as you see."

Flying-Officer Chambers said: "I see what has to be done, sir. But I'm afraid I don't understand it in the least." He turned to the professor. "I don't see what makes the thing go off. Do you think you could explain it to me, in very simple language?"

They retired into a vacant office and sat down at a bare deal table. The professor took a pad of paper from his case. "First," he said, "do you know how a thermionic valve works?"

"More or less."

Legge sketched rapidly upon a sheet of paper. "Well, there's a valve. That's the grid."

They worked on for two hours. At the end of that time Chambers was mentally exhausted, though he had firmly in his mind the principles of the device. He leaned back in his chair, studying the pencilled circuit diagrams.

"I see," he said. "The milliammeter is what I've got to watch."

The other nodded. "You must watch it all the time," he said gravely. "The modulator should maintain the current at about twenty-five milliamps. If it goes higher you must throw this switch." He laid his pencil on the paper. "That breaks the primary circuit."

"If I don't do that, I suppose the current will go on rising till the thing goes off."

"Yes. You must watch it very carefully and throw your switch immediately."

The pilot laughed. "Fun and games for everybody if I don't," he said.

The civilian was silent for a minute. He had lain wakeful in his bed for the last two nights in the grey dawn, tortured by a vision of what might happen if the current in the circuit were allowed to rise. And this young man now called it fun and games for everybody!

He said: "I've been thinking a good deal about this current rise. I had arranged with Wing-Commander Hewitt to put the switch on the instrument panel just by your hand."

Chambers said: "That's what the new thing on the panel is, I suppose?"

"Yes. But now I think it would be better if we send up somebody with you to watch the milliammeter and throw the switch immediately it starts to rise. In fact, I think I'll come myself."

The boy looked up at the professor. "I don't see that's necessary. It's only just to throw the switch if it goes over twenty-five, isn't it?"

"Yes. But you'll have the machine to fly. This thing will want watching very carefully."

"I'll put the machine on to the auto pilot. I shan't have anything to do except to watch." He paused, and then he said: "How quickly will it go up, if it's going?"

The professor turned to the litter of papers in his bag, picked out a sheet, and made a little calculation. "For the battleship, I should expect it to go up at the rate of ten milliamps in three seconds."

"And it goes off at forty milliamps?"

Legge nodded.

"Well, that's four and a half seconds. Time enough to get your hair cut."

"Nevertheless, I think another man in the machine would be a help."

The pilot faced him, colouring a little. He was twenty-three years old, but he had not yet quite got over blushing.

"I'm damn sure he'd be a bloody nuisance."

There was a momentary silence. The professor said:
"Well, it's as you like."

"There's two things that I'd like," said Chambers.
"One's an armoured seat in case that bloody bomb goes
off under my backside. The other is a beer before lunch.
Let's go over to the mess."

Over the beer he spoke about the armoured seat to
Wing-Commander Hewitt. "I've got very simple tastes,
sir," he said. "Just a can of beer and a young woman to
take to the pictures. My carpet slippers and my old
arm-chair. But I would like the old arm-chair to be a
steel forging, if we could arrange it."

The wing-commander nodded. "Bring it right down
behind the legs and up behind the head."

"Something like that, sir."

"About three-eighths steel plate." The wing-commander considered for a moment. "I'll send Martin over
to the Dockyard and get them going on it right away."

For the next two days they worked on the machine.
The seat was delivered from the Dockyard in thirty-six
hours; the pilot watched the men as they installed it. It
was a quiet, reflective time. He spent a few hours more
with the professor from Cambridge, and gained a clear
impression of the unseen influences around the ship that
would release the weapon if all should go well. He
was interested and cheerful, looking forward to the
trials.

He said once to Hewitt: "What's the programme, sir,
if this thing works all right?"

"We're fitting up three squadrons with it. The manufacture is in progress now."

"So all we've got to do now is to find out the adjustments and then we're all ready to go?"

"That's it. There'll be a bit of training to be done,
of course."

The pilot was entirely satisfied. "Give Hitler a bit of a sick headache when we start on him with this," he said, with satisfaction. "Have we got to wait till Tuesday before making a start?"

"The battleship won't be ready till Tuesday."

"We could start on a cruiser."

"The battleship is the least sensitive to start on."

The boy said: "I don't mind starting on a cruiser, if it means we could get ahead this week."

The wing-commander said: "I think we'll stick to the programme."

"All right, sir. In that case, can I take Sunday off?"

"I should think so. Get some exercise."

"I'll walk her till she drops." The wing-commander laughed.

That was on Friday. He went to the snack-bar that night, picked up Mona, and took her dancing. She said:

"We've got to be back earlier tonight, Jerry. My dad was cross as anything when we got home at two o'clock."

"Did he beat you?"

"Don't talk so soft. Of course he didn't."

"I believe he did. You'd better show me the marks."

"He'd beat me all right if I showed you where the marks would be, if there was any."

He let the vicious circle drop. "I'd just as soon get home to bed in decent time myself for the next few days. About Sunday."

"What about it?"

"Can you walk?"

"If I've got to."

"You've got to walk on Sunday. I've not got enough petrol to go riding round all day."

She laughed at him. "Who said we were going out all day on Sunday, anyway?"

"I did. I'm getting sandwiches from the mess."

"Where are we going to?"

He considered for a minute. "I think we'll take the car to South Harting and leave it there, and then walk up on to the Downs."

"It'll rain."

"If it does you'll get wet. That won't hurt you."

They went and danced again. He took her home when the place closed at midnight, kissed her soundly in the car, and drove back to Titchfield. In his bedroom he turned on the wireless and listened for a time to a station that was dedicated to Enlightenment and studied the handbook of instructions for the manufacture of the caravel. Then he got into bed and slept at once.

Sunday was fine, a windy sunny day of late February. The little car drew up outside the furniture shop at half-past ten, the hood down for the first time in several months. Mona was waiting ready in her room. She shot downstairs and out of the door into the car before there could be any questions from her father; Chambers let in the clutch and drove away with her.

In the shop her father and mother stood in the background among the furniture, looking out of the window, seeing, though themselves unseen. They saw their daughter get into the car, saw the boy greet her, watched the car move off.

Her mother said: "That's the one what gave her the ship. . . ."

The old warrant officer said: "He's a proper young officer, that one. Not like some you see about."

She said: "I've never known Mona go so regular with anyone, Stevie. I think she's ever so serious about him."

He said, a little gloomily: "It's no use crossing her."

"But I think he looks nice."

"Oh, aye," he said. "But he's an officer. She'd never learn his ways."

"I dunno, Stevie. Mona's very quick." She turned to him. "You wouldn't mind if she come back one day and said they wanted to be married?" She was an incorrigible optimist.

"No," he said thoughtfully. "Not if that's what they wanted. In the old days, if an officer married a barmaid he sent in his papers. That's what they used to do."

She said: "Things is different now, what with the war and everything."

He admitted that. "But if she wanted to do that, we'd see no more of her, Ma," he said. "Officers is officers, and the lower deck's the lower deck."

She was silent. The same thought had been lurking in the back of her mind.

"Give them a fair crack of the whip," he said a little heavily. "Our ways ain't officers' ways, and never will be."

The little car made its way out of the town into the country beyond. Mona asked: "Where are we going to?"

He said: "South Harting. My doctor says I've got to get some exercise."

"You and your doctor! What are we going to do when we get there?"

"Leave the car at the pub and walk to Cocking over the downs."

"How far is that?"

"About seven miles. And," he said firmly, "seven miles back."

She stared at him. "I can't walk that far."

"Let's see your shoes."

She drew one up for him to see beneath the instrument panel of the cramped little car; he peered down at it, and swerved violently to avoid a lorry. They were broad-toed walking shoes. "I got them for the holiday camp last year," she said.

"They're all right. You'll walk fifteen miles and like it."

"I've never walked so far before."

"You walk that far every night round the floor of the Pavilion."

"Don't be so silly. That's dancing."

"I'll borrow a mouth-organ from the pub and you can dance to Cocking, then. But that's where you're going."

They came to South Harting presently, a village close beneath the down, a place of thatched cottages in one long street, a village pub with the spacious rooms of an old coaching-house, and a church that stood among elm-trees. Chambers parked the little car beside the stocks outside the church. "This," he said, "is where we start to walk."

He was wearing uniform, as he had to. He had put on his oldest tunic and slacks, spotted with indelible oil-stains from the aeroplanes he flew, and faded with much cleaning. He slipped his forage-cap into his hip pocket, and he was ready to walk. The girl wore a blue jumper and an old tweed skirt.

She stared at the hill above them. "You're not going to walk up that?"

"My doctor says I've got to. It's part of the treatment."

"I think you ought to change your doctor."

They set off up the hill.

Three hours later they dropped down a muddy lane into Cocking, another hamlet underneath the down. They had seen a herd of deer, four squirrels, and a woodpecker, and had attempted—unsuccessfully—to have a ride upon a sheep. With the muddy winding of the track over the downs and through the woods, they had walked a good deal farther than the seven miles that he had guessed; they dropped down into Cocking tired and foot-sore and hungry and thirsty and happy.

Mona asked: "Where do we go now, Jerry?"

He said: "To the pub, of course."

They found the village inn, a modest one devoted to

the local farm labour. In the private bar they ordered beer and shandy at a table covered with linoleum, and unpacked their sandwiches, egg and sardines and ham. He had taken pains over the provision of the sandwiches, had explained to the grey-haired sergeant of the W.A.A.F. in the mess that his young lady was rather particular. She had said, in motherly fashion: "All right, Mr. Chambers, I'll see to it that she gets what she likes." It was by a narrow margin that she had not called him "dearie".

The sandwiches did not satisfy them; they topped up with a plate of bread and cheese from the bar and a few chocolate biscuits.

Presently they began to walk again, more slowly this time, towards South Harting by the lanes that ran beneath the downs. They got back there by tea-time, having tarried a little while to try a pig with chocolate biscuits.

At the "Ship" in South Harting they demanded tea, and were shown into a large upstairs sitting-room that overlooked the village street. A bright fire made it cheerful. They washed in an adjoining bathroom; presently they sat down to their boiled eggs and tea and cake, refreshed and pleasantly tired.

Chambers said: "I'm not going to change my doctor, not for you or anybody else. It's been a good day, this."

The girl nodded, her mouth full. "I've liked it ever so," she said presently. "Are your feet tired?"

"Not too bad. Are yours?"

She nodded. "I got heavy shoes on."

"Take them off for a bit."

She bent down and unlaced them, kicked them off and stretched her toes. "That's better."

He said: "You ought to do this oftener. I'll speak to my doctor about your feet. He'll probably say you've got to have a walk like this every week."

"What about my church?"

"There's no church like the open vault of heaven. Ruskin or Thoreau or Walt Whitman or somebody might have said that."

"If they're friends of yours they'd say anything. But, really and truly, I've enjoyed this ever so. I'd like to come again, next week or any time."

He was silent for a minute. "I don't know about next week," he said. "I shall be working pretty steadily from Tuesday onwards. When we start, we shan't knock off for the week-end."

She said: "You and your work! I believe you just play about, out at that aerodrome."

He grinned and said: "Have another doughnut."

She shook her head. "I've finished."

He took one himself. "Honestly," she said, "what do you do all day?"

He eyed her for a moment. "I can tell you one thing that I did last week."

"What's that?"

He said: "Made my will."

This was quite true. He had been to Smith's, the booksellers, and had bought a will form in an envelope for sixpence. He had read the instructions carefully, as carefully as if they had been for the circuit of his wireless set or for the rigging of his caravel. Then he had sat down and had written what he wanted to say upon the ruled lines of the form, without erasures or alterations. He had folded it over and got a couple of the batmen to witness his signature. Then he had sealed it in an envelope and put it at the back of the drawer in which he kept his collars.

Mona stared at him, uncertain whether to believe him. "No kidding?"

He munched the doughnut. "Not a bit. Show it you if you like."

She was puzzled, uncertain of his mood. "I don't believe you made a will at all." People didn't make wills till they were old, about to die.

He took a drink of tea. "Well, I did. I can't show it to you now, because I haven't got it with me. But I'll tell you what's in it."

She was silent. There was something that she didn't understand.

His eyes smiled at her. He said: "Like me to tell you?"

She said quietly: "If you want to, Jerry."

He said: "I left everything to you."

In the short evening of the winter day it was already dusk. In the long room it was getting dark; the flickering firelight was already brighter than the windows. Outside the trees massed blackly against the deep blue sky, which seemed to pale towards the whale-back of the downs. It was quiet outside in the village street. Quiet and cold.

Mona said softly: "What did you do that for?"

He grinned at her, a little embarrassed. "It's not enough to bother about," he said. "There's a couple of hundred pounds in War Loan that Aunt Mollie left me. That's all there is, really, except things like my wireless set—and the car, of course. That's worth about thirty quid."

There was a silence. She leaned towards him, puzzled and distressed. "But, Jerry, I don't want your money. Honest, I don't."

"I hope you're not going to get it. I shall be very much upset if you do."

She stared at him. "But what did you want to make a will for, anyway?"

He leaned back in his chair. "Well, somebody's got to have what I've got. In case I should get killed or anything."

"So you thought you'd leave it all to me. . . ."

He nodded.

She got up from the table and came round to his chair. She stood by him, looking down at him as he leaned back, balancing on the back legs of the chair with one leg crooked beneath the table.

"Why me?" she said gently.

He began fingering the bottom edge of her jumper, and he was silent for a moment. Then he looked up at her. "Because we've had a fine time," he said, "ever since we met. Because you were so frightfully nice to me after I sank *Caranx*. You know, you did a lot for me then. I wanted to do something, if I could, to pay back what I owe you. Even if I was to do myself a bit of no good."

Her eyes moistened. "You don't want to talk like that, Jerry."

He grinned. "All right—let's drop it. Let's talk about something else."

Her mother had quite rightly said that Mona was quick. "That's right," she said. "Let's talk about what happens if you live to be ninety." She laughed down at him tremulously. "You're trying to make out you owe me something. If you die, I get two hundred quid and your car."

He was uncertain what was coming. "And my wireless set," he said. "You mustn't forget that. I got Chungking the other night."

"But that's all if you're dead. What do I get if you live to be ninety?"

With the hand that had been fingering her jumper he smacked her seat. "A bloody good spanking. You can have the first instalment of it now, if you like."

She looked down at him. "What do I get?" she repeated.

"If I told you, you'd slap my face and start out to walk home."

"It's twenty miles. I couldn't walk that far."

"You'd have to take a bus."

"There aren't any buses." There was a short pause, and then she said: "You'd better tell me, Jerry."

He jerked forward in his chair and got up. He took her hands in his and stood there looking down on her, blushing pink. Her eyes were hardly higher than the stained and drooping wings upon his chest. "All right," he said, "I'll tell you. If this was peace-time and things were ordinary, I should want you to marry me, Mona. But I don't want that."

She said in a small voice: "What do you want then, Jerry?"

He laughed. "Your mind runs in a groove," he said. "I don't want that one, either. I want to go on as we are."

She was silent.

He said: "I've not got a lot of use for people who think they're going to get bumped off next week, and so they take a running jump into a honeymoon. If I got married I should want to have a kid or two and see them growing up. And if I couldn't see beyond the middle of next week, I'd just as soon lay off it altogether."

"I feel that way, too. It wouldn't be like being married if you didn't have kids."

He grinned. "They'll want people like us when this war's over."

She looked up into his face. "There's one thing I don't understand," she said slowly. "All this you say about you're going to be killed. What's it all about?"

"Indigestion, I should think. I've been missing my Eno's."

"Talk sensible for once, Jerry."

"It does happen from time to time, even in the best-conducted wars."

"Is this what you do at Titchfield very dangerous?"

He slipped an arm around her shoulders and drew

her to him. He wanted to make her understand, to see the matter in its true proportions.

"Look," he said. "There's a little bit of risk in every sort of flying in war-time, just as there is for ships at sea. When I was at Emsworth three chaps from my squadron fell into the drink. A month ago I was over Germany, down as far as Leipzig. This new job isn't any more dangerous than any of the other things. But in a war, in any sort of job, things do sometimes happen. That's why I made that will."

"I see."

There was a long pause. Presently she said: "I dunno if it's going to be so easy for us to keep on the way we are now, Jerry."

He was silent. The feel of her shoulder warm beneath his hand had put the same idea into his head.

She turned in his arms and looked over to the window. "If we found we couldn't, I don't want to jump into a honeymoon the way you said. It wouldn't do. I'd rather that it was the other way."

Gently he turned her back to him. "Is this what they call an improper proposal in the Sunday papers?"

She giggled. "I suppose it must be."

"You mean, you'd rather that we went away together somewhere for the week-end or something?"

"That's right."

"I wouldn't know how to set about it."

"Nor would I. But we could learn."

They looked at each other and laughed.

Chambers said: "I'd have to get a book about it and read it up. I suppose I'd have to get a wedding-ring for you, and then we'd go to a hotel and register as Mr. and Mrs. Smith."

"We'd want to have an engagement ring as well. It'ld look awfully fishy if I went with just a wedding-ring."

"A very new one, too."

"That's right. Wouldn't it be awful if we got found out?"

He said: "They can't do anything to you for that. The police, I mean."

"Not even if you register with a false name? In wartime?"

"I'm not so sure about that one. They might not like that very much."

"They could be terribly nasty, anyway."

He laughed down at her. "I don't think very much of your idea," he said. "It's too risky and too complicated. It'ld be a damn sight simpler to be old-fashioned and get married, and have done with it."

She said: "I don't want to do that."

He asked gently: "Why not?"

"I dunno, Jerry. . . ." There was a pause, and then she said: "It wouldn't do. I'd like to go on like we are. But if we found we couldn't, then I'd rather we was Mr. and Mrs. Smith for a bit."

He said very quietly: "Every word you utter goes like an arrow to my heart. A barbed arrow, I should say. You know, you're the Bad Girl of the Family. The Scarlet Woman."

She smiled a little. "You do say awful things."

"Added to which," he said gently, "my pride's cut to the quick. Here I am, Lord Jerry of Chambers' Hall, Chambers, Chambershire, and you spurn my suit."

She did not laugh. "That's it," she said softly.

He stared at her. "I believe you've got this wrong," he said. "Are you thinking of our families?"

She said honestly: "That's right. We aren't really the same sort, Jerry, and being married is for ever. We'd want to be terribly careful, or we'd be unhappy all our lives. Both of us."

"I am being careful. I haven't been so careful since I first went solo."

"Talk serious. I mean it."

"I know you do."

"Well then. . . ."

She turned in his arms and faced him. "Look, Jerry," she said, "let's talk sensible. You know how I feel about you. You can have anything you want from me—honest, you can. And there's never been anyone before, either."

"I know that," he said.

"But I don't want to marry you—not for a long time, anyway." She looked down. "It wouldn't do."

"Why not?"

She said: "I wouldn't marry you unless I could talk like the other officers' wives, and dress like them, and play tennis, and that and—and sort of *think* like them. I can't do any of them things. If we got married now we'd be happy for a month, and then we'd be unhappy ever after. That's not good enough."

He was silent for a minute. Then he said: "You're wrong. You won't be an officer's wife, not when the war's over. I shan't be able to stay on in the Air Force— not with the *Caranx* business on the record. And in the war, it doesn't matter a hoot."

She looked up into his face. "You'll stay in the Air Force," she said, "and you'll go right up to the top. You'll be an Air Vice-Marshal before you leave, or something of that. You will, Jerry—I know."

He grinned at her, but there was moisture in his eyes. "Fat lot you know about it," he said. "Look, Mona. I want you to marry me, at once."

"I dare say you do," she said. "But I'm not going to."

They argued for a quarter of an hour and got no further. Presently she said: "It's getting very dark, Jerry. If we're going to get on the road before the black-out, we'll have to go."

He took her in his arms and kissed her. "Next week," he said, "I've got to do a little work. I'll have to get to bed early each night; I can't be late. I'll make a date to come and take you dancing on Monday of next week for certain. If we get a day of bad weather I'll come in during the day, but don't count on that. Don't be worried if I don't turn up till Monday week."

She said: "That's a long time to wait, Mr. Smith."

"Lord Jerry of Chambers' Hall to you. I'll have no *lesé-majesté.*"

She laughed up at him. "Mr. Smith to me."

VII

"I DON'T see what he's getting so worked up about," the pilot said. "He's only got to watch. God help him if he ever got into a real jam."

The wing-commander turned and glanced with the pilot at the civilian pacing nervously up and down in front of the aeroplane. "He feels responsible for this. He took it very badly when the Navy cut the time short. Since then he's been working long hours on his distribution curves."

The pilot said: "He looks as if he'll have a litter of them any minute."

Professor Legge had a headache. He walked up and down before the aeroplane, anxious and fretting. From time to time he went round to the tail and got into the cabin, inspecting the last adjustments that the electricians were making to the apparatus, bothering them with his evident anxiety.

He had worked hard for the last week, too hard for his health. Unaided, he had covered in a week the research which he had estimated would take six weeks. He had covered about half the ground that would have been necessary to ensure safety for the enterprise. Now the trials were upon him, and he could do no more.

In the mental fatigue and strain from which he suffered he had lost a great deal of his sense of proportion. He had slept, in the last week, for a total of about thirty hours. He had been compelled to go to Cambridge to collect certain data, and he had visited the aerodrome three or four times. For the whole of the rest of the week he had sat in the sitting-room of his Southsea flat plodding through endless computations

with slide rule, graphs, and the little black compto-
meter. His wife had helped him very much. She had
brought him tea and biscuits at intervals of two hours
all through the night, had given him aspirins to help
him sleep, had slept little more than he had in the week.
This she had done without any understanding of the
work, because for reasons of secrecy he had told her
nothing. All he had said was that he was terribly afraid
that they might have an accident, because the Navy
were in such a hurry. For Mrs. Legge that had been
sufficient.

Now on the morning of the trial, fretting and apprehensive as he waited for the adjustments to be finished,
he blamed himself most bitterly that he had not worked
harder, had not got through more in the time. Passing
through London on his return from Cambridge he had
slept a night at his club. He had got to London no later
than half-past eight at night, having travelled and
worked since dawn. There had been a train down to
Portsmouth at nine-forty-seven, which would have got
him to his flat in Southsea before midnight.

He might have got in three or four hours' more work
before going to bed that night. Instead, he had given
up and slept at his club, travelling down next day.
Those hours now were lost for ever. They might have
made a difference. There might be some new factor
only a few hours ahead of him, some presage of
disaster.

He tortured himself with the thought that he could
have worked harder, got through more, if he had not
been lazy. His laziness might mean the death of this
young man.

Wing-Commander Hewitt came up to him. "Pretty
well finished now, I think, Professor. The car's waiting.
It's about time we went down to the pier." They were
to watch the trial from a trawler.

The civilian hesitated, irresolute. "Just one moment," he said. He walked quickly round the machine and went into the fuselage again. The wing-commander waited patiently till he reappeared.

"All right?"

"I think so. Just let me have another word with the pilot."

They crossed the grass to where Chambers was chatting to the flight-lieutenant. "You *will* remember to keep looking at the milliammeter the whole of the time?" Legge said. There was a note of entreaty in his voice. "That really is very important indeed."

Behind him the wing-commander winked at the pilot merrily. With a grave face Chambers said: "I understand that, sir. It's all right up to forty milliamps. If it goes over that I throw the switch."

Legge said: "That's it. It will be quite all right if you do that. Mind, it ought not to go over twenty-five." He hesitated, and then he said: "I wouldn't let it go quite to forty. Say thirty-eight."

"Very good, sir. I'll cut the switch at thirty-eight."

The professor sighed. "That's better, perhaps. You are quite happy now about what you've got to do?"

"Quite all right, sir. I understand everything perfectly."

The wing-commander said gently: "I think we'll have to get along now, Professor."

"All right." Legge turned to the pilot again and smiled with attempted cheeriness. "All the best."

The pilot grinned. "We'll go out on a blind tonight if this thing works all right, sir."

He watched the wing-commander and the civilian as they walked over to the car. He turned to the flight-lieutenant by his side. "And we'll go to the bloody mortuary if it doesn't. What about a beer before lunch?"

In the trawler a small party of naval officers were

already waiting. Captain Burnaby was there, and greeted them affably.

"Good morning, Wing-Commander. Good morning, Professor Legge. I hope we're going to see a good trial today."

The civilian licked his dry lips. It was incredible that these officers did not seem to realise the risk of absolute disaster staring them in the face. He said: "I hope so, too."

Burnaby turned to the Air Force officer. "Everything all right, Hewitt?"

"Quite all right, sir. The machine is ready to take off now."

"Very good." He turned to the R.N.V.R. officer in the little wheel-house. "You can cast off, Captain."

The trawler slid away from the quayside and headed for the Solent. Half an hour later they were passing through the Gate; in the open sea outside the island the trawler began rolling. It was a grey, cold day with clouds down to about fifteen hundred feet. As soon as the vessel left the quay the naval officers all bolted down below and crowded into the little cuddy, filling it with their gossip and tobacco smoke. Legge followed them, but the motion of the vessel, the smoke, and the tension of his anxiety combined to drive him up on deck again into the cold, salt air. He stood in a sheltered corner watching the flung spray drive past him from the bows, cold and miserable, and feeling rather sick. Presently the R.N.V.R. officer invited him into the wheel-house; he sat down on a bench inside the door behind the helmsman and went on torturing himself with mental calculations of the influences round the battleship.

An hour later the trial took place.

The trawler lay rolling head to sea; everyone was now on deck. Most of the officers held field-glasses in their gloved hands; Legge had no glasses, but the captain of the trawler lent him his own. Half a mile away the battleship lay, practically stopped, rolling very slightly in the trough of the sea. Above her, circling around, was the twin-engined monoplane.

Captain Burnaby said: "All right. Give him the light."

A signalman began flashing at the aeroplane with an Aldis lamp. In answer a red flare detached itself from the machine and floated slowly down against a cold grey sky. Hewitt said: "He's ready now."

The aeroplane withdrew a couple of miles to the south, then turned and flew straight for the battleship. Legge watched, tense and apprehensive. The naval officers watched with interest, tempered with unbelief.

The machine came on . . . and on . . . and on. Nothing happened. Sick with anxiety, Legge watched it fly over the ship, turn slowly, and fly back towards the south.

There was a general relaxation and a few faint smiles. Somebody said aloud: "The bloody thing won't work."

The minutes crawled by. The machine returned, flying a little lower. Again it passed over the ship and nothing happened. Again it turned towards the south.

Captain Burnaby turned to Legge. "What do you think can have happened, Professor?" he said. There was a grim set to his face; he did not like to be trifled with.

"I've no idea." The suspense was unbearable.

Hewitt said: "The pilot's probably just being very careful."

Again the monoplane approached the ship. But this time that happened which was meant to happen.

The machine roared down upon the trawler in a power dive, pulled out twenty feet above her mast-head and went rocketing up from her in exultation. On her decks the tension was snapped; everyone was talking at once. Burnaby said: "I do congratulate you most heartily, Professor. And you too, Hewitt. It went splendidly."

The civilian said weakly: "Thank you, sir." Above everything he wanted to go somewhere and sit quietly and rest. He was desperately tired, too tired to be pleased with the success.

The naval officers stood around in little groups discussing in low tones. What they had seen disturbed them very much. Ships were their homes, their livelihood, their very lives. It hurt them and distressed them to see a ship treated in the way that that one had been treated.

Somebody said ruefully: "There wouldn't have been much left of her if that stuff had been loaded."

Another said, with doubtful optimism: "I should think the multiple pom-poms would have got the machine. . . ."

The discussions ranged in low, uncertain tones all the way back to harbour.

The trawler made fast to the quay at about four o'clock. Burnaby said to Hewitt: "I'll come up with you to the aerodrome, if I may. I should like to see the installation in the aeroplane."

"By all means. We're going back there in the car."

They drove up to the aerodrome. Hewitt and Burnaby went straight into the hangar to the machine; Legge turned aside and went to the pilot's office to find Chambers.

The pilot was reading a novel at the bare wooden table. He got up as the professor came in.

The civilian said: "That was a great success, Chambers. Everyone was very pleased."

The pilot blushed a little. "I'm glad of that, sir. It seemed to go all right."

"It went very well indeed. What was the matter on the first two runs?"

Chambers said: "On the first one the milliammeter went right up, sir. It went to somewhere between thirty-two and thirty-six. It was jumping about a bit, so I switched off."

A cold hand clutched again at the professor's heart. There was no ending to the tension of this job.

"What happened on the second run?" he said quietly.

"On the second run it didn't work at all. The milliammeter stuck round about eighteen. It never got over twenty, and nothing happened."

This was terrible. Legge's half-formed theories of the distribution round the ship went crumbling into dust. They were just blundering in the unknown.

"And the third time?"

"The third time it went perfectly, sir. The milliammeter got up to twenty-five quite a long time before and stayed there steadily. I didn't feel it go at all. I just saw the ammeter go back to zero."

The Cambridge man said absently: "It all went very well. The Navy thought it was wonderful. In fact, I don't think they liked it much."

The pilot laughed. "I don't suppose they did. Hitler could give them a sick headache if he had it."

"Yes. As soon as we've got this to work, we'll have to concentrate on the defence against it."

"How can you do that?"

"Increase the influence from the ship or oscillate it rapidly."

The pilot thought for a minute. "That would mean my milliammeter would go all haywire?"

The professor nodded. "The explosion would take place in the aeroplane."

The pilot laughed. "Bloody good fun. You can get another pilot when you start on those experiments."

The civilian smiled faintly. "I shall want a lot more

time for pure research before we can begin on that."

Outside in the hangar Wing-Commander Hewitt crawled out of the fuselage on to the stained, greasy floor. Captain Burnaby followed him and adjusted the gold-peaked hat upon his head. "I do congratulate you again," he said. "It's very neat, and certainly it seems to work."

The Air Force officer nodded. "Would you like a word with the pilot, sir? I haven't heard his story yet."

"Yes, I'd like to see the pilot."

The wing-commander sent an airman to the pilot's office. Legge came with Chambers out into the hangar. They walked round the tail of the machine and came face to face with Burnaby and Hewitt.

The wing-commander said casually: "This is Flying-Officer Chambers, the pilot, sir. Captain Burnaby."

There was a terrible pause. The pilot slowly became crimson, blushing to the roots of his hair, embarrassed and furious with himself for blushing. The naval officer stood staring at him, four-square, the grim eyebrows knitted in a frown, the square jaw set firm. He did not offer to shake hands.

He said at last: "Good evening, Mr. Chambers. Do you feel satisfied with the trial today?"

The pilot said in a low tone: "Yes, sir." He cleared his throat. "I think it went all right."

The grey eyes bored into him. "And do you feel competent to carry on and complete the series of trials?"

The pilot said huskily: "Yes, sir."

The captain swung round on his heel. "I'd like to have a word with you alone, Wing-Commander," he said. They walked together out on to the tarmac.

Professor Legge turned to the pilot. "That was very queer of him," he said.

"He's a queer fellow."

"You knew him before?"

The boy nodded. "I suppose he's telling Hewitt all about it now," he said. There was a note of resignation in his voice. "I sank one of his bloody submarines last December."

The civilian stared at him. "You sank a submarine— a British one?"

The pilot nodded curtly. "It was miles out of position. I took it for a German."

"Oh . . ." The professor said no more. He felt himself in the presence of a service quarrel that was far above his head, and which he could do nothing to resolve. What the pilot had told him, so curtly and so shortly, was entirely shocking, and must obviously have created the bitterest feelings in the Navy. It was difficult to suppose that Burnaby would consent to the trials proceeding in the hands of Flying-Officer Chambers. And with that thought there came to the professor the swift corollary that he would get more time. The trials could not proceed if the pilot were to be changed; they would be held up for a few days, and in those few days he could press forward with his calculations. It might still be possible to mitigate the frightful risks that they were taking.

On the tarmac the two officers paced side by side in silence for a few minutes. At last Hewitt said:

"I didn't know a thing about this, Captain Burnaby. If I had I'd never have accepted him for this work. I can't think what Postings were about."

The naval officer reserved a grim silence. He would not say what he was thinking of the organisation of the Royal Air Force.

The wing-commander went on: "At the same time, there he is and we must make the best of him."

The naval officer stopped dead. "I hope you don't propose that these trials should continue in his hands? In our view he's completely irresponsible."

The wing-commander turned and faced him. "I'll tell you what our view of that is tomorrow morning, sir," he said coolly. "In the meantime I'll get on to the Coastal Command right away and find out all about him. Probably I'll go over tonight and see them at Emsworth."

"The trial tomorrow must be cancelled."

The Air Force officer said: "Not by us. We shall cancel it if we find our pilot is unfit to do the work. If not, we shall be ready to proceed tomorrow morning in accordance with the *pro forma*."

There was an angry pause. At last the captain said: "Do you consider him to be a fit pilot, then?"

The wing-commander said directly: "I've not made up my mind, and I must see my A.O.C. If you had asked me that an hour ago I should have said that I thought him a very suitable pilot for the job." He paused, and then he said: "His conduct of the trials to date has been both serious and competent."

The captain gave him a long, reflective look. "I can't deny that," he said at last. "At the same time, the trials have only just begun. We very much object to going on with him."

Hewitt nodded slowly. "I see that. Will you leave it with me for this evening, Captain? I must find out his record, and I must see his late C.O.; after that we'll make up our minds. We'll run no risks by using a bad pilot for sentiment. But to change him will set back these trials a week, and I'm not going to do that because you don't like his face."

"No," said Burnaby. "But in our view he's not responsible."

"I understand that, sir. Tell me, where can I get hold of you tonight?"

"I live at Shedfield." The wing-commander took down the telephone number.

"Very good, sir. I'll get in touch with you upon the telephone after I've been to Emsworth."

He saw the naval officer to the grey-blue car with the airman chauffeur, watched him drive away. He turned back towards his office, but Legge was at his elbow.

The professor said: "Could you spare me a few moments?"

"Of course." They went into the office together.

The civilian said: "I've been talking to Chambers." He told the wing-commander of the vagaries shown on the milliammeter. "That means the distribution round the ship is very far from what I had assumed. I'm afraid it means we simply don't know what we're doing."

"But the thing worked all right, Professor."

"I know it did—at the third shot." There was strain in the civilian's voice. "But don't you see—if he hadn't switched off on the first run it would have gone off in the aeroplane."

The wing-commander nodded. "I see that. But after all, that's what we put the switch there for."

Legge picked up a pencil from the desk and rolled it absently between his fingers. "I've got to tell you that I think this programme is extremely dangerous. We simply don't know what's happening."

Hewitt said: "We're finding out very quickly."

The other could not deny that. "Going at it in this way we learn a great deal in a short time. But the risk is enormous."

There was a short silence in the office. At last Hewitt said: "If we stopped the trials completely for a week— how would that suit you?"

"It's what I should like best. A fortnight would be better."

The wing-commander smiled. "I couldn't give you more than a week, and then only if the pilot had to be changed. The Navy don't like Chambers."

"I know. He told me about that."

"What do you think of Chambers, Professor?"

"I think he's a very good lad. Too good to be treated as we're treating him in this programme."

The wing-commander sighed. "I can't do anything about the programme," he said heavily. "We made our decision at the last meeting that we'd do it this way, and nothing's happened since to alter that decision. But if we have to change the pilot, that does give us breathing space."

Legge left the office. Hewitt sat down at his desk, rang for the clerk, and signed the papers in a couple of files. Then he put on his hat and coat and walked back to the hangar in the fading light. On the road he met Chambers going towards the mess.

He stopped. "I want a word with you, Chambers. Come back to my office."

In the office he said: "Captain Burnaby told me about the spot of bother you had in the winter."

The pilot was angry and defensive. "Yes, sir."

The wing-commander said: "I hadn't heard of it before, and I'm very sorry it's arisen now."

"Yes, I got posted away to Yorkshire. Then they posted me back here." He hesitated. "Does Captain Burnaby want another pilot?"

Hewitt said: "This is an Air Force station, not a bit of the Navy. We work in with the Navy and, in general, we do what they want, but only if it's reasonable. I want to go to Emsworth tonight to see Air-Commodore Hughes."

"He'll give me a good chit, sir. There was a lot of doubt about that submarine. I still think it was a German."

"The Court of Enquiry didn't, Chambers."

The pilot said bitterly: "It was a naval court, sir."

There was a short silence.

The wing-commander said at last: "What on earth possessed you to come back here from Yorkshire?"

The boy faced him. "The usual thing," he said. "There was a girl down here, sir, who'd been decent to me that I wanted to see again. And that's the truth of it."

The wing-commander sighed. There was no answering that one.

Captain Burnaby drove back to the Dockyard in the Air Force car, dismissed it, and walked up to his office, that old-fashioned, Georgian building attached to Admiralty House, with ships in repair in docks all round about it. He was angry with the Royal Air Force. He knew that it had been the merest chance that had made Chambers into the test pilot for these trials, but it seemed to him to be one of those chances that should not happen in a well-regulated service. To him it was the inefficiency of the Royal Air Force once again, an inefficiency that existed largely in his own imagination. In his opinion nothing that the Air Force did was right; the Coastal Command never would become efficient until it became a sub-department of the Admiralty. The daily rubs that must occur in the liaison between two fighting services irritated and inflamed his views; he was inclined to suspect antagonism to the Navy where none existed. He was accustomed to work long hours, never sparing himself; the strain of war was telling on him, making him difficult.

He worked for a couple of hours, then left his office and walked down to the Unicorn Gate, where his car was parked. In the black-out he drove slowly through the town and out into the country, a heavy pouch of official papers at his side. Forty minutes later he turned into his little country house, put the car into a small wooden garage and went indoors.

He lived in a modest style, as he had done all his

life. He had married twenty years before, just after the last war; for most of that twenty years he had lived in furnished rooms and scantily-furnished flats. It was not until he had achieved the brass hat of a commander that he had been able to afford a regular maid to live in the house. He had two children, a boy of seventeen and a girl of fifteen, both at boarding-schools; their school fees made a heavy drain upon his income. When he had been promoted to captain he had moved to the little country house at Shedfield without quite realising how much it would cost him; in consequence he had not yet escaped from the gnawing of anxieties about money. He did not regret the move; it was proper that a captain should live in the country, and his wife's delight in the garden was a pleasure to him. But the wages of the second maid, and of the part-time gardener, were a burden and a difficulty to him and did not help his attitude towards the Royal Air Force.

Enid, his wife, came out to meet him in the hall. "Had a good day?" she asked.

He slung his gas-mask down into a chair, and laid the pouch beside it. "No," he said. "The trials went all right. But you remember that young Air Force cub, who sank *Caranx*?"

"Yes."

"Well, he's back again. The Air Force have made him pilot for these trials."

"Oh, Fred, I *am* sorry. Whatever made them do a thing like that?"

He turned away. "I never know what makes them do these things. I told them that they'd got to shift him out of it."

He turned away to go and wash. She said: "Come down and have a drink. Dinner's nearly ready."

"In a minute."

They sat down together to dinner, served by a maid

with fat red hands, who breathed heavily as she handed
the vegetables. He told his wife a little of the successful
trial that they had had, enough to please her without
violating the Official Secrets Act. She told him about
the garden, about the crocuses that were beginning to
appear and about the snowdrops. He saw very little of
his garden in the winter months, because he left the
house soon after eight and did not return till after dark.
It pleased him to hear her talk about it.

They went into the drawing-room after dinner and
sat down before the fire, with coffee. They listened to
the nine o'clock news on the wireless, and turned it off
again. Enid got out her knitting; presently she said:

"I don't know how I shall get through this month,
Fred. Do you think you could let me have another five
pounds?"

He raised his eyes from the buff paper he was reading. "Where's it all gone to?"

She said: "There seem to have been a lot of things
this month."

They had been married twenty years. He knew when
she was trying to conceal a small expenditure.

He frowned at her. It was the same frown that had
made him cordially disliked in the Royal Air Force, but
long experience had robbed it of all terror for her. She
said placidly:

"Repairing Jim's motor-bike was one thing."

He was mildly irritated; if there had been an accident
his son should have told him. "I never heard of this.
What happened to it?"

"He ran into the back of the milk-cart during the
holidays, and buckled the front wheel and the forks."
She knitted on in soft contentment. "I told him not to
bother you about it, because it was just after *Caranx*,
dear."

He said, irritably: "I can't go on paying out for that

motor-bike like this. If Jim has accidents, he'll have to save up out of his allowance and get the thing repaired."

"He couldn't have done that. It cost six pounds fifteen. But it's all right; I paid it out of my own money. I told him he wasn't to bother you by asking for the money for it."

"Well, how does that make you short now?"

"I had to have some new shoes and things, and there wasn't any money left in my account, so they had to come out of the housekeeping."

Her tortuous reasoning in money matters was no novelty to him. "Jim's got no business to go running into milk-carts," he said. "He's got to learn that damage has to be paid for. If he can't pay for it, he'll have to sell his motor-bike and find the money that way."

She laid down her knitting. "Don't be too hard on him, Fred."

He stared at her, surprised. "I'm not being hard on him, my dear. But he's got to learn."

She said quietly: "I know he's got to learn. He has learned already, from running into the milk-cart. He'll never do that again. There's no point in making him miserable by making him sell his motor-bike." She paused, and then she said: "You know, you *are* hard on young people, Fred."

He was silent. As a young lieutenant, when he had first been married, he had thought what fun it would be to have a family, to watch his children growing up. It hadn't worked out quite like that. A trip round the world with royalty had intervened, then a three-years' commission on the China station. He had been home for a year, and then there had been a commission in New Zealand. A couple of years in the Mediterranean, followed by another spell in China, had filled all the twenty, busy years. In the pressure of work that falls to a successful officer he had had little time to get to know his children. He knew very little of their nature, or the reasons why they did odd things that seemed to him to be so silly.

"Am I hard on them?" he said.

She gathered up her knitting, got up, and crossed the room to him. "A little bit," she said. She kissed him gently on the forehead. "You're a good father, but you don't know a lot about the young." She smiled at him. "I think I'm going up. Don't sit up late."

He said: "I'm expecting a telephone call and I've got a few things to look through." He indicated a heavy pile of buff files lying on the empty pouch. "I shan't be very late."

She left him and he heard her moving about overhead. He sat there working quietly by the dying fire until the telephone rang by his side. He picked up the receiver.

"Hewitt here," it said. "I'm speaking from Emsworth. I'm just leaving, Captain Burnaby, and as Shedfield's on my road I thought I'd look in and see you, if you're still up."

"Certainly, Come in and have a whisky, Wing-Commander."

"I'll look in just for a minute. I'll be with you in about half an hour."

He rang off and the naval officer settled down again before the fire. The papers on his knee failed to hold his mind. His thoughts drifted to his son, the boy that he considered to be so full of promise, who went and did a silly thing like running into the back of the milk-cart. Perhaps Enid was right in saying that he didn't understand the young. These accidents that seemed to him to be so criminal, so desperately wrong, perhaps there were just—youth. It might well be that no further punishment or persecution was required, that the collision with the milk-cart was its own lesson.

It was quite true what Enid said; he didn't understand the young. A great part of his life had been spent in dealing with them, moulding them into the old naval form in the old naval way. He was too good a technician not to realise that methods must change with the years. His methods had not changed since he had left Dartmouth as a midshipman. He had continued blindly on the old, worn tracks of rigid discipline because he lacked the understanding to thrash out a method of his own for dealing with young officers.

He sat there, deep in thought, before the dying fire. It had hurt him to be told that he was hard.

Presently he heard a car upon the gravel of the drive outside. His servants had both gone to bed; he got up and let Hewitt in himself. In the drawing-room he poured out a whisky and soda for him.

The wing-commander said: "I won't stay long, Captain. I've been dining at Emsworth with Air-Commodore Hughes, and we had a long talk about Chambers. The air-commodore feels that as this is a naval trial we must be guided by your wishes. In view of his past record, if you feel that you'd like a change of pilot we are quite prepared to make it."

The grim bushy eyebrows drew together in a frown. "Give my compliments to Air-Commodore Hughes," the naval officer said, "and tell him I appreciate that very much. But as a matter of fact, I've altered my decision. I want that young man to continue with the trials."

VIII

THE trials were resumed next day at the appointed time. On Chambers his reprieve had a tonic effect. He had gone to bed miserable and resentful, planning yet another transfer, this time to a single-seater squadron, which he thought could never, under any circumstances, require liaison with the Royal Navy. At midnight he had been roused by a batman, who brought him a signal confirming that the trials would proceed as ordered, and that the Navy had agreed to Flying-Officer Chambers as pilot. A great surge of relief came over him and he slept well, with pleasant thoughts of Mona. In the morning he went straight to the wing-commander's office and heard of the surprising change in Captain Burnaby. He did not understand it, nor did anybody else, but the new atmosphere that it implied was very welcome.

Chambers put all other matters out of his head and concentrated on the work in hand, keen and enthusiastic for the coming trial.

Professor Legge had got the news by telephone about midnight, and he received it with the deepest disappointment. He had spent the evening relieved and rested. His wife had seized upon the respite that a change of pilot was to give him, and had made him take an evening off from work. They had dined together in the snack-bar of the Royal Clarence Hotel on a grilled steak and a fruit salad; the professor had been able to detach his mind sufficiently from distribution curves to take note of the pretty barmaid serving drinks to the young officers across the bar. From the "Royal Clarence" they had gone on to a movie, where they had seen a film called *Blondie Gets Her Man*. For seventy-five minutes all thought of battleships, of electronic influences, and of explosives had been swept from his mind. He had laughed almost continuously throughout the film, and he was better for it. They had returned to their little flat in Southsea in the black-out happy and amused. Mrs. Legge had persuaded him to go to bed at once in order that he could be really fresh to recommence the work next morning. He had agreed willingly, and had gone to bed anticipating a long, restful night of sleep.

At midnight the telephone rang, to tell him that the trials would proceed next day according to the programme. He slept very little after that.

At nine o'clock he went on board the trawler in the dockyard, worried and resentful. There were more naval officers than ever this time, by reason of the success of the experiments the previous day. Legge said to Hewitt:

"I thought this trial would be postponed. Is it still Chambers flying the machine, or have you got another pilot?"

Hewitt smiled. "Burnaby took a less extreme attitude after all. So we didn't have to change from Chambers, and the trial could proceed."

The professor laughed shortly. "That's very unfortunate from my point of view. I hoped that we were going to get a bit more time."

The wing-commander nodded. "I had that in mind as well. But I'm afraid it's not panned out that way."

There were three trials to be carried out that day, each with the battleship. Between each trial it was necessary for the aeroplane to go back to the aerodrome for loading up. All day the trawler lay and rolled a mile from the battleship, while a protective screen of three destroyers kept guard to seawards on the alert for submarines. Between each trial the civilian sat in the wheel-house, cold and apprehensive and rather sick.

The first trial worked satisfactorily at the first attempt. There was great satisfaction till the machine came out for the second trial, when the device failed to work for three successive runs over the battleship, functioning at the fourth attempt. On the third and last trial it worked at the second attempt.

The trawler went back to harbour, and the battleship steamed out to sea in the falling dusk, bound for some unknown destination. She had other things to do besides serving as a lay figure for the trials of a secret weapon. No other battleship was to be available for a fortnight; in the meantime trials were to go on with a cruiser.

As the trawler steamed back to harbour, Burnaby held a little conference with Legge and Hewitt in the reeling chart-room. "It works perfectly when it does work," he said. "It's a pity that it isn't more reliable."

Legge said: "That isn't fundamental to it, sir. It can be made reliable as soon as we find out exactly what the forces are to operate it. But at the moment we're trying to do the exploration without records, and with an explosive charge on board the aeroplane."

Burnaby said directly: "Do you feel that we shall not be able to get it ready for service in this way?"

Legge said: "No, I don't feel that. I think this way is far the quickest method of getting it ready for use in war. But I do think that we're taking some appalling risks."

Hewitt said: "We did decide to take them, after a good deal of thought."

The civilian said: "I know. I suppose I'm not used to this sort of thing."

Burnaby said, rather unexpectedly: "None of us are."

It was practically dark when Legge and Hewitt got

back to the aerodrome. Chambers was waiting for them there; together they went through the results with him. "The milliammeter went up over thirty-five on the first and third run of trial two," he said, "and on the first of trial three. I switched off each time. I can't see why it didn't work all right the second run of trial two."

There was a long silence. The civilian studied the pencilled sheet of the pilot's notes carefully and methodically.

Hewitt said at last: "Does that mean anything to you, Professor?"

The other said slowly: "I think so. I'd like to work upon this for a bit. It's quite clear we want different modulation for the battleship, and while we're at it we might drop the frequency a bit. How long did Burnaby say that it would be before we had a battleship again?"

"A fortnight."

"That's good. I think we should be able to be more reliable by then."

Chambers turned to Hewitt. "A signal came through from the dockyard about the cruiser, sir. They want to know if the trial tomorrow is confirmed."

The wing-commander turned to Legge. "Is that all right, Professor?"

"Is what all right?"

"To go on tomorrow with the cruiser."

The civilian looked at them over his spectacles. "The current will rise quicker if it's going up at all. That's because of the smaller absolute size of ship, you understand. There won't be much longer than two and a half seconds for throwing the switch."

Chambers said: "If there's two and a half seconds, that's all right, sir. I had time to eat a banana today."

"Two seconds is a very short time, Chambers," Legge said seriously.

The pilot laughed. "It's the hell of a long time when

you're sitting with your hand upon the switch, wondering what that bloody little needle's going to do," he said. "No, seriously, sir—I think it's quite all right."

Hewitt said: "You're the sole judge of that, Chambers. If you feel that time is rather short, just say so, and we'll have to tackle it some other way."

The pilot said: "Two and a half seconds is quite long enough to throw that switch out, sir. As a matter of fact, there is no other way to do this, is there?"

"Only by exploring and plotting the air all round a typical ship of this size."

"Well, that's absurd. I mean, it 'ld take a month of Sundays to do that. No, this is perfectly all right for me."

They discussed it for a few minutes longer, sketching a little in pencil on a pad. Finally, Hewitt said: "All right, we'll have the ship tomorrow. I'll make a signal to the dockyard. We've got her till the end of the week."

The pilot said: "That's fine. We should be able to get somewhere with it in that time."

They dispersed. Legge took the pilot's notes and went back in his car to Southsea, driving slowly in the dark, with a new horror to sit by his side. To him, two seconds was a desperately short time. He was a man of middle age and his reaction times were getting longer with the years; it was difficult for him to place himself in the position of the pilot, who could operate the switch in one-fifth of a second. Disaster stared him in the face, and drove him to his calculations for the cruiser as soon as he got to his flat. The battleship problem was relegated to a corner of his mind. He had a shrewd idea now of the source of all their difficulties with that and he could see the means of overcoming them; when next they went out to a battleship the thing would work right every time. But that was now no longer of the first importance. In one night's work he must now cover the ground of three months' steady research upon the cruiser if an accident were to be made reasonably impossible. No man living could do that, but he must do what lay within his power.

Immediately he settled down to work, with blue-prints, pad, and calculating machine.

Chambers went back to the mess, and up to his bedroom. He had a little electric stove in his room at Titchfield that he had bought at the local ironmonger's and had adapted furtively to work from the lighting circuit; it overloaded the circuit, but warmed the room beautifully. He turned on this and tuned the wireless to the Columbia system; for a few minutes he listened to an agricultural expert answering queries about hog-disease in Iowa. Then he got out the caravel and spent a happy hour shipbuilding.

He dined in the mess and played bridge for an hour or so, winning three and twopence. Then he drank a pint of beer and had a game of shove-halfpenny with a flight-lieutenant. By ten o'clock he was retiring to his room; he was sleeping quietly by eleven. He slept till after seven in the morning.

Mona, on her part, spent the evening in the bar, as usual. She was still vaguely dissatisfied, though less restless than she had been before Jerry had returned from Yorkshire. She still thought it would be nice to be in the perfumery department of a big shop, but you couldn't do everything. She knew very well that matters could not be static now between Jerry and herself; she might end up as Mrs. Chambers or she might end up as Mrs. Smith; beside either avocation the perfumery paled into insignificance. If her life was in fact to be linked with Jerry's she did not want his friends to know her as a girl that he had picked up in a shop. In a confused way she had certain social grades defined and ordered in her mind. She would do him less harm in his career if she married him as a barmaid than if she married from a shop, or so she thought.

These reflections mitigated the snack-bar of the "Royal Clarence" to her. She was tired of the smell of beer and of the stickiness of vermouth, but she was able to bear with it phlegmatically.

That evening was fairly slack, being the middle of the week. In the seven months that had elapsed since the beginning of the war she had come to know a great many young naval officers by sight, habitués of the bar, young men serving on ships based upon the port, who came there for a grill when their ships were in. That evening there was a little party of new faces, a lieutenant-commander, R.N., two lieutenants R.N.R.—men of thirty-five or forty, these, hard-looking toughs—and a young sub in the R.N.V.R. This party joined up with a little group of minesweepers; their gossip very soon told Mona that the newcomers were off a salvage ship.

The salvage men drank whisky. They talked a good deal of the war in Finland, recently concluded; one of them had spent a good many years in Baltic ports. They talked of football pools, and of magnetic mines and how to sweep them up. This last discussion was in very low tones, so low that the barmaid only heard a few words here and there. From that, by natural transition, they went on to submarines.

A trawler officer said: "I was at Sheerness the first three months. The destroyers were at them every day, then. But it's eased off now. Down here, we don't get hardly any. One a week—not more."

One of the R.N.R. salvage men said: "They're still getting a good few around the estuary. Not like they were, of course, but still—a few. We picked up one of them off the Goodwins, 'bout a month ago."

"Picked it up?"

"Yah. Took it into Dover."

The trawlerman said: "Get any of the crew?"

The other shook his head. "There was plenty of them in it, but they were dead. It had been depth-charged all to hell—the hull was split in three places. We reckoned she'd been going home upon the surface in the night, and hit the sands about low water. Then up comes the tide before she can get off, and drowns the lot."

The trawlerman said: "What's everybody drinking?" He turned to Mona: "Same all round, lady."

She busied herself with the whiskies. Somebody else asked: "Did they learn anything useful from the submarine?"

"I don't know about that. We went off on another job. I only know that there was one bloody funny thing we found."

"What's that?"

The man turned to the lieutenant-commander. "Tell 'em about the torpedo-tubes, sir."

The naval officer smiled slowly. "Only one tube," he said. "I went in at the first low tide to see if any of the tubes were loaded."

One of the R.N.V.R. officers said: "Grisly sort of job."

"Yes—it was rather." He was silent for a minute, thinking again of that eerie journey through the black cavities of the dead submarine, flashing an electric-torch before him. The structure had dripped salt water on him at each step; it had smelt abominably of fuel oil, salt water, chlorine, and corruption; it had been slippery and very dark.

He said: "I opened the back doors of all the tubes. One of them was full of fuel oil."

"Fuel oil?"

The officer nodded. "I opened the door and it all came out, all over the floor and my boots and everything."

One of the trawlermen said: "How did that stuff get into a torpedo-tube?"

The other laughed. "That's not the end of it. What do you think came out with the oil?"

One of the R.N.V.R. officers, fingering his third whisky, said gravely: "A nest of field mice."

The naval officer said: "Well, you're wrong. Most of a British rating's kit."

They all stared at him. "In the oil?"

"In the oil, in the torpedo-tube. There was a hat, and a couple of jumpers and a shirt, and a pair of bags, and a lot of Portsmouth City Council tram-tickets, if you please. All sorts of stuff."

They were incredulous. "But how did that get there?"

The salvage officer laughed. "It's one of their tricks. They keep a tube full of fuel oil and British sailors' stuff. If they get in a tight corner they discharge the lot, blow the tube through with the compressed air. We see a lot of oil and air come up and stop our depth-charges. Then we see a British matloe's hat floating in the oil, and we get all hot and bothered and stop bombing altogether. And while we're dithering about it, he gets away."

"How long have they been doing this?"

"God knows. We've only just cottoned on to it. This one on the Goodwins was the first definite case we found of it."

Somebody said: "They're up to any bloody sort of trick you like."

Somebody else said: "I've heard of periscopes being stuck in a floating barrel, but I never heard of that one."

Behind the counter the barmaid stood motionless, staring at them. It was the clothes that came up in the fuel oil that had decided the Court of Enquiry upon *Caranx*; Jerry had told her so. But for that they would have given weight to what he said about there being no identification marks. The officer had said that they had only recently come to realise the floating clothes to be a German trick. What if it had been going on some time? What if the submarine that Jerry had sunk had really been a German one, as he had thought?

She must see Jerry and tell him.

The officers went to their meal, and she went on with her work, absently, in a dream. She served one gin and French to a subaltern who had asked for three beers, and she served two bottles of Guinness instead of two small whiskies to a couple of marines. Then she broke a sherry glass.

Miriam said: "That's the third glass gone this evening. Mr. Harries, he won't half be cross."

"Sorry," said Mona. "I was thinking of something else."

There was more in it than just the clothes. There were other funny things that she had heard. What was it she had heard about the slick, with oil all coming up? Porky something. Porky . . . Porky . . . Porky Thomas. That was the name. Porky Thomas had sailed through the slick with the oil coming up, but she couldn't remember that he had said anything about clothes. But Porky Thomas had said it was just off Departure Point, and it wasn't off Departure Point at all. She had asked Jerry that, and he had said it was much more towards the Island.

But someone else had said something about a submarine that had been sunk off Departure Point, surely? In a newspaper—a newspaper cutting about contraceptives. The one that that young officer had had— Jimmie, Joe . . . James—Mouldy James. That said a submarine had been sunk just off Departure Point, and on the same day, too. But Jerry was quite sure it hadn't been anywhere near Departure Point. It seemed all nonsense, any way you looked at it.

Somebody asked for two beers and a gin and Italian. She served them correctly, and began to rinse some glasses. That newspaper cutting must have been all wrong. After all, it was only an American paper, and they weren't half so good as English papers. Everybody knew that. It was obviously wrong, because it was wrong in another place as well. It said that *Caranx* broke into two bits when she was sunk, so that the bow and stern came up separately, both at the same time. That was all wrong in the paper; Jerry had told her just what happened. *Caranx* had sunk by going right up on one end, and going down straight, like that. The two ends never showed at the same time.

You couldn't believe anything you saw in foreign papers, anyway. What with the different way of sinking and the different place, it might have been a different submarine, the way they wrote about it.

It might have been a different submarine.

She stook stock-still for a moment. That was possibly the truth of it. They were sinking them the whole time. But then Porky Thomas should have known, and all the officers that were talking about Porky Thomas, that same evening. Or was it the next evening? She had forgotten. Funny they hadn't said about another submarine that had been sunk, the day that Jerry had sunk *Caranx*. And Mouldy James, he hadn't seemed to know about it, either.

But that was quite silly. If nobody had known about a second submarine being sunk that day, who was it sunk it? Jerry hadn't sunk two. Whoever sunk the second one must have known.

Well then, there couldn't have been a second one at all. But then, that seemed to be all wrong, too.

A rush of orders came upon her then, and drove the matter from her mind. It was something terribly important that she must talk over with Jerry when she met him; she felt sure he would be able to resolve the puzzle for her, and explain what it all meant. In the meantime there was a crowd of thirsty officers to serve, and she must get on with her job.

She left the "Royal Clarence" at about a quarter-past ten and went home. Her father and her mother were still up when she got home, sitting in the little kitchen, one each side of the fire.

Her mother said: "We just had a cup of tea, dearie. Make yourself a cup; it's still hot in the pot."

She shook her head. "I don't mind a cup of cocoa." But there was no cocoa, and she prepared to go upstairs to bed. She paused at the foot of the stairs. "Dad," she said. "You couldn't sink a submarine without you knew it, could you?"

He took off his spectacles and stared at her. "Who couldn't sink a submarine?"

"I mean, if a submarine got sunk, somebody would know who done it?"

"Should do, girl. Who's been talking to you?"

She said: "Nobody special. It's just what I heard in the bar. There was one sunk, and no one seems to know who sunk it."

"Sunk in the Channel? In these parts?"

"Off Departure Point, they were saying."

"Off Departure Point." He ruminated for a while over this conundrum. "The only thing would be, if it had been sunk by another German submarine, by mistake, like. Nobody would know then who done it."

She shook her head. "I don't think that makes sense. It doesn't matter. I was only wondering, because they was all talking about it."

He said: "That's the only way I knows as it could happen without anybody knowing."

She went up to her room and got into bed, the problem still in the background of her mind. Jerry would put it right for her. It was five more days before she met him, unless the weather were to turn bad suddenly. But there was not much chance of that; in fact, it was unusually fine for the time of year.

Still, five days would soon go.

She slept.

Psychiatrists say that when you go to sleep with something on your mind, some difficult problem, your subconscious mind continues working at it all night through. Mona woke up at about three in the morning and sat bolt upright in bed.

It wasn't *Caranx* that Jerry had sunk. It was a German, a German with British sailors' clothes in her torpedo-tubes. *Caranx* had been the other one, sunk off Departure Point.

The pieces of the puzzle fitted then, each one of them in its own place. Jerry had been absolutely right when he had said he had seen no identification marks upon the hydrovanes. Of course he hadn't; it was a German submarine, as he had thought. It was steering the same course as *Caranx* from Departure Point, perhaps to try and make its way into Portsmouth. But it was late; it couldn't have known *Caranx's* time schedule.

In the little, shabby bedroom over the furniture shop the truth of a naval tragedy came to the light. The German had sunk *Caranx* off Departure Point. The Dutch skipper in the newspaper had said the British sunk a German submarine, but that was wrong. He had seen *Caranx* sunk, perhaps torpedoed by the German, as she moved upon the surface.

That was why Porky Thomas said he saw a slick, with oil coming up, just off Departure Point. He *had* seen such a slick; he had steamed through the oil that came from the torn, shattered hull of a British submarine, and he had never dreamed of it.

This was the truth, naked and undeniable. The submarine that Jerry sunk had itself torpedoed *Caranx* an hour previously.

She lay reclining on her pillows for half an hour, turning this theory over in her mind. It must be true;

there was no other way of it. And with that conviction, there came to her deep happiness. She could help Jerry, really help him in his work, in his career. He had not said much to her of the setback he had suffered, after that first evening. Then he had said that he was afraid he wouldn't be able to stay on in the Air Force after the war. She knew what that would mean to him; the end of his career. No more doing the work that he had chosen, that he was good at.

But that was over now. He hadn't sunk *Caranx*, and she'd prove it. Mouldy James and Porky Thomas and everyone should be brought in to help.

She lay back quietly, desperately happy. If she could help to rid him of the slur of having sunk a British sub-marine, it wouldn't matter quite so much, perhaps, if he married a barmaid. With *Caranx* and a barmaid both upon his record, he'd never be able to stay in the service after the war. But if it were shown that he had really sunk a German submarine, then things were different. A German submarine would be an asset on his record, sufficient to outweigh even a barmaid, if she were very careful always to talk nicely, and to learn to do the right things with a visiting-card. And that should not be very difficult to learn.

It was not Mona's way to lie awake. When she was happy, she usually went to sleep, and she was sleeping quietly before so very long.

She caught her father in the shop next morning, after breakfast. "Dad," she said, "what would you do if you was me?"

"I dunno, girl."

"You know Jerry—Flying-Officer Chambers, what takes me dancing sometimes."

"I see him once," he said cautiously.

"Did you know about his trouble, Dad?"

He shook his head.

"He sunk a British submarine, with bombs, when he was on patrol. That's what the Court of Enquiry said, but it's all wrong, Dad. Honest, it is."

His brow darkened; he was first and foremost an old naval petty-officer. "Let's get this right, girl," he said quietly. "What is it that you say he done?"

"He sunk a submarine called *Caranx*, so they said. But he didn't do it, really, and truly."

It took him ten minutes to extract the story from her. It would have taken anybody else half an hour, but he spoke her language and could understand her processes of thought. In a quarter of an hour he had completely absorbed the whole story; he sat there rubbing his chin thoughtfully.

She said: "What ought I to do, Dad? I mean, some-one ought to know about it."

He said: "In a ship the officer of the watch would be the one to tell. But with this—I don't know, I'm sure."

She was silent.

"It's not as if you know anything, really," he said. "It's just what you suppose."

She said stubbornly: "I don't see that, Dad. Seems to me that it's the only way it could have happened." There was a pause, and then she said: "That Court of Enquiry never saw Porky Thomas or Mouldy James, or anyone. They never even knew about the clothes in the torpedo-tube, because that's only just been found out."

"I dunno what to say," he said weakly.

"Somebody ought to be told."

"The only chap to tell would be the young chap him-self. The one what takes you out."

She stared out of the shop window to the street out-side. "I'd rather tell someone different. He might not want to go raking it all up again. But it's something that they ought to know."

"I don't know, I'm sure," he said.

That morning the trawler went out again, with Burnaby and Legge on board, and a number of naval officers. As they went, Legge, tired and worried, lectured to them on the modifications that he proposed to put in hand for dealing with the battleship. They could not all follow his reasoning, though one or two were able to discourse with him intelligently. In half an hour he had satisfied them completely.

Burnaby said: "This seems to mean, then, that we're practically home. When you get the new modulator installed, we're ready for war."

The civilian said hesitantly: "I think we shall be very near that stage. But only as regards the battleship, you know. There'll be another set of conditions altogether for the cruiser."

Burnaby said: "I quite appreciate that, Professor Legge. But as regards the battleship alone, we're very nearly ready for service use?"

Legge said: "I think that is so."

The naval captain said: "I do congratulate you, Professor, both on the thing itself and on the speed with which you've brought it along."

The civilian flushed a little. "I wish we didn't have to take such risks."

"I know. But the solution for the battleship has justified the risks of accident."

Legge said nothing. He could not bring himself to agree with that. In his private view, these officers were too impatient for results. Granted that the country was at war and that this device was needed more than most, he could not feel that this slapdash method of full-scale experiment so loved by the services was reasonable or scientifically right. He knew very well that an accident in the early stages would have turned them all against him, would have killed the weapon stone-dead in their minds. The possibility was now removed by the partial success that he had had with the battleship, but that did not affect his view that basically the method of experiment was unsound. They would have done better to have spent more time upon research.

The trawler reached the area allotted for the trials and met the cruiser. For half an hour they lay rolling a few hundred yards apart. Then the bomber appeared flying from the land, the cinema photographers made the final adjustments to their cameras, and the Aldis lamp flashed for the trial to commence.

The machine approached the cruiser and flew over it. Nothing happened. It passed above the ship and began to turn away; on the trawler the officers relaxed the intensity of their observations.

Burnaby said: "That will be the modulation again, I suppose, Professor?"

Legge said: "I should think so, sir. We must expect it to be a matter of trial and error, just as with the battleship."

The monoplane approached the ship again, flying steadily upon an even keel, but on a different course.

This time the device worked.

The monoplane swept down upon the trawler, circled round her very low, the pilot waving merrily as she turned, and made off towards the land. On board the trawler there was great satisfaction. True, it had not worked first time, but it was generally realised that that was just a matter for adjustment. Professor Legge was treated with considerable respect. They made way for him in the little cuddy of the trawler at lunch-time to give him the best seat at the little table; a second trial was to take place at two o'clock.

Back on the aerodrome, Chambers reported to Hewitt: "It worked all right, sir, at the second shot. They're loading up again now for the trial this afternoon."

The wing-commander nodded. "Any particular reason why it didn't work the first time?"

"None at all, that I could see, sir." He paused. "As a matter of fact, it didn't go a bit as the professor said. You know he said that the current on the milliammeter would go up suddenly, in two and half seconds?"

The wing-commander said: "Yes. He was very worried about it."

"Well, he's got it all wrong. It just went creeping up, very slowly—much slower than the battleship. It must have taken seven or eight seconds. I switched off when it got to thirty-six."

"That's funny. He was all wrong about the rate of rise?"

"Yes, sir. It went up very slowly." The pilot hesitated. "Do you think we ought to let him know?"

"Send him a code signal by radio, you mean? We can't send that in clear."

They glanced at each other. They had both had some experience of code signals in the hands of wireless operators in training. It might very well take three or four hours to get an intelligible answer to a cable of that sort.

The pilot said: "I should think it would be all right if we just carry on. After all, it only means there's that much more time to cut the switch."

The wing-commander said: "That's all it can mean. I should carry on, and tell him tonight."

"Very good, sir."

Chambers went off to the mess for a quick lunch. At the table somebody asked him: "How's it going?"

"Not so bad," he said. "Did the cruiser a bit of no good this morning—or would have done if the thing had been real."

Somebody else said: "The Navy are all hot and bothered over it."

"And well they may be."

He walked back to the hangar. The machine was not quite ready; he put in his parachute-harness and his Mae West and stood waiting on the tarmac. It was a fine, breezy, sunny afternoon; cold with the blustering cold of March, but invigorating with the promise of summer to come. The flight-lieutenant came and stood by him.

"Bloody nice day," he said, "Going to flirt with death again?"

Chambers grinned. "Nice day for the ceremony. I always think rain spoils a funeral."

"How's it going?"

"Not so bad. I think we've got it pretty well whacked now."

The flight-sergeant came up to them. "All ready now, sir." The pilot turned and got into the machine.

Presently he took off and flew towards the coast, on the alert for other aircraft. As he passed out over the beach at about a thousand feet he was turning over in his mind the morning's trial. He had a firm impression that this hit-and-miss business of experiment was quite unnecessary. There was some means of procedure that they could adopt, somewhere, somehow, that would make this rather tricky method of experiment obsolete. Some combination of the height and speed and modulation, and frequency which would ring the bell each time, delivering the stick of chocolate with accuracy and regularity. He had a feeling that the problem contained within itself a neat and accurate solution, and a safe one, too. He knew that Professor Legge had the same instinct, but neither had been able to formulate it in words.

Presently, far ahead of him upon the sunny corrugated sea, he saw the cruiser, with the trawler lying at a little distance from her. He closed them rapidly and circled round above the trawler at about a thousand feet. In a minute the white flashes of the Aldis lamp showed from her bridge; he turned away and flew south for a couple of minutes, getting distance for his run towards the ship. Then he turned again, and made for the cruiser.

He switched on current to the apparatus at the main switch and pulled over the safety-switch. The milli-ammeter showed sixteen or seventeen; that was about normal at the beginning of the run. He glanced quickly at the cruiser to check the direction, ruddering slightly to maintain his course.

Then he glanced back at the milliammeter. Still only about eighteen; it wasn't rising as it should.

The run was going to be another failure.

He shot another quick glance at the ship, corrected slightly with his feet, and back to the dial of the ammeter.

The needle wasn't there.

For an instant, perhaps the fifth of a second, he was bewildered; then his hand began to move towards the switch.

At the same moment he saw the needle in a different place, right up at the far end of the scale. It was over fifty.

Quick as he moved his hand, the current passed along the circuit-wires more quickly. He never heard the detonation, nor felt the burst of flame. He saw, but did not feel, the structure of the cockpit dissolve round him.

He felt no pain.

He saw the port engine fall out and go down, trailing a plume of black smoke in its fall. He saw the flaming wreckage of the wings collapse and leave him, and he saw, but did not feel, the fuselage rear up and go into its long, uneven plunge tail first towards the sea.

He thought: "This is being killed."

And then he thought: "My God, we've been a pack of bloody fools."

Clear in his mind was what they should have done. It was so easy, such a simple little trick. It would have freed the trials from all risk. It would have saved his life.

He was being killed and nobody would know. Another pilot would come forward and would carry on the trials and he, too, would be killed. And then another, and another one. He could have stopped all that, but he was being killed.

As the wrecked fuselage plunged tail first into the sea, one thought was paramount, pervading every fibre of his being.

He must, *must* try and live, to tell Professor Legge.

It is a horrible thing to see an aeroplane destroyed by an explosion from within.

On the trawler the naval officers stood stupefied. The detonation blew the belly of the machine out downwards, and a sheet of flame shot outwards from the fuselage, coloured a cherry-red against the pale-blue sky. The big monoplane staggered, practically stopped. Then a round mass that was an engine fell from the port wing and went down to the sea, leaving a great plume of black smoke behind it in its fall.

The wrecked bomber put its nose up and the port wing burst into flame. Then the wings crumpled up and the whole port wing parted from the fuselage, and hung for a time suspended by the hot air of its own combustion. The remnant of the fuselage and the starboard wing dropped backwards in a tail slide, and plunged down to the water, gathering speed at every moment of its fall.

It hit the sea a few hundred yards from the cruiser, with a resounding crash and a great sheet of spray. It bobbed up to the surface in the middle of the foam of its own fall, and began sinking fairly slowly. Above it the port wing hovered flaming, dropping streams of blazing petrol to the sea. Then it, too, began to fall, quicker and quicker, till it hit the sea a little way away.

A motor-pinnace splashed down heavily into the water from the cruiser, turned, and made for the sinking wreckage.

On the bridge of the trawler, Captain Burnaby stood staring at the disaster. He moved once to speak to the captain; the R.N.V.R. lieutenant jumped for the telegraph and rang it to full speed. The trawler turned slowly and made for the floating wreckage.

Burnaby stood staring at the wreck through field-glasses, grim and silent.

By his side, Professor Legge stood white and sick, gripping the rail before him with both hands. He had seen a boy killed before his eyes, a boy that he had known, talked to, consulted with, a young man that he had admired for his light-hearted courage. And his one reaction was a feeling of relief.

Relief that it was over. The long, grinding tension of anxiety was finished, for the worst had happened. There would be no need now to lie awake at nights, worrying desperately if there were no more that he could do. There would be no more arguing and pleading with the officers for a more cautious programme and no more rebuffs. This marked a period.

The tension of anxiety was snapped. Unnoticed, a tear trickled down his cheek to his moustache, but he only felt relief, an immense thankfulness that it was over.

The motor-boat was now beside the wreck.

IX

IN the snack-bar that evening, Miriam said: "I don't
know what's come over you. You're looking pleased
as a dog with two tails tonight. What's it all about,
anyway?"

Mona tossed her head. "Nothing to do with you."

The other smiled. "It's that Air Force officer you go
out with. Meeting him tonight?"

Mona shook her head. "He can't get off till next
week."

"Well, then, what are you so pleased about? Got
another one?"

"Don't talk so soft. It's nothing like that."

Miriam sighed, unbelieving, and broke off to serve a
couple of whiskies. The evening progressed along the
usual lines. The bar was moderately full; as the months
went by the proportion of women in the bar tended to
increase. The W.A.A.F.s and the W.R.N.S. seemed to
come more frequently; sometimes they came with naval
or Air Force officers, but frequently they came in little
groups of two or three of their own service. Then they
would sit at a table by themselves, rather self-conscious
in so masculine a place, drinking with care and feminine
economy.

About eight o'clock Mona nudged Miriam. "There's
those Wren officers you know. The one in the middle,
what you said was the daughter of the officer at the
Navigating School."

Miriam looked across the room. "Why, that's right,"
she said. "That's Miss Hancock. I don't know who
them others are with her."

"What's that Miss Hancock like? Do you know her?"

The other shook her head. "I never spoke to her. My cousin Flora was in service there—that's how I know her. Flora said she was all right. A bit stuck up, like. But all officers' daughters get like that."

Mona said: "I suppose they do. Would she mind it if I went and spoke to her, do you think?"

The other girl stared at her. "Whatever for?"

Mona regretted she had made the suggestion. "Just something I was thinking about," she said weakly.

Miriam looked at her kindly. "She's all right," she said. "She won't bite your head off." In her own mind, she had a very good idea what Mona wanted to talk to Miss Hancock about. She wanted to get into the Wrens, and she wanted some help. That was what she had been so excited over earlier in the evening.

"All right," said Mona, with determination. "I'll go and try."

The white-coated waiter came with a tray for three glasses of light sherry for the Wrens. Mona said: "Look, Jimmy, I'll take that along."

Miriam said: "Here, what about the bar?"

"Give a hand in the bar, Jimmy. I won't be a minute." She took the tray and carried it over to the three Wren officers in the corner. She put the glasses down carefully on the table before them, wiping the foot of each with Jimmy's napkin, and waited while one of them fumbled in a purse with finger and thumb.

She took the money and said: "Please, is one of you ladies Miss Hancock?"

The middle girl looked up. "I am Miss Hancock," she said. She spoke with a public-school voice, clearly and very definitely. Mona was a little damped.

She said diffidently: "Do you think I might speak to you alone, please?"

The Wren stared at her with amused astonishment. "Of course you can," she said at last. She got up from

her chair, saying to the others: "Look after my drink."
She turned to Mona. "Where shall we go?"

There was nowhere they could go privately, except
the ladies' room, and that was probably full. Mona said
weakly: "Just anywhere, I suppose." They moved a
little way aside from the other two, watching Second-
Officer Hancock with curiosity.

The two girls faced each other. "What is it?" asked
the officer.

Mona said: "It's just something I overheard, Miss
Hancock. You know, we hear a lot of talk in the bar
here of an evening—this and that, you know. Sometimes
you just don't know what to do for the best, whether to
tell anyone or let it go. Or who you ought to tell."

"What did you hear?"

"It was about a submarine called *Caranx*."

The Wren frowned. *Caranx* was a sore subject at
Admiralty House, the source of a great deal of bitter-
ness. "What about *Caranx*?" she asked sharply.

Mona said: "They all said that she'd been sunk by
one of our own aeroplanes. But I don't think that's
right, honest I don't."

"There was a Court of Enquiry that went into the
whole thing very carefully."

Mona tossed her head. "Precious fine Court of
Enquiry, if you ask me. They never heard what Porky
Thomas had to say, nor Mouldy James, neither."

Miss Hancock was startled and impressed. "Who are
they—Porky Thomas and Mouldy James?"

"They're naval officers what come here of an evening
and talk free when they've had a beer or two. Off the
minesweepers, I think they are—both of 'em."

"Do they know something about *Caranx*?"

Mona hesitated. "All they know is what they saw,"
she said at last. "There was another submarine sunk
that same afternoon, besides *Caranx*."

The Wren officer fixed her with a cool, level stare. "You're not making all this up?"

"Honest, I'm not. Porky Thomas saw the oil coming up from the bottom the next morning, and Mouldy James had a cutting from an American paper describing how the second one was sunk, and it was that same day. And then there was the clothes, too."

"What about the clothes?"

"There was a salvage officer here only last night saying about the Germans carrying our sailors' clothes in their torpedo-tubes, to shoot out if they was depth-charged. I don't know his name, but he was off one of the salvage ships."

"I see."

Miss Hancock was silent for a minute. Around them the crowd moved and chattered with all the clamour of a bar at nine o'clock at night. She was impressed; the girl seemed to know something. Certainly she knew a great deal more than it was right for any civilian to know in war-time. It would probably turn out that it was all imagination; on the other hand, it was just possible that there was something in it. Miss Hancock had seen and filed the minutes of the Court of Enquiry; she could remember nothing about any other submarine or about clothes being carried in torpedo-tubes, for that matter. She knew very well the bitter feelings that had been raised by the affair of *Caranx* between men over-strained by war. If it were possible to show, even by inference, that *Caranx* might not have been sunk by our own action, the gain in unity would be enormous.

"What's your name?" she said at last.

"Mona Stevens."

"Look," said the Wren officer, "we can't talk about this here. When can you come to Admiralty House—tomorrow?"

Mona said: "I'm on duty here from twelve till two,

and then again from six till ten, Miss Hancock. I could come any time between."

The other said incisively: "I come off watch at six bells. Could you come and see me then at the side entrance to Admiralty House? The signalman will show you the office."

The barmaid looked at her helplessly. "Please—what time did you say?"

"Three o'clock in the afternoon. Come in at the main gate of the Dockyard; I'll tell them to expect you. You'll have to sign the book."

"All right, Miss Hancock. I'll be there."

"I wouldn't talk about this too much."

"I won't do that."

Mona picked up her tray and went back to the bar. The Wren officer rejoined her friends. One of them said: "You had a nice little heart to heart. What was it all about?"

Miss Hancock was silent for a minute. Then she said: "She's got an idea into her head which might be important. You know, there's no proper organisation for civilians who get to know things. They never know whom to see about it."

"What are you doing?"

"I told her to come to Admiralty House tomorrow afternoon."

Two miles away, in Haslar Hospital, Sister Loring was going on duty. She was the night sister in Block B, Floor 2; each night at nine o'clock she came to take over from Sister MacKenzie, the day sister. Sister Loring went straight to the floor office and took off her cloak, hanging it on a peg. There was a trolley there loaded with the grim appliances for a transfusion. She gave it a cursory glance, patted her hair before the mirror and adjusted her cap, and crossed to the desk. The record-sheet was there, made out in MacKenzie's angular, crabbed handwriting. There was no sign of MacKenzie.

The night sister glanced at the sheet. Everything seemed much as she had left it before, except for one new case, multiple injuries and burns. That would be the transfusion, no doubt. The record showed an injection of strychnine, one-sixteenth of a grain, at eight-forty—twenty minutes previously.

There was a quick short step outside. Sister Mac-Kenzie came into the office, and a glance told the night sister that she was in a blazing temper. Her mouth was set into a thin, hard line of disapproval; her high, angular cheek-bones glowed pink.

"'Evening, Sister," said Loring. "Got a new accident case, I see."

"We have that," said the Scotswoman dourly.

The other glanced at her curiously. "Who is he?"

"A young air pilot. Been up to some daft fool trick, nae doubt."

"Bad?"

"Aye, he's bad all right. And if you ask me, Dr. Foster's oot to make him worse. I doot he'll die before the morn."

The night sister nodded slowly. Such things were not a novelty to her. More interesting was the rancour of the day sister against Surgeon-Commander Foster.

"Fractures, I suppose?"

"Aye—twa ribs and the right thigh. Maybe the pelvis, but it's early yet to say. Burns on both hands and arms. Shock, of course."

The night sister glanced at the trolley. "When's the transfusion?"

"I dinna ken—you'd better ask that Commander Foster. I'll tell you when it should have been, and that's two hours ago. Maybe the doctor will let him have it in another two hours, if he's with us still."

"I see he's had strychnine."

"Aye, and a heavy dose. Did ever you hear the like! The laddie comes in here conscious and all excited, and they give him strychnine!"

The night sister nodded; it did seem to be a very odd treatment for shock. She would have said morphia, to put him to sleep, to rest while the shock spent its force. She wrinkled her brows. Strychnine, surely, would make him still more conscious. It sounded absolutely crazy.

"What on earth are they playing at?" she said.

The day sister shrugged her shoulders in eloquent silent disapproval. "There's another thing," she said, with evident restraint. "A thing ye'd never guess, if ye was to guess from now till New Year's Day."

"What's that?"

"He's got a visitor."

"A visitor!"

"Aye—a business visitor. And there the laddie is, at this very minute, talking eighteen to the dozen about engineering and the Lord knows what!"

Sister Loring stared at her. "But what on earth possessed them to let a case like that have a visitor?"

"Ye may well ask that. I'm coming to think this place is turned into a mad-house. There have been Navy officers and Air Force officers and all sorts here this evening, talking with the doctor. Such craziness I never met in twenty years of service."

A gleam of light came to Sister Loring. "Is this visitor an officer?"

"Not a bit of it. There might be reason in it if he was. It's just a civilian of some kind."

"How long has he been with the patient?"

Sister MacKenzie glanced at the watch upon her wrist. "Eight and a half minutes. Commander Foster said ten minutes was the time he was to have, but I'll no let him stay that long. It's time he was off oot of it."

She left the office and marched a little way along the corridor to a single room. Loring followed her; they entered with quiet precision learned from the long years in the wards.

The Scotswoman said: "Your time is up now. Will you please go away?"

In the bed the patient turned his head with difficulty. "I want a minute or two longer, Nurse."

"And ye're not going to have it." She turned to the civilian. "I have asked you to go away," she said, with icy dignity. "Will ye please go at once?"

Professor Legge got to his feet. "Don't worry," he said to the still figure in the bed. "I've got it all now."

There was no answer from the bed. Legge turned away; the sister marched to the door and held it open for him. He went out; in the passage he turned back to her. "What are his chances?" he asked softly.

She was still very angry. "One half of what they were before your visit," she said. "And that's the truth I'm telling you."

She turned back into the room and shut the door in his face. Professor Legge went heavily towards the entrance. There was no ending to the pain and anxiety of this work.

Half an hour later Surgeon-Commander Foster straightened up above the bed and removed his gloves; a nurse wheeled away the trolley and Sister Loring finished the bandaging. The surgeon said in a low tone: "Now the morphia injection, Sister. Half a grain."

"Yes, doctor."

Presently the surgeon went away. The sister stayed for a while with the nurse, tidying the room and making all ready for the night. Once as she bent over him to adjust the bedclothes the patient said: "I want Mona to have my rabbit."

She smiled at him. "You go to sleep," she said. "I'll

see that Mona gets your rabbit. But you're not to talk any more."

There were few other patients in the ward, and she was with him most of the night.

Next day, at three o'clock, Mona was at the Dockyard gate. The policeman greeted her affably and made her sign the visitors' book. He compared the name written in the book with a pencilled list.

"That's right," he said. "Admiralty House. You know where that is, do you?"

"Turn to the right, don't I?"

"That's it, miss. Big house on the right-hand side, with pillars in front, just before you come to the arch. You can't mistake it."

She walked on and came to Admiralty House, standing in the middle of the Dockyard with a mown sweep of grass in front of it. One or two old cannons graced the entrance, with one or two symmetrical piles of cannon-balls; the brass was very brightly polished, and the long flight of steps that led up to the main door were very white. The perfection with which the big old house was maintained externally gave it a queerly masculine effect; it exuded discipline. Mona was slightly intimidated.

She saw a side door and went in. A naval signalman came forward. "I want to see Miss Hancock," she said.

He took her to a very small office on an upper floor; with a typewriter and many files and dockets of papers. "'Afternoon," she said. "You got here all right?" She cleared a bundle of papers from the only other chair and offered it to Mona.

The girl sat down upon the edge of it, a little nervously. "Yes, thank you," she said.

There was an awkward pause.

Miss Hancock leaned back in her chair. "Well, what is it?" she said at last. "You told me that you thought another submarine had been sunk on the same afternoon as *Caranx*."

"That's right."

"But how did you come to know that *Caranx* had been sunk at all?" Miss Hancock had thought of that one in her bath that morning.

Mona had anticipated it. "They was talking about it in the bar the night it happened," she said. That was true enough, although she hadn't heard what they said.

"Who was talking about it?"

"All the naval officers, I think. They all seemed to know."

Miss Hancock was silent. It was extraordinary how these things got around. People talked too much.

She said: "Tell me again what Porky Thomas saw. What's his real name, by the way—and his rank?"

Twenty minutes later she tapped at the next door but three along the corridor, and then went in. Commander Sutton looked up from his desk, red-faced, red-haired, and jovially plump. "Ha," he said, "what are you doing here? I thought it was your watch below."

Second-Officer Hancock was patient with him. The reference to her watch below was part of a long-standing ridicule, aimed at the naval talk affected by the W.R.N.S. It had reached its culmination the week before, rather offensively in her opinion, when he had found her making tea. "Tea!" he had roared for all the corridor to hear. "Sailors don't drink tea! You want a tot of rum! That's the stuff to put hair on your chest!" Since then there had been a coolness in the office.

She said: "There's a girl in my room that I'd like you to see, Commander."

He said: "Is she pretty?"

She raised her head a little higher. "I don't know if you'd think so. But she's got a story that I think you ought to hear."

He stared at her, slightly more serious. "Who is she, anyway?"

"She is the barmaid at the 'Royal Clarence', in the snack-bar."

He burst into a guffaw of laughter. "Of course I'll see her. Anytime—anywhere. Lead me to her." He sobered himself and then said: "Where is she now?"

"She's in my office."

"Go and get her. I say, do you know that one—'My Lord, there is a maid without'?"

Miss Hancock said frigidly: "I know that one, Commander. I'll go and get her."

She went back to her own office. "I want you to come and see Commander Sutton," she said. "He's just along the corridor." She hesitated, and then said: "You mustn't mind his way. He thinks he's funny."

She need not have worried. Commander Sutton reserved his pleasantries for young women who considered themselves his superior in the social scale; with his inferiors he was both courteous and polite. He got up from his desk as Mona came into the room. "My name is Sutton," he said. "How do you do, Miss Stevens?" He indicated a chair. "Would you sit down?"

He offered her a cigarette, which she refused. "Well now," he said jovially, "what's this all about?"

Miss Hancock said: "It's about the *Caranx* accident, Commander. Miss Stevens thinks another submarine was sunk on that same afternoon, off Departure Point, and that that one was really *Caranx*."

"Oh . . ." The plump officer lit his cigarette with care and laid the match down carefully in the tray. Then he stared across the desk at the barmaid, and all joviality was gone. "What makes you think that, Miss Stevens?"

Mona said in a small voice: "It's like this. I work in the 'Royal Clarence' in the snack-bar."

"I know you do," he said gravely. "You've served me there."

She smiled weakly. "Yes, sir. And you know how people get to talking of an evening when they meet old friends. Not but what they're very careful, but they forget about the girl behind the bar." She looked up at him. "We get to hear ever such a lot of things—you wouldn't think."

He nodded without speaking.

"Well, the day after *Caranx* was sunk all the naval officers—the young ones, I mean—they seemed to know all about it. And they was arguing where it happened. And somebody said that somebody called Rugson had told him that it was off Departure Point, in Area SL, I think it was."

The naval officer absently wrote "Rugson" on his blotting-pad. "Departure Point is in Area SL," he observed.

"That's what they said. And they said that an officer called Porky Thomas had sailed through a lot of oil coming up from the bottom just off Departure Point, and that he told Rugson."

"This was the same day?"

"No, sir. That was the next morning, after *Caranx* had been sunk."

"I see. It's all a bit second-hand, isn't it?"

Mona said: "I beg your pardon?"

"I mean, somebody told somebody something, and he told somebody else, who told somebody else over a drink. It's not very good evidence, is it?"

Mona looked him in the eyes. "I didn't think nothing of it till I saw a newspaper that an officer called Mouldy James had." She smiled. "I'm terribly sorry I don't know their proper names—Porky Thomas and Mouldy James. I only know what people call them."

"That's all right." He wrote the names upon his pad. "Do you know if they were R.N. or R.N.R.?"

"R.N.V.R. they were—both of them. They had wavy rings."

"I see. And what was in this newspaper?"

"It was an American newspaper—just a cutting, you know. It said that the captain of a Dutch ship had seen a submarine sunk in the Channel, off Departure Point. It was on December 3rd, the paper said. That was the day that *Caranx* was sunk, wasn't it?"

He eyed her seriously. She seemed to know the hell of a lot about *Caranx*. "I think it was," he said.

"It said another thing in the paper. It said that the submarine broke into two bits, with the bow and stern showing at the same time, like. But *Caranx* didn't do that. She went down upright with only the bow showing."

"I think she did," he said. This girl would have to be investigated.

"That's what made me think there might have been two of them, you see," said Mona. "And then only the night before last there was some officers from off a salvage ship in the bar, talking about submarines. And what they said was that the Germans carry British sailors' clothes in their torpedo-tubes sometimes and fire them out to make us think that we're attacking a British one."

The red-haired officer opened his eyes a little. "They're doing that now, are they?"

"That's what he said. So then I got to wondering which of them was which, and if it really was the English one that"—she hesitated—"that our people sank. So I came and saw Miss Hancock."

"I see."

There was a short silence. The commander sat motionless, staring at his blotting-pad. Presently he said: "It's been very good of you to come and put this to us, Miss Stevens. Very public-spirited. Now, I'm going to ask you to wait for about half an hour in Miss Hancock's office while I see if I can get hold of any of these people——" He glanced at the pencilled names upon his pad. "Then we'll have another talk."

He smiled at her affably, and she went out with Miss Hancock. The commander waited till the door was shut then lifted the telephone from his desk.

"I want the file on *Caranx*—the Court of Enquiry," he said. "Send the signalman up with it."

In a minute or two the signalman came in, a grey-haired sailor. The officer said: "Signalman, did you see a lady come in a little while ago who wanted to see Miss Hancock?"

"Yes, sir."

"She's with Miss Hancock now in her office. I don't want her to leave the building. You'd better stay at the foot of the stairs."

"Very good, sir."

The red-haired officer turned to the file. Ten minutes later he closed it and sat for a few moments staring out of the window at the elm-trees in the middle of the Dockyard, at the rooks building in them. It was quite possible that there had been a second submarine. The evidence given to the Court was not inconsistent—in fact, it all pointed the same way. It would explain the very positive evidence of the pilot that there had been no marking on the hydrovanes, and it would explain why *Caranx* had answered no signals for an hour and forty minutes before she had supposedly been sunk. She was already at the bottom of the sea.

He opened the file again and re-read the censure of the pilot in the findings of the Court. If this new story should turn out to be the truth, it meant the pilot had done well. Very well. In fact, he must have sunk the German that sunk *Caranx*. The Court would have to be recalled to reconsider its findings—to eat its words.

But now, what about this girl? He did not believe
her story for one moment, that she had overheard the
details of the sinking of *Caranx* by conversation in the
bar. She knew the details far too well, almost as if she
had had that very file of papers in her possession. There
had been a leakage of information, a very serious leakage. Somebody who knew the whole thing had been
desperately indiscreet, and not the least important part
of the investigation would be to find how that barmaid
got her knowledge of the proceedings of a secret Court.

He tucked the file under his arm and went down-
stairs. He went into the office of the secretary to the
Commander-in-Chief with a beaming, careless smile.
He said to the paymaster-captain: "Jumbo got anyone
with him?" In his younger days Admiral Sir James
Blackett, K.C.B., had played centre-forward for the
Navy.

"I don't think so. I'll just see, if you like."

"I wish you would."

The paymaster-captain went through the inner door
behind the glass screen that led to the Commander-in-
Chief's study. In a minute or two he reappeared. "Will
you go in?"

He went through to the study. Admiral Blackett,
white-haired and pale-faced, six foot three in height and
massively built, was seated at his desk. A bright fire
burned in the grate; the room was painted white, with
tall windows. A large oil-painting of Admiral the Earl
St. Vincent hung above the fireplace.

Sutton said: "I've got the file on *Caranx* here, sir.
Rather an odd thing has just happened about that."

The Commander-in-Chief frowned. *Caranx* was still
a sore subject. "What is it?" he asked tersely.

Ten minutes later he said: "Is the girl still here?"

The red-haired commander said: "She's upstairs, sir.
I thought it better not to let her go away."

"Quite right. You might bring her down. I'd like to get to the bottom of this. I'll see if I can get hold of Burnaby." He lifted a telephone and spoke to his secretary.

Commander Sutton said diffidently: "Should I ring up Rutherford over at Fort Blockhouse, sir?"

"I think you might. Ask him to come across."

Ten minutes later Commander Sutton brought Mona downstairs. "The Admiral wants to see you himself," he said. "He's quite a nice old stick."

Mona followed him obediently; inwardly she was terrified. She would have got away if that had been possible, but she was caught in the grip of the machine. She steeled herself with the thought that they couldn't eat her, anyway. She thought of Jerry, flippant and debonair. She must go through with it for his sake and face whatever came.

They went through the secretary's office into the study. The Commander-in-Chief was standing in front of the fire, a great tall man who dwarfed everybody else. He came forward as Mona came into the room.

Sutton said: "This is Miss Stevens, sir."

The Admiral held out his hand. "How do you do, Miss Stevens?" Another officer entered the room behind them. "Oh, Burnaby, this is Miss Stevens—Captain Burnaby." The captain bowed to the barmaid. "Miss Stevens has some evidence upon the loss of *Caranx*. I thought you might be interested to hear what she has to say."

The iron-grey brows bent together in a frown. "I should indeed, sir."

Commander Sutton intervened. "I have located Lieutenant James in T.174, sir," he said. "I think he is the officer that Miss Stevens knows as Mouldy James. The vessel is at North Wall. I spoke to him on the telephone, and he's coming down now."

He paused. "Rutherford is on his way over."

The Commander-in-Chief nodded. He turned to Mona. "Take a seat, Miss Stevens." He drew up an arm-chair for her before the fire. "Now, just tell us in your own words what you overhead during your work."

Mona went through her story once again. From time to time they interrupted her with questions, shrewd, penetrating questions. Their questions were not hostile; rather they were designed to help her memory. She found that with their aid she remembered much more than she thought she had been able to. Commander Rutherford came in while she was being questioned and took a chair by the wall.

Seated at the desk behind her back the secretary was taking notes.

Presently she got into difficulties.

It was Captain Burnaby who did it. He said: "There's one thing that I don't follow, Miss Stevens. This newspaper cutting that Lieutenant James had. Why didn't he report the submarine which was said to have been sunk?"

She said: "I don't think he paid much attention to it."

"Then why did he keep the cutting? Why did he show it to you?"

She hesitated. She could not tell these officers, these men who were old enough to be her father—she could not tell them a low joke about rubber, especially when it wasn't a very funny one. She said weakly: "I don't know."

The Commander-in-Chief looked down at her curiously. "He must have had some reason for showing it to you."

She was silent. At last she said: "I think he just showed it to me, like."

There was a short silence. To the officers her answer was unsatisfactory. It left an unexplained gap of motive;

it indicated something that she wished to conceal. Instinctively they all came to the same conclusion; that she had started lying.

Presently Sutton said:

"Where did you say that *Caranx*—or what we thought was *Caranx*—had been sunk, Miss Stevens?"

Mona said: "Just inside Area SM, wasn't it?"

"Yes." The commander smiled at her; he did not want to frighten her. "But how did you know that? Who told you?"

She said: "I heard them talking in the bar."

"You heard a great deal of detailed information in the bar, didn't you? I mean, about the area, and the difficulty that the pilot had in identifying the submarine, and the way she sank. And then the clothes that were picked up—you heard about those, too. Somebody must have done a lot of talking in the bar. Who was it?"

She stared at him in dismay. It would never do to tell them about Jerry at this stage—she'd get him in an awful row. She said: "It was just officers, I think."

"Several officers?"

"Yes—I think so."

The Admiral said quietly: "Do you mean that the loss of *Caranx* was discussed in every detail by a number of officers in the bar?"

She was miserably silent. Then she said: "I suppose so."

Captain Burnaby said: "Can you describe these officers to us?"

She shook her head. "I don't really remember them."

"But you remembered the others—Lieutenants Thomas and James." His frown was terrible to her.

"Yes."

"But you can't remember anything about the ones who told you about *Caranx*?"

She shook her head.

The Admiral turned to the secretary. "Take Miss Stevens to your office for a few minutes and make her comfortable," he said. "If you don't mind, Miss Stevens. . . ." Commander Sutton opened the door for her and she went out with the secretary.

"She's lying," said Captain Burnaby.

The Commander-in-Chief said: "Yes, she's lying some of the time. We shall have to check up on everything she has said."

Commander Sutton said: "I feel that a good bit of it is true."

Commander Rutherford said: "I agree with that, sir. Especially as regards the clothes. The fact that the clothes were soaked in fuel oil was always a mystery. Her story does at least explain that part of it."

The paymaster-captain came back into the room. "Lieutenant James is waiting, sir," he said.

"Tell him to come in."

Lieutenant James came in uneasily. In private life he was a young schoolmaster; all his life had been spent in schools and universities. He knew the atmosphere of Admiralty House very well; it was that of the headmaster's study. The fact that he had been called there, *ipso facto*, meant that he was guilty of some misdemeanour, and he would have been much easier in his mind if he could have recollected what it was.

The Admiral's first question did not reassure him in the least. The old man fixed him with a stony look and said:

"Lieutenant James, are you acquainted with the barmaid in the Royal Clarence Hotel?"

He was dumbfounded. "I—I go there sometimes,' he said.

"Did you ever show her a newspaper cutting?"

Recollection came to him. "I think I did once."

"Have you still got the cutting?"

He felt for his wallet. "I should have it, sir." He produced a slip of paper. "This is it."

"Let me see it." The young man gave it to him.

The Admiral read it through methodically, then passed it to Captain Burnaby. The others came to Burnaby and looked at it over his shoulder.

The Commander-in-Chief said: "What made you show this to the barmaid? Had you discussed submarines with her before?"

The young man was genuinely astonished. "Submarines, sir?"

"Yes, submarines, Mr. James. Were you in the habit of discussing submarines with this barmaid?"

A hideous vista of trouble loomed before the young schoolmaster. "I never did that, sir," he expostulated. "It was quite another thing. We were having a joke about the rubber."

"What was the joke?"

"I was with the contraband control when this ship was brought into Weymouth, sir. The captain said that his six hundred tons of rubber was for use in Holland as contraceptives, but he didn't get away with that."

The Admiral said dryly: "I imagine not, Mr. James." Commander Sutton chuckled audibly: it was the kind of joke he liked.

The young man said: "No, sir. I've got an uncle in Norfolk, Virginia, and he knew that I was in the contraband control. He sent me that cutting just for interest. As a matter of fact, it was more interesting than he thought. I kept the cutting as a souvenir."

"Why did you show it to the barmaid, then?"

"We were all laughing over it, and she asked what the joke was. So I showed it to her."

Commander Sutton smiled broadly. "And you told her what the joke was?"

"Yes, sir."

The Admiral said: "I see. Now, Mr. James, this cutting also mentions a submarine. Did you discuss that with the barmaid?"

"No, sir. Not at all."

"Have you ever discussed this submarine story with anybody?"

"No, sir. I never thought about it much."

They asked him a few more questions and sent him away, very much mystified. The Admiral laid the cutting on his desk.

Commander Sutton said: "I think that clears up one point, sir. She was lying when she said she didn't know why he showed it to her, but that's quite natural when you come to think of it. She didn't want to talk to us about contraceptives."

The Commander-in-Chief said: "That may very well be the case."

Captain Burnaby said: "We still have the major point, how she came to know anything at all about *Caranx*. She was clearly lying when we asked her about that. I must say, I'm not satisfied. There's been a very serious leakage of information, either from somebody who attended the Court of Enquiry or from somebody else who had access to the papers."

To the red-haired, red-faced, jovial Commander Sutton there came a sudden thought. It came to him because he was perhaps the youngest in years and in spirit of the four of them assembled in the room.

He said: "I should like to clear up this rubber point once and for all, sir. She'd probably tell me alone, when we should have difficulty if all four of us were questioning her. May I go and ask her one or two questions about that?"

The Admiral said: "By all means."

Commander Sutton found Mona sitting disconsolate

in the secretary's office behind the glass screen. He beamed at her. "Lieutenant James has just told us a funny story," he said cheerfully. "He said that there was a low joke about rubber in that newspaper cutting, and that that's why he showed it to you."

She said: "That's right. I didn't like to say in front of the Admiral, and all."

He said merrily: "Well now, I think that's rather funny. You know, we all thought you were hiding something terrible."

"I wasn't, honestly. Only that."

He sat down on the arm of a chair. "Look, Miss Stevens—do you mind if I ask you rather a personal question? You needn't answer it unless you want to."

She said: "All right. . . ."

"Are you engaged—or going about a lot with anybody in particular?"

She looked down. "Sort of," she said at last.

He smiled down at her, full of quite a genuine sympathy. "He's in the Air Force, isn't he?"

She was silent. It was no good trying to deceive these officers; they were too clever for her.

"Is he a pilot?" he said gently.

She nodded without speaking. They knew everything.

"Is he the pilot who sank *Caranx*?"

She raised her head. "He never did," she said angrily. "You and your precious Court of Enquiry tried to make out he did, but that's all wrong."

He smiled at her. "We only want to get to the bottom of the thing," he said. "We can't do that if you hold out on the essential facts, because then we don't know where we are at all. Look, tell me the whole of it. First of all, what's his name?"

"Chambers," she said. "Jerry Chambers. I don't mean that—I mean Roderick Chambers." He waited patiently while she collected herself. "He's a flying-officer."

"And you're engaged to him, are you?"

"Not properly. Sort of half and half."

He thought for a minute. It was all becoming clear as crystal now. "I suppose when he was in trouble over *Caranx* he told you all about it."

"He had to tell somebody," she said. "Who else was there for him to talk to? You was all against him."

"I'm not blaming him, or you, or anybody," he said. "I'm trying to help. Tell me, did you ever hear anything about *Caranx* except from Mr. Chambers?"

She shook her head. "Only from Jerry. They was talking about it a little in the bar the night it happened, or the night after, but not so that anyone could hear."

He smiled at her. "That clears up everything, Miss Stevens. Will you come in with me and tell this to the Admiral? I'll help you."

She got up reluctantly and followed him back into the study. It was awful; she didn't know what Jerry would say. But she was powerless to contend against these men.

In the study Commander Sutton said easily: "I think we've cleared up where the leakage came from, sir." He smiled. "Miss Stevens is engaged to Flying-Officer Chambers, the pilot who was responsible for sinking *Caranx*—or what we think was *Caranx*."

The Admiral stared at her with creases round his eyes that indicated the possibility of a smile. "So that is where the leakage came from?"

Mona was silent, confused. Commander Sutton said: "Yes, sir. Miss Stevens has assured me that she had no other source of information."

Rutherford said: "Well, that seems to clear up all the difficulties."

Captain Burnaby said nothing. One perfectly appalling difficulty was opening before him.

The Commander-in-Chief said: "I agree with that.

Now we can set to work and analyse the evidence."

He turned to Mona. "I'm going to ask you to wait a little longer," he said. "Would you like a cup of tea?"

She said shyly: "Yes, please."

"Come along with me."

He opened the door for her that led into the main hall of Admiralty House, white, and very high, and pillared. "I think they're having tea in the drawing-room," he said easily. "My wife will want to meet you."

He opened the door. In the large, well-proportioned room a tea-table was drawn up before the fire; a solid, comfortable tea served in the old aristocratic style. A middle-aged lady with grey hair brushed back from her forehead was sitting on a sofa in the act of pouring out; another, possibly a sister, sat opposite to her upon the far side of the fireplace. Two children, a boy and a girl of school age, were digging into the bread and jam.

The grey-haired lady looked up as the Admiral came in. "Ring the bell for another cup, Jim dear," she said. She saw Mona behind him. "Oh . . ."

The Commander-in-Chief said: "I haven't come to stay. I want you to meet Miss Stevens, Muriel, and give her a cup of tea. Miss Stevens has just been very useful to us, so be nice to her. I'm going back to my conference."

Lady Blackett smiled. "Do come and sit down," she said to Mona. She made room beside her on the sofa. She had become accustomed to the unexpected in the way of visitors since she had become hostess at Admiralty House. She did not know in the very least who Mona was, but then she had not known a great deal about the young Siamese prince that she had had to entertain the day before, or the twenty-three American journalists the day before that.

The Admiral said: "I don't suppose we shall be very long," and went back to his study.

He noticed at once that Rutherford was missing. Burnaby said: "He's telephoning from the next office, sir. He won't be a minute."

In a few minutes Rutherford returned, a little red in the face. "I just had an idea. I should have thought of it before. One of the caps that was picked up when *Caranx* went down was an ordinary rating's cap with the initials A.C.P. inside the band."

"Well?"

"It just struck me to ring up Blockhouse and find out if there was a rating on *Caranx* with the initials A.C.P."

The Admiral nodded. "Was there?"

"No, there wasn't, sir. There was a man called Porter, an engine-room artificer, but his names were Thomas Edward."

There was a short silence. Captain Burnaby said at last: "So apparently that cap did not belong to anybody on board *Caranx*."

Rutherford said: "Apparently not. It was careless of me not to have thought of this before."

Commander Sutton laughed. "Well, that's another one."

The Commander-in-Chief moved over to the table; they grouped themselves around him. "It's interesting, but it's a minor point. The first thing that we must establish is the position where this other submarine was said to have been sunk."

They sat down at the table and went into conference.

Half an hour later the Admiral rose from the table. "That's all then." He turned to Rutherford. "I shall leave this in your hands, Commander. Make your arrangements direct with Commander Hobson for the divers." He turned to the secretary. "See that Hobson is informed."

The two commanders made as if to leave the room,

but Captain Burnaby hesitated. "There's just one more thing, sir," he said.

"What's that?"

Captain Burnaby was not easily put out, but he had not felt himself in a position of such difficulty for many years. "It's about the Air Force pilot who sank *Caranx*, or what we thought to be *Caranx*," he said.

"What about him? You mean the one that is engaged to this girl here?"

"Yes, sir. He happened to be the pilot who was doing the trials upon the R.Q. apparatus yesterday. You remember, there was an accident."

"That was the same pilot, was it?"

"Yes, sir."

To the two commanders this was so much Greek; each guarded his own secrets and knew little of the secrets of the other departments.

The Commander-in-Chief said: "He's in Haslar, isn't he?"

"Yes, sir. He's pretty bad."

"Dying?"

"I wouldn't like to say. He got through the night better than they thought he would." The captain hesitated, and then he said: "He behaved very creditably. He insisted upon seeing Professor Legge in hospital last night to tell him what happened."

The Admiral nodded. It was the sort of thing that one expected, but still good to see. "I don't suppose that did him any good."

"No, sir. The hospital were very cross about it."

There was a short silence.

Commander Sutton said: "I don't think the girl knows anything about that, sir."

"No," said the Admiral. "She'll have to be told."

The same thought had been in all their minds. Each of them had shied away from it, a desperately unpleasant business that each hoped would fall to someone else.

Burnaby said: "It isn't really necessary to tell her now, sir. It will get through to her in due course in the usual way."

There was a little pause. Then the Commander-in-Chief said: "No. She'd better be told tonight. She's deserved well of us, and so has the pilot."

He turned to them. "Leave that with me, gentlemen," he said firmly. They recognised their dismissal and left the study.

Outside the evening was closing in. A steward came in quietly and closed the shutters and drew the heavy curtains across the windows. The Admiral turned to his desk and picked up the telephone. "Get me Surgeon-Captain Dixon in Haslar Hospital."

He looked up from the telephone and said to the steward: "Ask Her Ladyship if she would come and see me in here for a moment."

Lady Blackett came into the room as he was putting down the telephone. "Did you want me, Jim?"

He got up to meet her. "I wanted a word with you alone. What's that girl like that I landed on you?"

She opened her eyes a little. "She's nice, Jim. Not quite from the top drawer, you know. But she's got a very nice mind."

"Pretty, isn't she?"

"I think she's very good-looking. Who is she?"

"She's one of the barmaids at the Royal Clarence Hotel."

She nodded; she was not surprised. "I thought it was something like that. We had quite a heart to heart. She's half engaged to somebody in the Air Force—an officer." She smiled quietly. "She was working up to ask me if she ought to marry him, but she didn't get as far as that."

He nodded. "Is she up to scratch?"

"I think she is. I wouldn't mind receiving her. Things aren't like they used to be when we were married."

He turned back to the fire. "There's a bit of trouble about that Air Force officer of hers," he said. "Flying-Officer Chambers. He was on one of the experimental jobs that the people at Titchfield are doing for us. There was a crash yesterday and he got very badly hurt."

She said quietly: "I'm very sorry."

"Yes. I've just been on to Haslar. He got through last night all right, but he's still very ill. Multiple injuries, burns, and shock. I don't quite know what to do about this girl."

"I'm sure she doesn't know anything about this."

"No. Should we tell her, do you think? It's not as if she was his wife."

She said: "I think we ought to tell her."

"That's what I thought. Normally, I wouldn't bother with it; I'd let her go away and find out in the usual course of things. But these two have deserved well of us, both of them."

"You'll give her a pass to go and see him in Haslar?"

"Of course." There was a pause, and then he said: "Is she alone in the drawing-room?"

"Yes."

He moved towards the door, a great massive figure in naval uniform, with heavy rings of gold braid on his arms, with three rows of medal ribbons on his shoulder.

She stopped him. "Let me do it, Jim," she said. "I'll bring her in to see you for a minute presently." She smiled gently. "This is the sort of thing that I can do a great deal better than you."

In the tall, spacious drawing-room Mona sat alone before the fire. From three of the four walls long portraits of bygone admirals in uniform looked down at her, clothed in the fashions of an older day. Presently she got up and began looking round; over the mantel-piece she read the legend on a picture: "Admiral Earl Howe." Each of the pictures had a title under it; some of them she could remember vaguely from her history-book at school.

Jerry, she knew, would get up to the top of his pro-fession. A hundred years hence Jerry's portrait might be hanging on a similar wall in some far-distant, similar drawing-room. She wondered what the wives of all these admirals had been. Had any of them been bar-maids? If she married Jerry, would he ever have his picture on a wall like that?

The door opened, and she turned to meet the wife of the Commander-in-Chief.

Lady Blackett came forward to the fire. "Sit down, my dear," she said a little nervously. They sat down together on the deep, brocaded sofa.

"I'm afraid I've got bad news for you," she said.

X

ALL morning the Dutch ship plugged along up-Channel, driven at twelve knots with a rumbling mutter from her Diesel engines. They had passed the Lizard in the night; at dawn they had been inspected by a low-flying monoplane of the Coastal Command. The name *Heloise* and the Dutch colours painted on her side had satisfied the aeroplane; the pilot had waved cheerfully at them and had flown on his way.

They passed the Start at ten o'clock and went on keeping a sharp lock-out for submarines. Once three destroyers passed to the south of them, steering west and going at a great speed.

On the bridge Captain Jorgen stood scanning the waters. He had slept little during the night; it was unlikely that he would leave the bridge before his vessel docked at Rotterdam. He was nervous of submarines. Without respect for neutrality the Germans had been sinking Dutch ships at sight in recent weeks: a policy that was difficult to comprehend. In successive voyages since the war began the *Heloise* had brought from America a considerable quantity of goods that had been destined for Germany. Not all had passed the contraband control, but a good deal had slipped through.

His first officer called his attention to a ship ahead of them as they drew near to Portland. He inspected it through glasses; it had the unmistakable outline of a destroyer. Moreover, it was steaming to meet him. He swore softly to himself. For the last two voyages he had had a navicert issued in New York, but that did not prevent the British from stopping his ship for further inspections.

Presently the destroyer began signalling to him with a lamp. "What ship is that?" Viewing him from the bow, she could not see the letters painted on his side.

He answered; there was nothing else to do. Back came the signal: "Request you proceed to Weymouth for examination."

Angrily he signalled back: "Have navicert, therefore no examination necessary."

Curtly the answer came: "Proceed to Weymouth." The destroyer took station on his quarter and accompanied him in. Her bow guns trained on him discouraged argument.

At half-past two the anchor rattled down in Weymouth Bay; the throbbing of the Diesel engines died away to rest. The captain stood on the bridge, staring angrily at the motor tender coming towards them from the harbour mouth. He nursed a sense of grievance. His ship carried a cargo of general merchandise, most of which was quite genuinely destined for consumption in Holland.

He gave an order, and a pilot's ladder rolled down the vessel's side. The tender drew alongside and made fast; he went down to the head of the ladder to meet the officers of the Control.

The first to come over the side was a lieutenant-commander in the R.N.V.R., that he remembered from his previous examinations. "Well?" he said coldly. "What is it that you want?"

The other said: "We shan't keep you longer than an hour or two, Captain. May I see your papers?"

Jorgens shrugged his shoulders. "It is no business for you," he said. "Nothing whatsoever to do with you—you understand? Still, you are here, and I have nothing to conceal. You may see the papers—alle, alle, including the navicert which is supposed to make me free from these delays."

Another officer climbed over the bulwarks, wearing the brass hat of a commander in the Royal Navy. The first officer said: "Captain Jorgen—may I introduce you to Commander Rutherford."

"So." The Dutchman bowed stiffly. "You are also of the Contraband Control?"

Rutherford said: "No—I belong to another branch of the Service." He looked around. "Could we go into your cabin, Captain? I shan't keep you long."

"As you like." He turned and led the way to the deck-house.

The commander laid his hat and muffler on the table. He took out his wallet and extracted a small piece of newspaper. "Would you take a look at that, Captain, and tell me if you've ever seen it before?"

The Dutchman opened his eyes a little wider. "Ja," he said. "I have this in my book also. My book of cuttings, you understand. So, exactly the same. It comes, from the *Star* at Norfolk, in America."

"That's it," said Rutherford. "Tell me, is this account of the submarine correct, Captain? Did you really see a submarine destroyed like this?"

"Truly. I have written it in the log."

The commander said: "My business is with submarines, Captain. May I see that entry in your log? We are anxious to find out everything we can about that sinking."

Jorgen reached down a volume from the shelf above his head and opened it upon the table. He turned the pages rapidly to December 3rd. "You are able to read Dutch?"

"No—I'm afraid I can't."

"So." The captain laid his finger on the page. "There —the date. The time, 1415, two hours and one quarter after noon—you understand? I will translate. It says: 'Strong detonation distance two miles on starboard side with indication of wrecked submarine. Sea moderate. Departure Point bears north thirty-six degree west.'"

Rutherford pulled an envelope from his pocket and noted on the back of it the time of the explosion and the bearing from Departure Point. "That is the bearing of the ship, I take it. Not the submarine?"

"Ja. I will show upon the chart the position of the submarine, if you wish."

"We'll have a look at that later. Tell me first, what do you mean by 'indication of wrecked submarine'? Did you see the submarine before the explosion?"

Jorgen shook his head. "It was sharp storm—what do you say?—a squall. With rain and a little wind. It may be that the submarine was up on the top of the sea, but we did not see because of the rain—you understand?"

The commander nodded. "Then passed the squall, all over. And at once we hear the explosion, that rattles the whole ship, very strong. We look, and we see a very big tower of water, and then we see the two ends of a submarine both at the same time above the water—like this." He indicated with his fingers.

Rutherford nodded slowly. "Did you see the ship that sank her?"

The captain said: "There was no ship at all. Not one in sight."

"What did you think made the explosion then?"

The Dutchman eyed him narrowly. "How should I tell you what made the explosion?" he said. "You know already everything about it."

The commander said: "If I knew everything about it I shouldn't be here, Captain. Tell me, what did you make of it?"

Jorgen shrugged his shoulders. "Some say one thing, some say another thing. For myself, I think first it is a mine, and then I think another submarine has fired a torpedo. Others think an explosion from inside. But who can say?"

"Did you see any sign of any other submarine?"

The captain shook his head. "It was rough weather."

Rutherford got to his feet. "Have you got a chart, Captain? Could you show me the position of the submarine as nearly as you can?"

"Ja. That I will do now."

They went into the chart-room, laid out the chart and drew rapidly upon it with ruler and pencil. "That is our course. There the position of the ship. And *there* the detonation."

The commander noted the position carefully upon his envelope, with the reasoning that led to it. It was several miles off shore, but it was on a shelf of the sea-bottom. There were only fourteen fathoms of water marked upon the chart. They could get a diver down there almost any time if it were reasonably calm.

He stayed for a quarter of an hour longer, poring over the chart, questioning the captain about the colour of the submarine, the general appearance, and the nature of the explosion. He got no more information than he had already gained. Once he said:

"When the bow went up you saw the bottom of the submarine, I suppose?"

"Ja—at the forward end."

"What colour was it, Captain? The underwater surface."

The other shrugged his shoulders. "The visibility was bad, you understand, and it was two miles away. The bottom was dark in colour. Black, perhaps."

"Would you say that it was rusty?"

"Who can say? It was black, I think."

The commander nodded.

"You didn't alter course to go and investigate?"

The Dutchman shook his head. "I have my course given to me in the Downs, to keep me clear of dangers. I cannot leave it. There may be mines."

That was quite true. Rutherford said: "You didn't report this to anybody?"

"Why should I do that? My country is a neutral, and your war is not our business. If I had been stopped and boarded by your Navy, then I would have said what I had seen. But I passed through your Control before that in the Downs."

Presently they were finished. "That's all, I think, Captain," said the submarine commander. "We won't keep you any longer." He glanced at the lieutenant-commander of the Contraband Control.

"His papers are in order, sir."

Captain Jorgen said: "You do not wish to keep me for examination?"

Rutherford said: "Not this time, Captain. We only stopped you so that I could have this talk with you about the submarine."

The captain smiled. "So," he said. "If my ship is not to be examined, we will drink Bols together."

Twenty minutes later the officers climbed carefully down the ladder to their motor-boat, not in the least assisted by the Bols. The boat sheered off and made towards the shore; on board *Heloise* men moved on the forepeak and the chain began to grind in at the hawse. Presently the engines rumbled out and regular, spasmodic puffs of fumes appeared from the exhaust-pipe in the funnel; then the vessel turned away and headed eastwards up the Channel.

That afternoon Mona crossed the ferry at the mouth of Portsmouth Harbour and walked up to Haslar Hospital. In the past week she had been twice before; the first time she had not seen Jerry at all. The second time she had seen him for two or three minutes only, a tired figure motionless in bed that smiled at her with his eyes and said very little. The sister had been with them all the time; she had left her present of grapes and come away.

She passed the gate and walked across the garden quadrangle, bright with spring flowers. She entered the hospital block and went up to the sister's room, carrying her bag of grapes. Sister MacKenzie looked up from the desk where she was writing up a temperature-chart as the girl came in.

Mona said: "Could I see Flying-Officer Chambers?"

"Aye, he's expecting you. Ye can see him for ten minutes today, and not one minute longer than that."

"How is he today?"

"He had a better night, the sister was telling me. He'll get along all right now, if he isn't wearied with his visitors."

Mona said: "I haven't got a watch. Would you tell me when it's time for me to go?"

The Scotswoman said: "Have nae fear of that. I'll come and fetch ye oot of it."

Mona walked along the passage and entered the room. She said: "Hello, Jerry."

He smiled at her from the bed. "Hello. You're looking very nice today."

She said: "Don't talk so soft. I brought you some grapes."

He was much better; there was no doubt of that. He lay in bed with both arms bandaged to the shoulder outside the bedclothes; his hair had been brushed and he had had a shave. He wore a vivid orange pyjama jacket, cut short at the sleeves.

"That's awfully nice of you, Mona. The last lot were grand."

"How are you feeling, Jerry? You're looking better."

"It hurts like hell when they do my arms."

She drew a chair up and sat beside him. "It must do. Still, you're looking better, Jerry."

"So I ought to. I've had Sister MacKenzie titivating me up for you for the last half-hour. Do you like my taste in pyjamas?"

"It's kind of cheerful," she admitted.

He grinned at her. "That's fine. You're going to see a lot of them."

"If you start talking like that I'll go away."

"I won't talk like that, then. I'll just think it."

She laughed. "That's worse."

She sat with him for a few minutes, talking of little foolish things. Presently he said:

"What do you think of my hyacinths?"

She turned her head. A large basket filled with moss and growing hyacinths, white and blue and pink, stood upon a table in the window. They gave a pleasant sense of comfort and habitation to the bare furnishings of the room.

"Who sent you those, Jerry?"

He turned his head upon the pillow to look at them; a puzzled frown appeared. "It's a damn funny thing— I can't make it out. The wife of the C.-in-C. sent them —Lady Blackett."

"Oh . . ."

He said: "I've never met the woman."

Mona said weakly: "I expect she sends flowers and stuff to every officer that gets hurt."

"I'm damn sure she does nothing of the sort. What's more, she's coming to see me tomorrow."

"Coming to see you?" This was terrible. She had given herself away so utterly to Lady Blackett.

"Yes. She rang up sister about an hour ago. She's coming tomorrow morning."

There was a short silence. Mona said at last: "They're

very pleased about what you done to have this accident, Jerry. That's one thing I do know."

"Are they? How did you hear that?"

She said cautiously: "There was a Commander Sutton talking about you. He got to know that we was friends."

"Do they think it was a good show, then?"

"They do, Jerry—honest. They think you did terribly well."

He said: "Well, that's something to set off against *Caranx*."

She ventured: "They're wondering about *Caranx* now. Commander Sutton was saying that there was another submarine sunk in the Channel that same day."

He stared at her. "Do you mean they think that there's a chance that the one I sank wasn't *Caranx*?"

She nodded. "Something of that. I know they're looking into it again."

"Damn it," he said, "I always knew that bloody thing was German." There was a pause, and then he said: "I bet this Lady Blackett knows all about it. Wife of the C.-in-C.—she's sure to know what's going on. I'll have to try and get a line on it from her."

Sister MacKenzie came into the room. "Time ye were gaeing along now," she said. "Ye've had more than the ten minutes."

Panic seized Mona as she rose to go. "Jerry," she said, "whatever Lady Blackett says, you're Mr. Smith to me. You won't forget that?"

He stared at her. "I don't know what you mean," he said. "But you've got that all wrong. I'm Lord Jerry and you're the Lady Chambers. Or you're going to be."

The Scotswoman glowered at them in uncomprehending disapproval. It was impossible to speak freely with her in the room, nor did Mona want to. "You can call me what you like, Jerry," she said. "But you'll remember what I wanted, just to be Mrs. Smith. That's all I ever wanted to be." She bent and kissed him; then very quickly she made her escape from the room.

Two days later, in the cold light of dawn, a trawler left the North Wall and proceeded down the harbour. Lieutenant Mitcheson stood on the bridge; as they passed *Victory* drawn up in her dry dock he called his crew to attention, as was fitting. One day in the future there would come Peace, a terrible day when they would take his ship away from him, and he would have to go back to selling haberdashery, or else to the motor trade. He put the thought away. There was, as yet, no sign of that bad time on the horizon. For months, perhaps years to come, he would have his three meals a day, his uniform, and his ship. He wished for nothing more.

On the well deck forward of the bridge a squat box with two wheeled handles was lashed down upon the hatch; by it the diver was smearing vaseline upon the screw threads of his helmet with loving care. The rubber suit was spread out on the hatch beside him with the long coils of hose and line.

In the little cuddy of the trawler an elderly, grey-haired lieutenant-commander of the regular Navy bent over a chart with Commander Rutherford. "That's the place where we put down the buoy," he said. "There's definitely something there—a wreck of some sort. We swept and caught it twice—once going east and west, and the other time north and south."

Rutherford nodded. "So you buoyed it."

"Yes. We put down a spar buoy."

"Any idea if it was a submarine?"

The other shook his head. "There was grey paint on the sweep wire when we got it in. That's the only thing. From that, I'd say she hadn't been down very long."

The commander nodded. The position that had been

buoyed was about half a mile to the west of the position
he had got from the Dutchman, but in poor weather
that sort of error might quite well occur.

The morning came up calm and sunny. The trawler
passed the Gate and steamed away up Channel, over a
calm sunlit sea. Two hours later Mitcheson said to
Rutherford, standing beside him on the bridge:

"There's the buoy." It stood up, a thread-like spike,
in the far distance ahead of them.

It was still an hour and a half before the time of slack
water, too early yet for a diver to go down. The trawler
drew up to the buoy slowly, manoeuvred for a few
minutes, then dropped an anchor. Then for a time she
slacked out chain, manoeuvring with her engines as she
did so; presently she dropped a second anchor. In half
an hour she was securely moored beside the buoy.

The diver's crew appeared from below and began
their preparations. A short ladder was made fast to the
ship's side, and the shot-rope was streamed beside it to
the bottom. With the deliberate care born of long
experience the diver got into his suit, the heavy boots
were strapped to his feet. The collar was laid upon his
shoulders as he sat upon the hatch, and the belt,
furnished with the knife and the waterproof lantern,
was strapped to his waist.

He was a fair-haired, serious man of about thirty,
smoking a cigarette. He said to his mate, now polishing
the windows of the helmet:

"If I'm down over dinner-time, tell cookie to keep a
plateful hot for me. And I don't want none of that fat."

"Or-right."

"What's he got for afters?"

"Plummy duff."

"I don't want none of that. Tell 'im I'll have a bit of
bread and jam."

"Or-right."

"Partial to a bit of bread and jam, I've always been," said the diver conversationally.

Commander Rutherford approached. "You've got it all clear, have you?" he enquired. "If it's a submarine, we want the nationality to be established definitely."

"Case it's *Caranx*, sir?"

"That's it. If you can get up to the conning-tower, *Caranx* had her name on it in raised letters, towards the aft end, about five feet from the deck. The letters were painted over, but you'd feel them with your hands."

"I got that, sir."

The commander glanced over the side. "Are you going now, or will you wait till the tide slacks a bit more?"

"All right if I go now, sir, I think." He turned to his mate. "Come on, let's have it."

They lifted the dome on to his shoulders and screwed it home. Through the front window he said to his mate: "Mind, I don't want none of that duff. Ask if he's got any stewed fruit, or anything of that."

"Or-right."

Two men began to turn the handles of the pump; the air hissed through the hose. His mate screwed the front window home and slapped the top of the helmet with his hand. The diver sat for a minute adjusting the air-valve by his ear; then he got up with an effort and walked two steps to the bulwarks. A couple of men helped him over the side on to the ladder.

He went down until the water rose above his head. Then, with the bright copper dome of the helmet showing as a little disc upon the water, he paused and adjusted the air-valve, that bubbled with a little splutter of white foam. Then in slow motion he reached out and grasped the shot-rope, stepped off the ladder, and was gone. The hose and life-line paid out slowly into the water.

On the trawler the time passed slowly. The bubbles which showed where the diver was wandered away to port and played about there, minute after minute. In half an hour they did not move more than fifty yards from one position. Presently they came back to the shot-rope, and a series of twitches gave the signal for a line to be sent down. A rope was lowered with a hook upon the end of it; to the hook a canvas bag was lashed with marline.

For half an hour longer the watchers on the trawler studied the bubbles wandering to the surface, and the vagaries of the air-tube and the ropes. On the bridge and on the gun platform in the bow seamen were posted to keep a vigilant look-out for submarines.

Once the old lieutenant-commander said fretfully: "How long is he to be down for?"

Rutherford said: "I left that to him."

The other was silent. He would have preferred to hurry the diver; it was asking for it to stay anchored off the coast like this. A submarine could come and take a pot-shot at them from far off, and they would be powerless to escape the torpedo. It was asking for trouble.

In the end there came a series of twitches at the hook-rope. At the bulwarks men began to pull it up. Rutherford and the lieutenant-commander went down to the deck; only Mitcheson stayed on the bridge to guard the ship.

The rope came up slowly, fairly heavily laden. A metallic rod, eight feet or more in length, broke surface with the hook. This rod was furnished at one end with a handle and a broken plate, through which it passed; the other end was twisted and broken. From the hook the bag was suspended, bulging with small articles.

These were all hoisted in and laid upon the deck. The diver's crew set to work to take in the life-line and the hose as the man came up the shot-rope. Rutherford and the other officer bent to examine what had been brought up.

The long rod passed through a broken plate close by the handle. This plate was engraved with the words STARBOARD CENTRE.

The officers looked at it rather sadly. It was no more than they had expected, but it revived the tragedy within their minds.

"What part is that?" said the lieutenant-commander.

Rutherford shrugged his shoulders. "Looks like one of the ballast cocks," he said. "We'll have to wait till we get back to Blockhouse to identify it positively."

They turned to the bag, unlashed it from the hook, and spread its contents out upon the hatch. Behind them the trawler crew came round in curiosity.

There were a pair of Ross binoculars with the broad arrow engraved on them, considerably damaged by sea water. There was a brass hand-wheel, the steel shaft of which was snapped off short; the brass rim was engraved with a double arrow and the words INCREASE and REDUCE. There was a double-ended spanner marked at one end 1″ and at the other 1¼″. There was a pewter coffee-pot of British naval pattern, and there were three table knives of the sort supplied for officers.

Rutherford said heavily: "Well, there's not much doubt about that, I'm afraid."

The other officer shook his head. "No doubt at all."

The diver came up the ladder presently, and paused with his head above the bulwarks. Two men assisted him over on to the deck; he sat down on the hatch. His mate unscrewed the front window and removed the helmet.

The diver rubbed a hand over his face, and brushed the hair back from his forehead. Then he saw Rutherford beside him. "It's a submarine, all right," he said.

"One of ours, too. See them words on the hand-wheel?"

The commander said: "Yes—I saw that. Is she very much damaged?"

"She's in two parts, sir—right in two separate pieces. You never saw anything like it. The stern is upright, more or less, and the bow over on the port side. I dunno where the conning-tower's got to. I didn't see nothing of that at all."

"You didn't see the name, then?"

"No, sir." He paused and then he said, "I reckon that's *Caranx*, all right. I reckon she got torpedoed, too."

"Why do you think that? It might have been a mine."

"It didn't look like any mine *I* ever saw, sir." The commander was silent; this man had seen many damaged ships. "It was more local, if you take me—more like a torpedo does. As a matter of fact, I did think I saw the tail of a torpedo crushed up underneath the aft part, at the break. But I wouldn't swear to that. I didn't go too near to all that broken stuff with the tide running round it."

"Where did you get these things from, then?"

"Out of the fore part, at the break. That bit was in the lee of the tide, if you get me, sir. I picked up everything loose I could lay me hands on."

Rutherford questioned him for a few minutes. Then he said: "All right. You can pack up your gear; I don't see anything to gain by going down again."

"Very good, sir."

The commander turned aside. His friends were very near him, Billy Parkinson, and Stone, and Sandy Anderson. Not very many fathoms from him they lay resting in the sea, the sea that in their lives had brought them so much pleasure and so much anxiety, so much joy and pain. His mind drifted to a surf-riding party at Hong Kong with Billy and Jo Parkinson and a dark girl that he might have married, but didn't. To a cottage on the

salt marshes near Bosham, where he had had a meal or
two with Stone and his wife, to a week-end with Sandy
Anderson upon a five-ton yacht in the Solent. In their
lives they had taken pleasure from the sea; that it now
wrapped them close could not be altogether ill.

He turned to the old lieutenant-commander. "Anybody got a prayer-book on board, do you think?" he said.
"We'd better read the service before getting under way."

The older man, his junior in rank, said: "I'll ask the
captain. But do you think it's wise to hang about here
any longer?"

They had been anchored there for more than two
hours, a sitting shot for any submarine. Rutherford
hesitated. "Tell the captain to get under way," he said
at last. "I'll read the service while he circles round the
buoy."

Presently the anchor winch began to grind in chain.
The diver, clambering out of the stiff rubber suit, said
to his mate in a low tone:

"Nip down and tell cookie to keep my dinner a bit
longer. He's going to read the bloody service."

"Or-right."

"Did you ask him about the stewed fruit?"

"He ain't got none." The diver made a gesture of
annoyance.

The second anchor broke surface; Lieutenant Mitcheson rang for half-speed ahead, and the trawler began to
move. She turned in a wide circle. Commander Rutherford went forward to the well deck and stood by the
bulwarks facing to the buoy. Then, in a level voice, he
began to read from Mitcheson's prayer-book.

The men stood round him with bared heads, awkward
and a little embarrassed. Rutherford read on steadily,
conscientiously, and rather badly. He knew that he was
bad at reading aloud. His friends had known that too;
he thought they wouldn't mind.

"I heard a voice from heaven, saying unto me, Write, From henceforth blessed are the dead which die in the Lord: even so saith the Spirit; for they rest from their labours."

The trawler turned from the buoy and set a course for home.

.　　.　　.　　.　　.

In the study in Admiralty House, Commander Rutherford made his report to the Admiral. Captain Burnaby was there, and Commander Foster, jovial and red-faced.

Rutherford said: "I think there is no doubt that the one off Departure Point is *Caranx*, sir. The long handle was part of the ballast controls, and the hand-wheel was the field-control to one of the motors. We identified that definitely."

Admiral Blackett said: "Was the other submarine really sunk? It's been established that she didn't get away?"

"We had a sweep made yesterday," said Captain Burnaby. "Commander Rutherford suggested that. There's definitely a ship there on the bottom, but it's too deep to get a diver down to her, except under very good conditions." He paused: "I think there can be very little doubt that she is the submarine that Flying-Officer Chambers sunk."

"I see."

The Admiral sat back in his chair. "As you would reconstruct the matter, then," he said, "*Caranx* was proceeding towards Portsmouth at two-fifteen in the afternoon, in a squall of rain. Probably, she was running on the surface."

Rutherford said: "Certainly on the surface, I should say. She sent a wireless signal at 1403."

"Yes—on the surface. As the squall passed she was

sighted by a German, which unfortunately was in a position to torpedo her, and did so."

The officers nodded their agreement.

The admiral thought for a minute. "The supposition is that, after that, the German took up the course that *Caranx* had been steering on, for Portsmouth. And that he ran upon the surface as *Caranx* had been doing." He paused. "Why did he do that?"

Commander Foster beamed, leaned forward, and said keenly: "He was a clever chap. He would have seen from her course that *Caranx* was making for the Gate, and he would have realised that aircraft and trawlers would have been warned not to attack her. He may have hoped to get right up into Spithead."

"So he proceeded on the surface, just as *Caranx* had been doing. He took a very bold course if he did that."

Commander Foster said: "I think he was probably a very bold man, sir."

Burnaby said: "That sounds like the truth of it to me. He was doing his best to behave exactly as *Caranx* would have done, in an attempt to get right close into the Gate."

Commander Rutherford made a grimace. "He might have done a lot of damage if he'd pulled it off."

The Commander-in-Chief nodded. "Yes, he might have done a lot of damage. Unfortunately for him, he took too long to make up his mind. He was late on his schedule."

Foster said: "It's a bit of luck that Air Force pilot got him." He smiled broadly.

Admiral Blackett leaned forward to the table. "Well, gentlemen, that seems to be the truth of it. I'm glad we've been able to clear it up; it's always very unsatisfactory when things are left unexplained. Now, is there any further business—any other points that anybody has to raise?"

Captain Burnaby raised his head. "As a matter of form, sir, the Court of Enquiry ought to be recalled to reconsider its findings. That's a small matter; I should think they'd run through it in half an hour. But I think it ought to be done."

The Commander-in-Chief said: "I shouldn't waste much effort over that. It affects nothing now."

Burnaby persisted: "They censured the pilot in their findings, sir. I think that should be rectified with as little delay as possible."

The Admiral said: "I had forgotten that. All right, see my secretary and get them recalled. You'd better get that done at once; we owe a lot to that young man."

Commander Foster laughed out genially. "First of all he gets a strip torn off for sinking *Caranx*, when what he really did was to save our bacon for us. Then we go and blow him up in Burnaby's experiments."

Burnaby said: "That's another matter altogether. We might consider that as well, sir, if you like."

Admiral Blackett said: "Just as you like. He seems to have deserved well of us on two counts."

Rutherford said: "How's he getting on, by the way?"

"Quite well," said Burnaby. "He'll be flying again in six months."

The Admiral leaned back in his chair. "For the submarine he deserves a mention in despatches. That's clearly in our sphere. Is everyone agreed on that?"

They nodded their agreement.

"For the experimental work, I take it that we owe him a good deal. That is so, isn't it?"

Burnaby said: "That is correct, sir. The R.Q. apparatus will be ready for service in a month from now. That's very largely the result of the risks he took. I think he should get something for that, too."

The Admiral said: "Haven't the Air Force got a

special decoration for that sort of thing? It stays in my mind that they've got something of the sort."

There was a doubtful silence. Foster said: "Is that the Air Force Cross?"

The Commander-in-Chief said: "I believe you're right. Pass me that Whitaker's Almanack from the desk."

He turned the pages. "That's the one," he said at last. "'For acts of courage or devotion to duty when flying, although not in active operations against the enemy.'" He paused. "That seems to cover it."

Commander Foster said: "Well, that's a matter for the Air Force, isn't it? It's their decoration."

Captain Burnaby raised his head and stared at him arrogantly, the grim, iron-grey brows knitted together in a frown, the jaw firmly set.

"I don't agree with you at all," he said. "This was a naval trial. The Air Force supplied the pilot and the aeroplane, but apart from that they had nothing whatever to do with it. The matter of a decoration is entirely in our hands. It would be most improper for the Air Ministry to put him forward for anything except upon our recommendation."

He turned to the Admiral. "I quite agree that he should have the Air Force Cross," he said. "I suggest we make a recommendation in those terms to the Air Ministry."

L'ENVOI

DUSK fell upon the convoy, making westward from the land. There were nine ships in all, guarded by destroyers ahead and astern. They steamed in long zig-zags at about fifteen knots, heading out into the Atlantic.

Flight-Lieutenant Chambers, A.F.C., stood by the rail with his wife. He leaned upon his stick, because he could not walk without it yet. It would be some months before he would be fit to fly again; in the meantime he had been posted to Trenton, Ontario, as a ground instructor.

In the six months since he had sunk his submarine he had changed a good deal. He was thinner and he had lost a good deal of his fresh complexion, replaced by a brown tan gained from lying out in his long chair at the convalescent home. He bore himself with greater confidence.

Mona, too, was changed. In her, the alteration was less physical than verbal. When it had become inevitable that she must marry Jerry she had left the snack-bar and had entered on a concentrated course of study. Her general education did not worry her; her native wit told her that she would get by as an officer's wife if she took pains with her appearance and her speech. It was the latter that she had concentrated on.

Madame Tremayne had been her stand-by, Professor of Elocution, Public Speaking, and Deportment. Madame Tremayne, whose real name was Susan Bigsworth, lived in undistinguished style in Fratton and charged two shillings for each individual lesson. Her chief clients were young women who aspired to be mannequins; Mona had known about her for some

241

time. She taught Mona a correct form of English that would have given her away more surely than her mother tongue. From her Mona learned to abandon the phrase "you didn't ought to do that" and to say carefully "you should not do that". It was some time before she acquired familiarity with "you oughtn't to do that".

They had been married for a week. In the swift movement of the war so much had happened in that week that their marriage had not occupied their thoughts a very great deal. They had anticipated a long period of sick leave which they had planned to spend in Cornwall on their honeymoon; instead of that they had received upon their wedding-day a posting to Canada. After the first shock they had welcomed it. When all their life demanded readjustment a further change meant little to them. They had their clothes and a few suitcases; they had no other ties to bind them to one place. They sold the little sports car with regret for fifteen pounds, parked the wireless set and the half-built caravel with Jerry's mother, packed the rabbit-lamp among Mona's stockings and sailed. They were inured to change. Buckwheat cakes and maple syrup for breakfast on the liner were just another thing.

Mona said: "Can you see the land still, Jerry? I can't, now."

"I think we've seen the last of it," he said.

She drew a little closer to him. "How long shall we be away in Canada, do you think?"

In the uncertainty of war he could not answer that.

"For all I know, we may stay there for ever." He smiled down at her. "Would you mind a lot if it turned out like that?"

She looked up at him. "I don't mind," she said. "When you start fresh, like getting married, I don't know that it makes a lot of difference if you change your place as well."

He nodded. It was nearly dark astern; there would be no more to be seen. In many ways he felt the transition more than she did. To her the move to a less formal country was in itself desirable; there would be less tendency to criticise her when she slipped in the word "like" unwarily, or referred to "something of that". Chambers had deeper roots in England than she had.

"We shan't see any more now," he said quietly. They turned and went below.

So let them pass, small people of no great significance, caught up and swept together like dead leaves in the great whirlwind of the war. Wars come, and all the world is shattered by their blast. But through it all young people meet and marry; life goes on, though temples rock and the tall buildings start and crumble in the dust of their destruction.

THE HISTORY OF VINTAGE

The famous American publisher Alfred A. Knopf (1892–1984) founded Vintage Books in the United States in 1954 as a paperback home for the authors published by his company. Vintage was launched in the United Kingdom in 1990 and works independently from the American imprint although both are part of the international publishing group, Random House.

Vintage in the United Kingdom was initially created to publish paperback editions of books acquired by the prestigious hardback imprints in the Random House Group such as Jonathan Cape, Chatto & Windus, Hutchinson and later William Heinemann, Secker & Warburg and The Harvill Press. There are many Booker and Nobel Prize-winning authors on the Vintage list and the imprint publishes a huge variety of fiction and non-fiction. Over the years Vintage has expanded and the list now includes great authors of the past – who are published under the Vintage Classics imprint – as well as many of the most influential authors of the present.

For a full list of the books Vintage publishes, please visit our website
www.vintage-books.co.uk

For book details and other information about the classic authors we publish, please visit the Vintage Classics website
www.vintage-classics.info

www.vintage-classics.info